Cloverlawn

Three Tales from the Block

Joe Taylor

Chapbook Press

Schuler Books
2660 28th Street SE
Grand Rapids, MI 49512
(616) 942-7330
www.schulerbooks.com

Cloverlawn - Three Tales from the Block

ISBN 13: 9781966196235

Library of Congress Control Number: 2025910599

Cover Art by Kiarra Lambert

Printed in the United States.

Table of Contents

Things Left Unsaid

<h1 style="text-align:center">1</h1>

Will Miller rose every morning at seven, performed a set of exercises that had not changed since his wife died, showered, shaved, and dressed, and ate a light breakfast. Then he would walk his neighborhood, greeting those he came upon and sometimes chatting. Lately, he had been stopping for coffee at the Kava Korner, a busy little shop six blocks from his home.

He would order his pricey medium-roast in a to-go cup—a better value, he thought—and sit at a small table in a back corner, from which he could watch the customers, mostly young people with laptops or with colleagues or enroute to their jobs. He would often bring a book, but he was not much of a reader. He might make small talk with another patron or with the proprietors, a young couple in their thirties, but at seventy-seven the oldest person in the shop, Will might expect to feel irrelevant.

He was surprised one midsummer morning to hear someone call his name. He looked up, a bit startled, at the bearded man before him.

"Sheldon."

"Hi, Will."

He had noticed a man at the cash register, but had not got a good look at the face. Now there was no mistaking him. Will rose halfway out of his chair, smiling, extending his hand. "Sheldon. Good to see you!"

"My wife is at the orthopedic office next door," Sheldon said. "What is that you're reading?"

"Oh, just a novel." Will showed him the cover. The book was in large print due to his declining sight, but Will was hesitant to reveal that fact.

"Mind if I sit down?"

"Course not. Last time I saw you was at the reunion, I think. That would have been about, what, twelve or thirteen years ago?" It was the first summer of Will's retirement. He and Joan had taken a trip to Yellowstone later that summer.

As Sheldon set his coffee down and settled awkwardly into a chair, Will noticed that he had not aged well since that reunion. Sheldon would be seventy-six now, a year younger than Will. He looked tired. The skin of his face was blotchy behind that beard. He had been chubby as an adolescent and was chubby still.

"It was 2010, I think," Sheldon said.

"They called it the Cloverlawn reunion," Will said. "Someone said we had sixty kids on that block. I think most of them showed up that day. Strange that so many of us kept in touch over the years."

"Not me," Sheldon said. "I probably heard about it through my brother."

True, Will thought. Sheldon never associated much with the neighbor kids. Will guessed that he was Sheldon's best friend on the block.

"Your brother, Melvin. How is he?" Will asked.

"Oh, that *putz* will never change. He is still *so* impulsive! And irresponsible. He's back living at our old place."

"On Cloverlawn? Wow, he might be the only one left."

"Melvin was homeless for a few years, lived in some tough places, and now he is, what, seventy-five? When our renters went to assisted living, we moved him back in."

"I hope it's working out for him," Will said. "You were in Ann Arbor, last we talked."

"We bought a condo in Southfield," Sheldon said. "To be close to our daughter. And I can keep tabs on Melvin." He looked down, and back up. "We could not make it to the memorial, Will, but I'm glad I got a chance to meet your wife at the reunion. Such a sweet woman. How long has it been since she passed away?"

"Five years this month." After Joan died, a woman at a group grief session remarked that it had been five years since her husband had died. Back then, Will found it strange that the woman was still attending the sessions.

"And you still have your home here in Royal Oak?" Sheldon asked.

"Yep. Going on forty years."

"How many grandkids?"

"Four. One in Flint and three out East, in New Haven. How about you?"

"We have five. My daughter in Bloomfield has two. The others are out of state."

Will and Sheldon reminisced about the old days in the neighborhood. They had not much chance to talk personally at the reunion, but Will felt then that the connection between the two was still there, which pleased and puzzled him. And now, after another span of time without contact, that feeling of mutuality was back.

"And your wife, how is she?" Will asked.

"Denise is invincible. She is in a reading club at the library, a Jewish ladies' club, and she stays busy with the kids and grandkids. I cannot keep up with her."

"And your mother."

"My mother has been gone since '93, Will."

"Of course," Will said, embarrassed. He knew that Sheldon's mother had long been dead. He had always been fascinated by Mrs. Weiss. He segued to a question. "What are you doing with yourself these days, Sheldon?"

"Well, Denise says I am not a joiner. I retired about six years ago, but I still have a few contacts from my department at the university. And I try to stay current with my reading."

"You mean philosophy? Didn't you teach it?"

"I did. But I don't have to concentrate on that anymore."

"I once thought you would end up a rabbi," Will said.

"Me, too. I sometimes regret that . . ."

"But now you get to switch gears, eh?"

"Switch gears. Yes, now I get to study whatever I like."

Will asked if Sheldon would join him for lunch sometime. "We could meet halfway," he said.

They agreed to meet in two weeks at the Coolidge Café in Oak Park.

*****

Will and Sheldon were born in the baby boom years after the world war. In 1950, their parents had bought identical new bungalows—three small bedrooms, one bath, no basements or garages or lawns or trees—and had become next-door neighbors. Sheldon Weiss's family were Jewish. The Millers were Catholic. Jews and non-Jews were living peacefully, even amicably, but with little intermingling. And on their block, Cloverlawn, Jews were a minority. Yet, the two boys were friends, if tangentially and intermittently.

They had never seen the inside of each other's houses, and their families did not socialize. It seemed to Will that Sheldon's parents did not allow their sons to play outside the house very often.

Sheldon took a yellow bus to Hebrew school with its name, Yeshiva Beth Yehuda, painted on its sides. Afternoons, the bus arrived at a time when other kids on the block were already home and out on the street. Sheldon would emerge from that bus carrying a bookbag over a shoulder. It was made of a heavy fabric, pulled tight with a piece of rope. If Will was near, the two would often sit on a curb until Shel's mother's shrill, European-accented voice was heard calling him and his brother to dinner from an open window. That voice, coming from a woman who was rarely seen outside the house, always sounded to Will frantic, desperate.

Will would walk or ride a bicycle to the Catholic school, Our Lady of Fatima. When he reached high school age, he attended the public school, Oak Park High. His family attended Mass on Sunday, but the Millers were not nearly as devout as the Weisses, who observed traditional daily prayers and studied the Torah. The Weiss males wore yarmulkes. They often walked to the nearby orthodox synagogue on Saturday.

Will was an average high school student and played on the football and baseball teams. After high school, he worked as a stock boy at the local market, which was Jewish-owned and sold Kosher as well as non-Kosher. He commuted to Wayne State, but with no career ambitions and little interest, lasted only one year.

A year behind Will, Shel went to Yeshiva College, a Hebrew University in New York City. Will was eventually drafted into the Army, and Shel, who had found his calling in scholarship, had little time or income for trips home. If they saw each other after high school, it was at a distance.

Then, twelve years earlier, they re-connected at the Cloverlawn reunion. They exchanged phone numbers at that reunion, promising to stay in touch. Sheldon's number was still stored in Will's cell phone's memory.

But neither Will nor Sheldon had followed up before that morning at the Kava Korner.

2

The Coolidge Café was a relic from the old neighborhood. It was once a delicatessen but had changed names and menus and been remodeled several times over. After parking his pickup, Will saw Sheldon through the window. As they greeted each other, Will noticed that Sheldon looked tired. He was wearing a white shirt and nondescript tie, the same tie, Will guessed, that he had worn at their prior meeting.

They ordered: Will a sandwich with a Greek half-salad, and Sheldon a meat-lover's omelet.

"What happened to your hand?" Sheldon asked. Will held out his left hand. It was a workman's hand, large and powerful-looking. A nail was missing from his ring finger. The palm was wrapped with gauze that left his thumb and fingers free.

"I was building a shed in my daughter's yard. Cut it on a piece of siding. It didn't need stitches, but it hurt like hell."

"But you did something constructive, mechanical. I could not assemble one of those sheds to save my life."

"Yeah, and I couldn't stand up in front of a roomful of grad students to save my own. I was blue-collar and you were the professor."

"Last we spoke, you said you once thought I would become a rabbi," Sheldon said.

"Well, you always wore the scull cap."

"True."

"And you seemed like the religious type. You went to Hebrew schools, and that Jewish college."

"I got into a graduate program in Jewish Studies. That led me into Jewish philosophy. But I got married, and I thought a doctorate in general philosophy would lead to a better job."

"So then you stayed with philosophy while at UM?"

"In a way, yes. But I am drawn to theology and Jewish philosophy. I've specialized in thinkers like Buber and Spinoza and Kant, but those pursuits can be spiritually lonely. Joyless, you know? I would rather be still and behold the creation than live between doubt and certainty. Do you know what I mean, Will?"

"I think so," Will lied. He knew nothing of Buber and those other guys, but it seemed like a good idea, if a strange one, to behold the creation. He was curious. It struck him that his life, spent working with his hands rather than his head, had been woefully stagnant, while Sheldon had outgrown him both intellectually and spiritually.

"Let me try to explain myself," Sheldon said.

Will was silent. He did not know that he wanted to hear more confusing philosophy talk, if that is what it was, but he gave Sheldon his attention.

"I want time to sit in contemplation, and I want to live out, to act in this world."

"So, uh, okay, what do you want to do?"

"The thing that needs to be done. The thing I was created to do."

Sheldon went on to say that he had spent most of his life in his head, and his head was tired.

Will picked at his napkin. His own head was tired of listening to this man, but he could not deny that Sheldon had looked him in the eye and was sincere. Will wondered if there was a time in his youth when he might better have understood what Sheldon was saying.

"Well," he finally said. "I've got a bicycle to fix and a bathroom that needs a coat of semi-gloss." The here-and-now always worked best for Will. He felt more comfortable in a world in which reflection was unnecessary. He considered himself to be a man with no time for nonsense, a man of action.

Back on Cloverlawn, Sheldon rarely spoke of his mother, and Will wondered why. Most of the neighbors saw her as harried, anxious, self-absorbed. When Will was ten, he heard that Elena Weiss had been in a concentration camp. She rarely left the house except in the car—Mr. Weiss drove her to the grocery store—or to visit the Gordons, an older Jewish couple who lived on the block. She ran as if in a panic to and from the Gordons in a housedress and noisy shoes.

During that time before holocaust museums, before the term "holocaust" was used as reference to the mass extermination of Jews, Will shook off the anti-Semitic feelings he had absorbed from his surroundings. His associations with Jews as an adolescent and his experience working in a Jewish supermarket had taught him to look beyond religion and culture—at the individual.

Mrs. Weiss, he came to think, would have been a teenager during the war in Europe. Since his early teens, Will wanted to know what she experienced, how she was doing. He thought of her not as Mrs. Weiss, but as Elena, the girl with the numbers he believed the Nazis had tattooed on her forearm. From a distance he looked for those numbers until he discovered that prisoners from only one concentration camp, Auschwitz, were branded in that way. Will would ask about Elena, but Sheldon would say he did not know, that his mother never talked about it. Will sensed, though he never understood why, that Sheldon was embarrassed about his mother.

Of course, Elena was long dead by now. They were all dead, the parents. Will did not mention her that day at the Coolidge. There was not time, and he was operating under the assumption that the topic of Mr. and Mrs. Weiss was not for him to initiate. He did not want to take that pleasurable lunch into awkward territory. They talked of their families, on the current political situation that often verged on chaos, and on the war in Ukraine, about which Sheldon was informed and articulate. Sheldon was animated in his condemnation of Vladimir Putin, whom he called "Stalin without the mustache."

The two men had grown up next door in different worlds and their lives unfolded in very different ways. Yet they had history, and enough in common to be interested in each other.

Interested enough to agree to meet again soon.

3

A few weeks passed. Will was the first to initiate contact and propose another lunch date at the Coolidge. Sheldon said he was glad to hear from him.

Will left home early enough for a detour on the steamy hot August day. The Coolidge was near enough to cruise through the old neighborhood. He had not seen the block in ten years. As he turned the corner, he was struck by the difference from the days of his boyhood.

Those summers had seen kids and bikes and toys on porches, lawns, sidewalks. Cloverlawn had been lined with saplings that gave no shade, no hiding places. The boys played versions of baseball, football, and hockey in the street until a car came along, which would wait until a path was cleared for it to pass through. Will remembered the after-dinner game, Kick-the-Can, that drew girls and boys, young and old, from up and down the block. Sheldon rarely participated in these games. His brother, Melvin, was more likely to be seen on the street, but was, like his brother, not athletic. Girls stood on the sidewalk in groups, tending to their dolls or their younger siblings. Moms were in the kitchen or, hands on hips, watching from porches or screen doors. The family cars and the men who drove them were away at work until dinnertime, and then home for the rest of the evening.

Now there were no cars on the street, no signs of life. The city trees that lined the curb were fully grown, their leaves hanging in the noonday heat. But the Colangelo's paper birch, cared for so fastidiously by Mr. Colangelo, was gone, as was the big oak on the Green's lawn. The busted up concrete driveway of Will's family home was now a shiny asphalt. The brick exterior had been painted white—not a good look, he thought—and the concrete porch floor and steps were covered with red outdoor carpeting that looked to

11

be fraying. Next door, the Weiss place needed work. The roof was in dire need of attention. The exterior trim was way overdue for a paint job. The garage door hung off its rail on one side. It seemed that Sheldon's brother Melvin had been neglecting it. Will resolved not to bring this up to Sheldon.

When he arrived at the Coolidge, Will pulled his old pick-up next to Sheldon's SUV. They had agreed on a one o'clock lunch to avoid the noon rush. They ordered sandwiches and began with reminiscences of the neighborhood before moving on to talk of work and family. Sheldon told of his hippie granddaughter, his concerns about her boyfriend's dreadlocks. Will told of his son James's teaching job in Flint.

"But he'll be a professor at Stanford in January." This was not exactly true. James might eventually become a full professor. Stanford had offered him a research position that would include some teaching, but he had not yet accepted.

"Stanford!" Sheldon said, impressed. "That is fine opportunity. You must be proud."

Will beamed.

Sheldon noticed Will's scar. "How is your hand?"

Will showed it to him, a three-inch scab surrounded by redness.

"Still healing," Sheldon said. "Is it sore?"

"Some," Will said. "A cut on the palm is hard to ignore, eh? But it's comin' along okay."

"You could have been a farmer. Or a dock worker." Sheldon held his own pale, fleshy palms out on the table, turned them over. "And I know you were in Vietnam. I haven't used my hands for anything other than holding a fork. Or a book. You were an electrician, by trade?"

"Sort of," Will said. "I did mostly electrical and machine repair. Lately I've been repairing bicycles for people."

"You have skills."

"Yeah, well, you and I went off in different directions, eh Shel?"

"We began in different places, too," Sheldon reminded him.

"Even though we were next door neighbors. And now we're nearing the finish line."

Will and Sheldon spoke about their relatives, friends, and past Cloverlawn neighbors. Sheldon spoke at length about his recently deceased mother-in-law, his wife's grieving process, and the long ordeal of disposing of the woman's home and furniture. When prompted, Will spoke lovingly of his deceased wife, Joan, but he felt uncomfortable about delving into subtle feelings or specific details. He was embarrassed about his inability to make changes to the home he had shared with Joan. Her clothes and other possessions were largely undisturbed.

Sheldon asked how long it had been since Will's father died.

"Let's see, 1997 . . . going on thirty years," Will said.

Sheldon nodded. "I did not know your dad. I would see him in the yard. And the light in the garage was often on at night."

"Yeah, he was always organizing in the garage, and he loved being in the yard," Will said.

"What was he like?"

"Dad was a quiet guy. I think he needed those times out back to have a beer and get away from the chaos of the house--a wife and three kids, everyone wanting a piece of him. He won a Silver Star with the Third Army in Europe during the war. He was in the Battle of the Bulge, and his unit liberated Buchenwald, the concen—"

"Buchenwald!" As Sheldon said it, Will realized he had pronounced the name incorrectly. "I have been to the Buchenwald Memorial. It was one of the oldest and deadliest of the camps. Elie Wiesel wrote about his time there. I remember you saying your father was in Europe."

"Dad never talked about it, but I think he was proud of what his unit accomplished over there. But my mom was the talker in our family."

"Your mother was a good woman," Sheldon said. "I remember one Halloween—what did they call the night then? Devil's Night--our windows got soaped. It wasn't such a bad thing in itself, but someone soaped swastikas and "go home, Jew" on one window. The next day, your brother and a kid across the street—Danny McPhail—they were scraping soap from our windows."

"Huh? Al and Dan soaped swastikas on your house?"

"No! But Al said your mother made them clean it up."

"I don't remember that," Will said. "Al and Dan were innocent? But my mom didn't want your family to have to deal with the mess."

"I think your mother was embarrassed for us," Sheldon said. "She wanted the swastikas removed regardless of the guilty party. My mother never forgot that."

"She suffered, didn't she, Elena, during the war?"

"You know she suffered, Will. You have always been aware of her injury."

"Yeah, well, I heard she was in a camp. And I could see . . . her time in the war affected her."

"I thought it strange that you often referred to my mother by her first name."

"Elena," Will said.

"But you were not on a first name basis with her. Did you ever actually speak to her?" Sheldon mopped his brow with his napkin and finished his water. Will sensed that he was irritated, all these years later. *I'd been disrespectful. Too familiar. But I was fascinated by that woman.*

"Your brother spoke of her as Elena," Will said, "I thought that made it okay."

"It was okay, Will. It just seemed . . . my brother had no boundaries whatsoever. He still has no filter for anything that comes into head. Our father called her Elena, so Melvin followed suit."

"I was immature, Sheldon."

"As was I. We came up in that wonderful white world of Cloverlawn, and we had yet to discover that it was—that it, and we, had problems.

"Oak Park was Little Israel, Shel, and I imagined your mother was, like, an example of all that went down under Hitler. But no one talked about any of that back then. My dad used to say that the world had gone crazy, but in the fifties? Everyone was trying to forget."

"You and I were friends," Will continued. "Still are. And you know I was . . . interested in your mom. To me, she was a . . . a saint." Will almost said martyr. He wondered if Jews had martyrs. Or saints.

They were quiet for a time. Sheldon pulled his wallet from his pocket and examined the bill.

"Sheldon, do you think I considered your mother to be a curiosity? A freak? Because I--"

"She was a freak!" He said it with undisguised anger. "She'd been traumatized by seeing her parents and her brother, and many others, led to their deaths. She spent two of her teenage years in a concentration camp."

"I . . .."

"She shoveled dirt over mutilated corpses, Will."

"I sort of . . . guessed . . . I'm sorry."

"I didn't know the details myself, not until I was in my thirties. She was a walking case of PTSD. How neurotic she was! How unlike a mother, how unable to be there for me. And for Melvin and our father. And even though my mother grew, and our relationship became more intimate, I know that her paranoia, her self-absorption, shaped me. Thinking about those days saddens me."

Sheldon sipped his water, wiped his lips and his brow with his napkin, before continuing.

"You were my only real non-Jewish friend from those days on Cloverlawn, Will, but for many Jews the war was not spoken about with outsiders. It was rarely talked about in our own families."

"The elephant in the room. We were all trying to forget," Will said. "My father fought in Europe. My parents never talked about the war. No wonder my father drank. But, my God, what Elena—your mother—what she lost! I didn't know about any of that, but I imagined as much."

"It was not only my mother, Will. My parents tried to shield Melvin and me, but the silence only created distance. They tried to block it out and see the upside, that they were fortunate to survive the war and emigrate to this country. Before I got into my teens, it dawned on me that I have almost no extended family."

"I see. But Elena grew? I mean, later?"

"Eventually, speaking honestly about her past became her therapy. In the early '80s, just before they left Cloverlawn, Denise and I were visiting from St. Louis, where I'd been teaching. Such a time it was! My father was ill, and Mel was in the Oakland County Jail, picked up with stolen property. Oh, that kid! One night, after Denise had flown back to Missouri, my mother—Elena, if you will— and I had a long conversation about . . . everything.

"I think her healing began with Vera, a woman from Cleveland who she had worked with in a forced labor camp in Poland. Vera was Catholic. Somehow, Vera found my mother in Michigan, and they began a correspondence. Elena--my mother--showed me some of Vera's letters, dating back to 1979 and '80. These letters prompted my mother to visit Vera. Later, she joined a group from her synagogue. They were all Holocaust survivors, sharing their stories."

"Elena was a survivor," Will said.

"But she was, as you say, wounded. Traumatized. And you may have been the only one outside of my family who was interested. I think the kids on Cloverlawn, as well as their parents, were afraid of her. Afraid of my family." He drained the remains of his water and raised his glass in petition to a passing waitress.

"Afraid? Maybe," Will said. "Maybe there was fear on both sides. Caution."

"Yes. My mother may have fostered that fear, if that is what it was. She did not want Melvin or me to get familiar with the neighborhood goyyum. Maybe she thought we would be bullied."

"Those swastikas. Did you ever find out who soaped you?"

"No. We had suspicions, but we never voiced them. We knew it was not you Millers. Sometimes Mel or I heard comments. As ugly as they were, I sensed they came from kids who did not understand what they were saying. I was more afraid of those who they got their ideas from: their parents, their teachers. My parents worried for Mel and me. But I think their fear was, in part, residue from their past lives in Europe."

"So, your mom was in a work camp . . .."

"Her neurosis didn't come from nothing."

"Again, I'm sorry she suffered. And your father . . .."

"Jozef. He had a story to tell, too."

4

As August became September, Will stuck to his routines. He would rise around seven a.m. and have a light workout before washing up and dressing for the day. He might have eggs and toast or granola. Then he would walk, and would often stop at Kava Korner.

On one cool September morning, he was restless. He sat at his usual corner table at the Korner. He had brought another novel, a modern Western, but it did not interest him. He read a few pages, and then a whole paragraph without comprehension. He closed the cover and looked up, surveying the shop's clientele: an obese woman in her twenties eating a muffin with her coffee; a man selecting a dozen donuts, probably for his office mates; a few students or home office types at their laptops; several young men dressed in suits, discussing business—finance, it sounded like—in a booth. Will looked, concealing his longing for the woman behind the counter, the beautiful co-owner, Grace. Her husband Tim was in the back room. *That lucky dog,* Will thought.

Grace seemed to always be smiling. Will suspected she was beautiful inside as well as outside, as Joan had been. Joan was not the type to camp out before a mirror. She wore little makeup and bought her clothes at thrift shops. It seemed to Will that she had an inner confidence or poise that was matched by a serene expression and relaxed posture.

And he had always known that she loved him. He wished that she was seated across from him now. The wish was a mix of longing and regret. *I could have loved you better,* he almost said aloud.

He thought of his children. A daughter, Teresa, lived on the other side of town. A bright, funny woman, divorced with no children, who had always been very close to Joan, but not so much to Will. Terry was a producer at the local public radio affiliate. Her friends seemed to be intellectuals and artists with whom he had little in common. Will's role was to keep Teresa's home, which she shared with another woman, in good repair. He called her once a month and maintained a friendly if not deep or intimate fatherly relationship.

Since Joan's death, one tradition Will and Teresa kept was an annual outing around Christmastime to a restaurant of Terry's choosing, often an older established diner, nothing too fancy or pricy. But Will had not been in contact with Teresa since he tore up his hand while assembling her lawn shed.

His youngest son, James, was a single dad, a math instructor at the community college in Flint. He had recently finished his PhD dissertation and would be accepting a position at Stanford if he could bring himself to take the plunge on a career move to the West Coast. It had been a few weeks since Will had driven to Flint to see James and his daughter, Hazel.

An older son in Connecticut, Patrick, was a busy lawyer with a wife and three grown children. Pat had invited Will for Thanksgiving, but Will, worried that his poor vision and declining reflexes were a warning against driving, was undecided. He had a serious aversion to flying.

Will often disagreed with his kids about history, religion, politics, and life issues in general. Pat and Teresa thought of him as "old school" to a fault; they pointed to things they thought were inconsistencies in his reasoning. Will had given up defending the Vietnam War, but always maintained some contempt for the "do-gooders" and "peaceniks" who protested it. And while his union job always gave him a decent living and good retirement benefits, he often ranted about union excesses. Will's contentiousness often contrasted with Joan's always loving, approving, nurturing, openness.

Will's brother, three years older, lived alone in a seniors' apartment in Traverse City. Al was eighty, a widower, getting feeble and losing his memory. He had telephoned Al on Labor Day. "How is Susan?" Al had asked. Will had to remind him that their sister had died of cancer a few years before.

He had work to do in the garage. Bicycle parts—a chain and a set of bushings for a waiting project—had arrived the previous day. But the bike could wait. *I don't want to be alone*, he thought, sitting amidst the hubbub at the Korner. He could stop in on his neighbor, a sweet lady whose husband had died some months earlier, but he sensed that this woman wanted more than the friendly chat he had in mind. Another neighbor, a retired shop rat like himself, was rebuilding a 350 Chevy engine in his garage. The guy would offer Will a Bud, and they might analyze yesterday's Lions' victory. But no, not today.

Will finished his coffee, then dialed Sheldon's number.
"That you, Shel? It's Will."
"Good to hear from you."
"Got plans for lunch today?"
They agreed to meet at the Coolidge.

*****

Oak Park had become more multicultural since the old Little Israel days. Will saw no yarmulkes on his ride to the Coolidge. He passed a group of Black school children and a bakery with Arabic writing on the storefront sign. The Star, a Jewish bakery that he remembered from his earliest childhood, was still in business.

The Coolidge was only a few miles for both Will and Sheldon, coming from different directions. It was a busy place with a mixed clientele, but it was quiet enough for conversation, and the specials were inexpensive. Will liked the Chili with onions.

Sheldon Weiss, the man sitting across from him, had serious bags under his eyes, a blotchy complexion, and an obesity issue. Will feared for Sheldon's eating habits. On this day in mid-September, Will opted for the Chili. Sheldon had a cheese omelet with hash browns and lots of salt, a side of bacon, and white toast. Will waited until after they finished eating. Then it came out.

"How is your health, Sheldon?"

"Very good. Why?"

"Just askin'. I had my annual checkup last week at the VA. I came out okay, but they want to put me on a cholesterol med. And the eye doctor wrote me a scrip for new glasses. Did I tell you I have a retina problem?" Will hoped that by revealing himself, he could prompt Sheldon to do the same.

"I didn't know," Sheldon said. "Is it serious?"

"Not yet, but it's a degenerative thing. I've been getting eye injections from time to time."

"Ouch. That must hurt."

"Yeah, but they say it helps. Along with a special vitamin and diet routine."

"That's good. You always seemed to be in great shape, Will. And the meds will help lower your cholesterol. I've been taking them for twenty-five years."

Will remembered Joan's cautions over cholesterol meds. He had not made up his mind about them, and his cholesterol was not high enough to dwell on it. He was more curious about Sheldon.

"You're otherwise in good health?" he asked.

"Oh, I have my aches and pains." Sheldon did not seem eager to elaborate, but Will waited. "I have a heart doctor, a pulmonary specialist, a urologist, and, let's see, an EENT doctor, And an optometrist. I am lucky to have good insurance for all that."

Will resisted the temptation to give advice. Over the years, Joan had become health conscious. He thought about how she had not only saved his life during darker times, before they were married, but she also took care of him and taught him to care for himself. Some of Joan's habits of diet, exercise, and sleep had become Will's habits and had served him well.

Something else had been on his mind. He thought, later, that it was why he had called Sheldon that morning. He did not want to come out and ask about Elena. He knew that Sheldon had complex feelings about her. He knew also that Sheldon was sensitive about his continued interest in her.

So he asked about Melvin.

"Melvin means well, but he has never been able to walk a straight and narrow path. He's a golem."

"Golem. A no-account?"

"Forgive my judgment, Will. But yes, I worry about him."

"When we were kids," Will began, "there was a certain charm to his . . . offbeat sense of humor. He would crack up for reasons that only he was aware of."

"Yes, that shrieky laugh was his default. But I think as he got into his twenties and it was time to make a living, get stable, all that, he did not have it in him. He could become homeless if he doesn't take better care of the Cloverlawn house."

"That house is in sore need of a roof, Sheldon."

"I have a roofer lined up for next month."

"Last I knew, Mel was hanging out at Family Rec," Will said.

"Melvin was a poor snooker player, but he did not go there to play. He would hang with these punks who he considered friends. If he was not there, he was playing the horses."

"I would see him at Hazel Park Raceway back in high school."

"How did he get in? How did you get in? I thought you needed to be twenty-one."

"It was easy. Kids would find an old guy to walk through the gate with." Sometimes on a summer evening Will and Chuck, and sometimes John Derry or Dan McPhail, would find a free place to park and a discarded racing form, buy a ticket or two for the last few races, and try to build on their few dollars. They played favorites and their favorite jockeys. They rarely won much, but they did not lose much, either.

Will continued, "I once saw Melvin scooping discarded tickets from the floor. Some bettors would drop a ticket if the payout line was long, or if the payout was only a dollar or two."

"I believe it," Sheldon said. "But when he got older and began making real money, he'd blow a paycheck at the track."

"He never grew up, did he?"

"Not really, and the only people who accepted him were *shtunk*, you know, punks, stinkers. Guys who either were not making a living or making it illegally. Shysters, petty thieves, misfits. I hate to say it, but Mel is on probation."

"Wow. At his age? What . . .?"

"Check kiting."

"Sorry to hear that."

"All I ask is he should take care of the Cloverlawn house and pay the taxes on it. I know the condition it's in, but the guy does not seem to have any pride. He does not eat well or take good care of himself. He is too old to be neglecting his health."

"Mel was a skinny kid," Will said. While Sheldon was always pudgy, his brother was his opposite.

"You should see him now," said Sheldon. "Weighs about 120 pounds, sopping wet."

"And he's retired now. On Social Security?"

"Yes. But his best job ever was stock boy in the produce department at Dexter-Davison Market."

"I worked there in high school and first year of college." His only year of college. Dexter-Davison had the best selection of kosher foods for miles around. Will remembered that the Jewish store owner and managers were suspicious of non-Jewish employees. They would double-check Will's counts of grocery stock, singling him out as a possible risk for theft. "I was long gone by the time Mel worked there."

"He worked at Dexter for five or six years. Then when they merged with Farmer Jack, the new management laid him off. He moved on to a couple of janitorial jobs at delis and diners. Katz's, Zuckerman's—remember Hy's?"

"Hy Horenstein's Deli. Sure. Hy kicked me out for life."

Sheldon laughed. "For life! You could not pay your tab?"

"It wasn't that. One of the waitresses accused me, John Derry, and Gary Braun and I-don't-know-who-else of stealing her tip. We had been playing poker, nickel-dime, and we counted our change on the table. We were punks, but we didn't steal tips. Hy stood at the door until we were out of there. He told us not to come back."

"Banned, at sixteen!" Sheldon said, laughing.

"Uh-huh. But Hy eventually forgot about it."

"Or he began to see you as a paying customer. Hy didn't much care for Mel, either. I think he worked there a year or two. When my father died, that was kind of the end for Mel. My parents always tried to help him. And no one ever loved him like my Dad did. Mel does not really have anyone now."

"He has you, Sheldon. Your dad? I only knew him as the guy who pulled in and out of your driveway every day. I don't think we ever made eye contact."

"His name was Jozef. Jozef Weiss. Yes, he kept to himself, but he was tzaddik, a saint. He did not live for himself, but for my mother and Melvin and me."

"Sounds like he was tied down."

"If you knew my father, you would have known that he was his own man. He had a strong sense of family, but that did not define him. He knew himself. Before he came to this country, he spent almost three years alone, holed up in a tool shed, working fifteen acres of land, alone."

"That sounds like solitary confinement," Will said.

"*Badad* is a Hebrew word for solitude that has a double meaning, Will. It can indicate, say, being ostracized or even banned from the community. It can also be a spiritual exercise. A purification ritual, if you will."

"What was it for your father?"

"I believe it was both. Surely Jozef suffered. He told me about the unpleasant conditions, to say the least, of his ordeal. But he got visitors from time to time. And his confinement saved him from—well, it saved his life."

"So he was a victim of the war, too."

"There were millions of victims, Will. But my father was also a survivor."

5

A week later, Will and Sheldon sat in the same booth at the Coolidge Café. They had already shared news about family and had reminisced about Cloverlawn.

"Your dad," Will said. "You said he had a story to tell. Was he hiding from the Germans?"

"The Soviets, then the Nazis. His experience was very much like my mother's. And like Elena, he shared the details with me, but not until his last years."

"I wish I'd known him. You said his name was Jozef. How did he meet Elena?"

"That part comes later. I did some investigating and some writing about my family after my parents died. I should tell you . . ." Sheldon hesitated, caught the waitress's attention, asked for more coffee and water. "Because both my parents suffered great trauma during the war, some of that got passed down to Melvin and myself. I can tell you I had lots of anxiety as a child. I was confused and insecure, like my mother. Part of *my* healing has been to understand who my parents were, how they suffered. So I compiled their stories. In this way I learned compassion for them and for myself."

"I can understand this, Mel. I know a bit about PTSD."

"Yes. You're a Vietnam Veteran. You might also know that many of the children of holocaust survivors, and perhaps some war veterans, are predisposed to anxiety. This has been borne out in studies. I believe Melvin and I fit into that category."

"Sure. It makes sense." Although he had never been diagnosed, Will had his own struggle with PTSD. He shared much of his Vietnam experience with Joan, and at her suggestion he once joined a therapy group through the Veterans Administration. He saw healing in that group, and was humbled by the honesty of many ex-

GIs, but reticence about sharing himself got in his way. Sitting across from Sheldon now, he was eager to change the subject.

"So . . . Jozef," he said. "I never knew his first name until the last time I saw you."

"Elena called him Joe," Sheldon said. "He grew up near Lviv, which was then part of eastern Poland."

"But it's an important city in Ukraine now," Will said.

"Yes, and the Russians are again at war there, eh? My father had a younger sister named Pen, or Penelopa. Well, after the Nazis invaded Poland, Russia was still in control of the area around Lviv. Joe's father--my grandfather---foresaw that war between Russia and Germany over Poland was coming. He sent my father and his mother and sister to Lithuania, which was thought to be safer. My grandfather stayed with the farm, at first. So at sixteen, my father was responsible for his mother, whose name was Nakia, and Pen.

"They went to Vilna, which at that time was called 'the Jerusalem of Lithuania' because it had, and I emphasize the past tense, a thriving Jewish culture. Schools, hospitals, and synagogues."

"Are you referring to Vilnius?"

"Yes. Vilnius was Vilna. Eventually the family found a room in a poor Jewish neighborhood in Vilna. After a few months of relative peace, rumors of a Russian occupation forced Joe to leave the city because he feared conscription into the Soviet army. He got work on a farm. He said it was not far from Vilna, where he could visit Nakia and Pen.

"In June 1940 the Soviets took control of Lithuania. They claimed that Lithuania *chose* to join the Soviet republics, but that was a lie. Most Lithuanians hated Communism and wanted to remain an independent state. The Soviets forced many Jews to join the Communist Party or be deported. So, thousands of Jews in Lithuania were sent off to Siberia. But some escaped."

"Joe escaped?"

"I'm getting to that. Nakia, like most Jews in Vilna, opted to join the Communist Party."

"But only to save herself."

"Yes, and her daughter. Pen was about twelve. Joe refused to join, but before the Soviets got around to finding him and deporting him, the Germans invaded. That was in June of 1941. So the Soviets were out, and the Germans were welcomed as liberators."

"I know what happens next."

"Yes. The Nazis persuaded the non-Jews that the Jews were to blame for the Soviet invasion."

It's those damn kikes, dad would say, Will thought. *I heard plenty of Jew-blaming from my own father.*

"So," Sheldon continued, "what happened next was mass executions of Jews, and many non-Jewish Lithuanians were willing collaborators."

"How . . .?

"Propaganda, Will." Sheldon drank eagerly from his water glass, and wiped at his mouth with a napkin. "The Soviet occupation had been *lethal.* Stalin sent tens of thousands to camps in Siberia. And the Jews were said to be aligned with the Soviets.

"So, early in the occupation," Sheldon continued, "the Nazis rounded up 5,000 Vilna Jewish men. They were to be sent to a work camp."

"But they weren't . . .." *Here it comes*, Will thought.

"They were taken to a place. It was in the country." Sheldon took a breath before continuing. "They were executed one by one, Will. Buried in mass graves. Next, the Nazis set up a ghetto. It was for the 'safety' of the remaining Jews."

As Sheldon spat out the word "safety," Will could not have missed that his friend's agitation was growing. A lecturer by trade, Sheldon could normally speak calmly and authoritatively about the

Holocaust story and the war story, but this was his father's story. Jozef Weiss's story.

"When I think of a ghetto, I think of the old Black Bottom in Detroit, or Watts in LA, or Harlem," Will said.

This put Sheldon back into lecture mode. "The term 'ghetto' goes back to Italy in the 16th century, Will. Ghettos were designated areas for Jews in Venice. By modern times, 'ghetto' became synonymous for Jewish areas all over Europe. But ghettos could also be towns, villages. Goring, the general who set up Nazi policy in Europe, wanted to cordon off areas to separate Jews from the population. The Warsaw Ghetto—"

"I've read about that ghetto."

"It was the largest. It held almost a half-million people. Germany set up over a thousand ghettos in Europe."

"So, Nakia and Pen were still trapped in this ghetto in Lithuania?"

"Yes. Nothing and no one could enter. Or leave. Nakia and Pen were cut off. Cut off from Joe. I've read and heard stories about that area. No food, bad water. Garbage piles so high, Will," Sheldon took a breath and paused, "so high that they blocked windows. No way to dispose of human *shit*. More rats than people!"

"I . . .."

"Only a few hundred Jews survived that hell-hole, Will. In April of '43, Himmler ordered it to be liquidated. Joe heard that Nakia and Pen had been sent to a camp. It was a death camp In Estonia."

"My God! What about his father?"

"My grandfather . . . I want you to know his name. Anszel Weiss. When the farm became unsafe, he escaped to the mountains. The mountains in the south of Poland were only loosely controlled by the Soviets and later the Nazis, who were more interested in farmland. But Anszel was never heard from again. No one found out what happened to him."

A waitress appeared. Sheldon, out of coffee and water again, ordered more. He had calmed down, but was slumped, elbows on the table, staring at his empty cup.

"Your grandparents. Your aunt," Will said.

"There were others. In my extended family."

"But Joe. He was safe on this farm?"

"Jozef Weiss, my dear father, stayed on the farm. The Soviets had confiscated it and split it up, giving shares to local peasants. When the Nazis took over, Joe was in danger of being killed or sent to the Vilna ghetto, but the Nazis were more interested in confiscating crops than searching the more productive farms for Jews.

"The original owner of the farm, who still had control of almost half of his redistributed land, put Joe, always the hardest worker on any crew, in an outbuilding on the far end of his property, near a wooded area and a creek. This shed—it had one tiny window and a large sliding door—was used to store farm equipment. That is where Joe lived from spring of '42, when the Vilna ghetto was established, until late '44. The farmer assigned him a section of the property, ten or fifteen acres, to grow lentils. He spent over two and a half years there, in near-isolation."

"And in fear of capture," Will added.

"I must stop drinking coffee," Shel said, raising his water glass for more. "Denise has an app on *her* phone for monitoring *my* caffeine intake."

"That's love, Shel."

"It's control."

"That, too."

"In telling you all this about my father, I'm thinking about the baggage he left Europe with. The losses. His parents. His sister. Other relatives and friends from Poland. Those years in the shed. And the sense of life that he came to America with, that he nurtured his family with. He never spoke openly about his ordeal. I had to pry it out of him.

"Wow," Will said, temporarily speechless. "He and your mother were my next-door neighbors on Cloverlawn. Little did anyone in my family know what they went through."

"You said your father was in the war, Will. Didn't he earn a Siver Star? Did he ever explain to you what it was for? And did he talk about his time in Europe?"

"No. He told me that he was at the Bulge. But I did some research on Silver Star recipients in the Third Army. Dad's name was not on the list, and I never saw the medal, so I don't know what to make of it."

"And he liberated Buchenwald," Sheldon added.

"There was that." But Will did not want to talk about Buchenwald. "I know that the war left a mark on my father. I think it made him angry. I wish he and I could have talked about all that."

"Jozef was no talker, either, as you know, but once he got started, he wanted me to know. He was always conscious, I think, that his life was an incredible gift, that any inconvenience, any problem, would be an opportunity. He never complained."

"You were lucky to be his son, Shel."

"I was. Joe survived the war, but by the time the Soviets were back in control . . . by 1945 . . .," Sheldon took a gulp of water, paused for it to clear his throat, "Lithuania had lost 95 percent of its Jewish population."

Will could see that the conversation was wearing on his friend, but he wanted to know more. "Did Joe go back to Poland?"

"He did. He was eighteen, I think, by then. He returned to a village that was empty of Jews. No one had heard from his father. A family of non-Jews had taken over his family's house and farm. The Soviets set up a legal process for recovery of lost property, but it involved bribery, Dad said. And it was time-consuming.

"So he filed the petition for the land and went to Lviv, which became part of Ukraine after the war. He said the language was not much of a barrier there because both the Poles and Ukrainians spoke a mix of eastern and western Slavic.

"He got a job as a helper in a butcher shop. That's where he learned the trade that he worked for the rest of his life."

"What about his petition to recover the farm?"

"He never got an answer."

"Is that where he met Elena? Lviv?" Will tried to pronounce it the way Sheldon had.

"I know, you want to know about my mother. Yes, they met in Lviv. But I need to get home. My mother's family's story is for another time."

Elena's was the story I'd hoped to hear today, Will mused.

The Coolidge was nearly empty. Waitresses were refilling salt and pepper shakers. Someone was noisily putting up dishes in the kitchen. Sheldon was drained. And his narrative had left Will all but speechless.

6

And then it was early October. Will had not been very productive of late. He watched his football Lions, who were on a rare tear. He painted the bathroom and tinkered in the garage, where a bicycle rebuild could always wait for another day. In the storage room and in a closet, a weeding project awaited him. Boxes and bags of Joan's possessions needed to be sold, donated, recycled, or, God forbid, trashed. This was the job that Will had been putting off. He would rather do anything else.

A few weeks before, his daughter-in-law out East had posted a poem on Facebook that began:

I know, you never intended to be in this world.
But you're in it all the same.
So why not get started immediately.
I mean, belonging to it.

Will was not your typical reader of poetry, but these lines, and those to follow, had stopped him. He wrote down the whole poem and put it in a desk drawer.

The poet went on to ask the reader to bless everything in the world. Notice it all, bless it all. The world is waiting, she said, and asked,

"Do you need a little darkness to get you going?"
Let me be as urgent as a knife, then,
and remind you of Keats,
so single of purpose and thinking, for a while,
he had a lifetime

Was she (the poet's name was Mary Oliver) speaking to a young person? At first Will thought so. But as he read on it became clear both the poet and Will's daughter-in-law, Pat's wife Jill, were speaking to him. Telling him, first, to belong. Not only to belong, but to bless everything—whatever that meant. Then to get off his butt and do something. He was reminded of the remark Sheldon had made about "beholding the world." Will had been puzzled by that idea. But the poet suggested to him that perhaps belonging to the world might begin with blessing it, holding it close, beholding it.

On his walk that early autumn day, Will counted steps, planned his day, and chatted with neighbors. But he also wondered about this man Keats, who thought he had a lifetime. Someone who died young. On returning home, he climbed the driveway to his rear door.

The two bushes along the garage wall were no longer green, but red—not red, but a shade of red, like a cranberry or a burgundy or dark grape. There were little clusters of dark berries. He had seen these berries—when? Every year, probably. But he had never *looked* at them. He pulled one off and chewed on it. Not very tasty, and he wondered if he would be sick from it.

Will had helped Joan plant those bushes a few years before she died. She had told him the name—it sounded Latin, he remembered—and why she wanted them in that spot: she could see them from the kitchen window. She delighted in watching them grow and change. But they often outgrew the space they were planted in, and needed to be hacked at and snipped several times every year to be kept from blocking his garage windows and taking over the entire wall. Other than trimming them, keeping them in control, Will had never noticed them.

He stepped back about ten feet and looked again, and smiled. Some branches poked up much longer than others. And the garage window was blocked again as the bushes grew wide and tall. But Will shook his head and stood and looked. He could almost see his wife in those bushes. Joan was smiling, too.

*****

On the 7th, a Saturday, Will drove up to Flint to watch the Michigan vs. Minnesota game with his son. James was an avid football and Wolverine fan. But Will was very interested in James's thinking about the Stanford offer. After all, this was an opportunity that his son might never have again. While he considered himself to be a good listener, Will hoped that James would ask for his opinion on the matter. James had told Will that Hazel, his fifteen-year-old granddaughter, would be away on a class hiking trip. Will was looking forward to the private time with James.

Michigan was way ahead by halftime, so James changed the channel.

"Hamas terrorists have launched a surprise attack upon Israel!" a news bulletin announced.

"Really!" James said, rising from his chair. Will was too stunned to speak.

"Forty people are known to be dead. Hamas has taken hostages."

James changed the station to CNN for more information.

"Israeli Prime Minister Netanyahu has announced that Israel is now at war with the militant group Hamas, which was thought to be dormant."

The football game was forgotten. As the afternoon passed, Will and James learned that the attack involved both rockets and armed gunmen, and that over 1000 Israelis, mostly civilians, some of them babies, were brutally slain. Over 200 were taken captive. The attack came on the anniversary of the Yom Kippur War of 1973. The world, especially the Hebrew world, was in shock. Israeli leaders swore that the consequences for Hamas would be great.

Will told James about his childhood friend Sheldon. "He has people over there. He'll be worried about them. And worried for Israel."

The game and the terrorist attack had given James an excuse to avoid discussing his thoughts about Stanford. Watching the disturbing images of the attack on television put that conversation on hold. On the drive back to Royal Oak, Will texted Sheldon: *I am following the news and thinking about you and Denise. I'll call soon.*

He called Sheldon the following night.

"How are you? How is your family?" Will asked.

"Thank you, my friend," Sheldon said. "Denise is concerned about her brother and his children who live in the south of Israel, not far from where the fighters crossed the border. And I have friends at universities in Tel Aviv and Haifa. So far, we hear that everyone is safe."

"Good. I've been watching the reports. It looks like Israel is punishing those bastards."

"I know this is war, Will, but I do not understand how punishing the people of Gaza will win a war against terror or bring back prisoners. You were in Vietnam. You know what a war against guerilla fighters is all about. They have ways of blending in with ordinary people. There must be a stern answer from Israel, but I do not believe that Hamas will be deterred by attacks on the people of Gaza."

"But if Israel doesn't get to the terrorists through the ordinary people they blend in with, how will they win this war?" Will asked. The siege of Gaza promised to stop supplies of food, water, and electricity to several million residents.

"The enemy is bigger than terror," Sheldon said. "I fear that indiscriminate bombing of the people of Gaza will fail. There needs to be human connection with the neighbor. In this case, education and commerce and basic human relationship can bring our adversary closer. Otherwise, the fighting will never end. So . . . I am praying for peace. That may sound naïve to you, Will, because Hamas is truly a ruthless and unforgiving enemy. But we need to break through the bombs and the ignorance."

Will had expected to hear his friend express anger, but Sheldon's comments stopped him.

"If you want to get together, Shel--If you want to talk, let me know and I will meet you."

"Thank you, Will. I'll get back to you when I can. We'll do lunch at the Coolidge."

7

Israel's military was telling the inhabitants of Gaza City to evacuate, to make way for a coming ground offensive. Meanwhile, the city was being levelled by bombs. By the end of the first week, Gaza's death toll was close to 2,000. Residents were fleeing south toward Egypt. A humanitarian crisis was well underway. Meanwhile, the toll of dead in Israel had risen to 1400, and Hamas was still holding over 200 prisoners, some of them Americans. Fears of a wider war involving Iran and other Arab states were mounting.

One afternoon that week, Will returned to Flint. James had not yet decided about the Stanford offer. He had once told Will that his student reviews were not very good, and that teaching was difficult for him. Will knew that James was never a personable guy, but he wanted this job for him.

He knew his son to be good and fair. And brilliant. James had been a quirky kid, never very popular with peers and just average in his high school studies, but he had an early and obvious ability with numbers and games that he developed in college and beyond. And now his genius in mathematics was recognized by Stanford. The clincher, for Will, was that the position was research-heavy and did not require a full load of teaching: perfect for his son.

Will knew nothing more about Stanford than that their football team won the Rose Bowl a few years back. But when he mentioned his son's job offer, a neighbor told him that Stanford had one of the best mathematics programs in the country, which made Will proud.

His granddaughter, Hazel, opened the door. "Dad isn't home. He called to say he had work to do in school. But I think he's with his girlfriend."

Will was glad to see Hazel. She had common sense, and an authentic way of speaking, while her father, he feared, lacked in both sense and speech. She was not afraid to have opinions. And share them.

"I think Dad's gonna blow it," she said after they had got seated, and after she had turned her music volume down to an acceptable level.

"You mean, he's not taking the Stanford job? Last time we talked, you were planning on California in January."

"I gave that man more credit than he deserves. But he's caving, Gramps. He's under the spell of a wicked woman."

Will laughed.

"It's not funny, man. I mean, Deb does not care about Dad. She's too lazy to get off her ass and—sorry, her fanny—and take a flier on the West Coast."

"How much time before he needs to let them know?"

"I don't know. A few days. It sucks."

They watched one of Hazel's TV shows. Will was put off by the emotionally intelligent characters and their snarky, over-his-head dialog, while his granddaughter seemed to be able to enjoy the show and fiddle with her cellphone at the same time.

He left before his son returned because he did not want to make the drive back to Royal Oak after dark. He felt that his vision was good enough, at least in his one good eye, but at night, not so much. On the way down I-75, he got a call from James.

"Sorry I missed you, Dad."

"I thought you might want to talk about Stanford."

"Hazel told me so, but I'm, uh, not ready to get into that. Not yet. I'm working on it, Dad. Trying to see my way through it. Can I give you a call in a few days?"

"Do you realize the chance you have here, son? You told me about Stanford's reputation, and the work you'll be doing there. What's the holdup?"

"Dad, wait. Please! You don't understand—"

"James, listen to me. Don't throw this opportunity away. Think of your future. Think of the chance to display your gifts. To share them."

"I can't listen to this, Dad. You are the last person I want to talk with about this stuff right now because you'll only want to have your way about it."

"That's not true." It was true.

"I'm hanging up."

*****

Sheldon met Will at the Coolidge the following Wednesday for a late lunch. Will noticed that Sheldon's razor had missed a spot on his chin. They made small talk while Will ordered a turkey sandwich on a croissant, and Sheldon put in for two chili dogs with the cheesy fries. After Sheldon squeezed a generous amount of ketchup on dogs and fries, Will asked, "How are you, Shel?"

"Thanks for asking. I'm fine. But most of my attention lately has been on this Gaza war. My wife found out from a cousin that her family is safe. I also heard from my old colleague in Haifa. He is also well, but he says everyone is very concerned."

"What's gonna happen? I mean, how do you see this thing ending?"

"It has been only a week and a half, but we know Israel can wipe Gaza and its people off the map, Will. It has the means to do this, and I fear that this response to the Hamas attack is only the beginning. But the Palestinian will to be free cannot be wiped out. And Iran is already making trouble in the region. It's a very unstable situation."

"And the hostages?"

"Hostages are not of value to Hamas, but they are only a bargaining chip. We can only pray that negotiations for their safety will continue. I want to see a cease-fire and a dialog. But I'm afraid Israel's government will not move in that direction."

Will noticed Sheldon's lapel pin, which he took off and showed to him. It was a shield. Old, with a long stick pin. "My mother—Elena, if you will—gave it to me. It belonged to her father. She said it was her only connection to him." He paused, looked down at the Star. "It was said that this shield belonged to David of the Old Testament. The six points of the shield signify north, south, east, west, the heavens, and the underworld. David's shield was his faith in God, protecting him in every direction."

"I can see why it would have been important to her," Will said. "The family connection. But the protection, too."

"Then, as now," Sheldon said. "But I see you, too, are wearing a medal of some sort." A chain was visible on Will's neck.

"I am," said Will. He reached into his polo shirt and pulled out a cross. "It's called a four-way cross. My wife bought it for me, long time ago." He disconnected it from its chain and handed it across the table to Sheldon.

"I see Jesus, I think, at the top. Who are the others?"

"Let's see," Will said. He took the medal back and examined it, unsure if he could remember the other figures. Joan had given him the medal twenty years or so ago. Since then, he had always worn it, but he never much thought about the figures represented on it.

"And that's, uh, the Blessed Virgin on the bottom. The sides are, let's see, maybe that's Jesus's father Joseph on the left, and I'm not sure about the other guy." The other guy was holding a staff; the Christ child sat on his shoulder.

"I believe that is Saint Christopher."

"Of course!" Will said. "My dad had a Christopher magnet on the dash of our family Ford."

"It's very nice," Sheldon said. "I think the cross is the most recognizable image in the Christian Church."

"Yeah, it's everywhere," Will agreed.

"And it seems to have served you well. I would say you have been blessed."

"Well, I had Joan. Now I have the kids and grandkids. My oldest son is a successful lawyer in New Haven. He has a beautiful wife and four great kids. I'm gonna visit them Thanksgiving weekend, I think." This was not true. Will had been invited out East, but had recently decided not to go.

"And another son will be a professor at Stanford. He's a brilliant guy with a fine teenage daughter. And then my daughter Teresa. She is a producer for a radio station downtown, a very accomplished woman. And that's about it."

After he spoke, he reached for his water and took a long swallow.

"You are a lucky man, Will. You've done some things right."

"Well, I had Joan. And we did okay."

Will never said anything about his father's temper or alcohol abuse, or his mother's inability to confront his father. Nothing about his decent but messy upbringing. Nothing about his problems during or after Vietnam. Nothing about his struggles as a husband and family man, or the tensions in his relationships with his kids. Nothing about wounds or losses, or little deaths.

8

They finished eating. More coffee came, which Sheldon accepted. Will declined, but he saw an opening for the question that had been on his mind since Sheldon came back into his life.

He hesitated, then said, "You told me your mother got some, uh, healing after she reunited with a girl from a work camp during the war. And you said she told you about it, the war, and what she went through. That her healing changed your relationship with her. I've been wondering about all that."

"I know. You've always been curious about my mother, haven't you? I began to tell you, but it is difficult to speak about, even though it's not my story. But I'm a product of my mother's story . . . as are my children . . . and even my grandchildren. The wounds get carried across generations. Over time and space."

Sheldon leaned forward and spoke. "It was not only the Jews, Will. Hitler also saw Slavs, Gypsies, Africans, gays, the disabled, and even many Catholics, as the *Untermensch*, the less-than-human. He wanted his own countrymen to settle and farm the rich fields of Poland and Ukraine, of Eastern Europe. That my mother's friend, Vera, was Catholic was not the problem for the Nazis, but she was a representative of the Catholic Youth League in her town, which was demonized by the Reich. Clerics or students or anyone who might oppose Nazism were a threat."

"So." Sheldon paused, dabbed his brow with a napkin. "Let me tell you about my mother, Elena--her last name was Gabo."

"Elena Gabo."

"Yes. She grew up in the Ukraine, near the Polish border. I swear, Will, between the Ukrainians and Poles, I do not know who suffered more. And the punishment came alternately from Russia and Germany. First it was Russia, the Great Bear of the East.

"My mother was from a simple farming family. They grew barley, potatoes, yellow turnips. They had chickens, too, she told me. She had an older brother, Pawel. When she was a girl, the Soviets came and took over the land. They confiscated the crops. My great-grandmother, her grandmother, died of starvation on that farm, which sounds impossible, but it is true. Elena was twelve years old when she lost her.

"Then the Germans invaded in 1941. They fought a catastrophic battle with Russia. The two sides competed to see who could punish and torture and mutilate the other. Germany took hundreds of thousands of Russian prisoners. They blamed the Jews for everything the Russians had done. In Kiev, they rounded up 33,000 Jews, Will. This really happened. They took them to a ravine, and executed them."

"My God! Was that Baba Yar?" Will had read about the war in Europe some years before, and was anxious to show off his knowledge.

"Yes, Babyn Yar. Jews, gypsies, communists, and Russian prisoners, 100,000 in all, were killed there.

"The story was the same in Lviv, a city that my parents had in common. My mother's family was taken there and herded like cattle with other Jews. Lviv—it was called Lwow at the time—was a big city with a large Jewish population. The Germans put all the Jews into one neighborhood. Another ghetto, eh? My mother said they put her father and brother—she cried when she told me this story, Will—on what they said was a work crew. But the work," and here Sheldon paused. "Forty years later, and Elena is crying. She said the work was the digging of mass graves. Graves that they were to be buried in. After they were shot."

"This is sounding a bit like your father's family's story," Will said.

"Yes, and I'm telling you what Elena told me, but this happened. It has all been documented. The Lviv ghetto had been destroyed by war, but the rubble became a last stop for Jews. Elena told me about the stench--rotting bodies everywhere. Food and water were scarce. In this ghetto, in Lviv, Elena's mother got sick—stomach pains, malnutrition. Elena took her to a clinic. The Germans—how's this for irony?—the Germans were taking the elderly, and many of the sick, *out* of the hospitals. To *shoot* and bury them. So that was the last she saw of her mother . . . the clinic." Sheldon smiled bitterly, and put his hands around his newly refilled coffee cup.

"But her brother," Will wanted to know.

"Pawel. My mother described him as very handsome and charming. Some Jewish children who had favorable physical traits, blond, blue-eyed, lean and strong of physique, were sent west to be 'Germanized.' One day, the SS came through the ghetto. They said they were inspecting random children for disease. But some of the Jews overheard talk. This or that boy would, for example, make a good gardener or a butler in a German home. So they took some of these kids, six or eight teen boys and girls who looked like they could pass for German. Carted them off in a locked wagon. Gave them a new identity. My mother never found out what became of Pawel after the war. He did not return to the farm. His real name was not listed in the rolls of the POW camps. Or the DP camps. It's possible that he blended into German society after the war."

"So, Elena was alone, then," Will said.

"Yes, and because she was relatively healthy, she was eventually taken to a nearby work camp called Janowska. At the time, she thought she was lucky. Many Jews from Lviv were being sent to Belzec, a death camp.

"For two years, she worked twelve-to-fourteen-hour days in a factory. Artillery shells and other German munitions were made there. At the end of her shift, she was bunked in a concentration camp. It was just across the road from the factory, she said.

"She told me some things about Janowska, Will. Inmates might be shot for a grimace. For being unable to sit up straight, or for not minding their work. Or for smiling. Or for not smiling, Will! Can you imagine? And their bodies were burned there at Janowska."

Will felt the need to acknowledge his friend, but was at a loss for something to say. He looked Sheldon in the eye, though, and nodded, and finally said, "I'm with you, Shel."

"Thank you, my friend. My mother told me about her living quarters. A room barely large enough for twenty beds, ten sets of bunkbeds. The beds had sawdust mattresses and a blanket, no sheets. So twenty girls, one toilet, a washbasin, and a few rags.

"The daily menu consisted of a cup of coffee or tea, 200 grams of bread from which mold and bugs needed to be removed, and one or two cups of cabbage soup. Sometimes carrots or turnips were added to the soup, which also had to be inspected for bugs.

"It was a labor camp *and* a death camp. My mother told me things, things that were done to young men and girls that I cannot repeat here. I can refer you to a book, *The Janowska Road*, written in the '60s by a survivor of that camp. The night Elena told me about her time at Janowska, she gave that book to me. It is a chilling document, Will. There was a commandant at Janowska who would shoot a prisoner in the head if he did not like the way he was standing or the way his Jewish star patches were sewn on his armbands or trousers.

"One of her coworkers in the factory was the Polish Catholic girl, Vera. This was the girl—the woman—who found Elena in about 1980."

"I wonder how? After all those years?"

"You *goyyum* talk about how we Jews stick together. Well, we have cultural organizations and synagogues, and some information on membership can be shared. But how Vera, a Catholic, got access to that information, I have no idea. I wish I had asked Elena when I had the chance.

"As Russian troops neared Janowska after the fall of Stalingrad and were about to liberate—again, I use that word with terrible irony, Will—to liberate the area in 1944, Elena and Vera were put on a crew that was forced to excavate and burn the corpses of those who had been executed."

"What she saw!" Will said, horrified. Horrified for Elena. "To prevent the Russians from finding those corpses?"

"The SS tried to eliminate the traces of what they had done. My mother told me that the Germans were ordered to liquidate not only the corpses but the corpse *workers* after a time, so that they would not live to tell the world about what they had seen and done. But one of the SS officers grew fond of Elena and Vera, too fond of these two teenage girls to shoot them. And the Germans were finally forced by the new Russian advance to retreat to the west."

"So what happened to the girls?"

"The Russians were as efficient in their ruthlessness as the Germans. Elena and Vera were placed in a Russian prison camp as suspected collaborators with Germany, but they were lucky that the war was ending. After their release, they traveled to Austria, where they found shelter in a camp for displaced persons that the Allies had set up."

"A DP camp," Will said. "I've heard about them. And that's where she met your father. . . Joe?"

"Not yet. She was repatriated after a few months, but she had heard that returning to the farm alone was hopeless. The Soviets were back in control. She no longer trusted the non-Jewish farmers or villagers. So she went back to Lviv, found a one-room apartment, and got work looking after children. My father left Lithuania and returned to his farm after the German retreat, but his farm was no longer his farm, so he also went to Lviv. He got his first job in a butcher shop there and was living in a home not far from my mother. The synagogue in that part of town had been burned to the ground, so Jews were meeting in a converted storefront. That is where Elena Gabo met Jozef Weiss."

"Your parents never blended in on Cloverlawn. They were outsiders, and so were you and Melvin, to some extent."

"Both my parents' families," Sheldon mused, "were from Jewish farming communities before the war. They were on strange ground on Cloverlawn. They had not learned how to live in an industrial melting pot."

"My family were farmers on both sides, too," Will said. "They migrated from Europe in the nineteenth century to farms in Illinois. But in the years after the First War, when small farms were failing, they moved north to work in factories."

"It *is* sad," Sheldon said, "to think our families had something in common, yet they never connected. I don't think anyone was to blame. Jews have historically been a somewhat insular people, drawn together in part by anti-Semitism. And after World War II we were suffering from a sort of cultural PTSD. It took time for the European Jews who emigrated here to assimilate. My parents had not only the trauma of their war histories, but they had come to a new country with a strange language and culture."

"I wonder about this war in Europe now," Will said. "They say Americans are tired of supporting Ukraine. But if Russia isn't stopped there, will Poland be next?"

"Maybe we in the USA are doing the same thing the rest of the world did in the thirties, while totalitarian states threatened in the East and West. If the truth is left unspoken to authority, to power, then the autocrats take over."

9

Toward the end of the following week, having heard nothing from his son or granddaughter in Flint, Will gambled that someone would be home. There was no use in calling ahead. James had not been answering his phone or returning calls from his father. Will's texts to Hazel were answered with one of those maddening automated replies: "Can't talk now" or "text you later," a "later" that never came. He understood that his son was angry at him for pushing him to accept the Stanford job. Will wanted to apologize, but more than that he wanted to know his son's plans. He both feared and hoped that James had accepted the position.

He arrived at the house early enough to spend a few hours and return home before dark. James let him in, but without a hug or handshake.

"Hazel is at band practice. I gotta pick her up in a half-hour."

"I'm glad to hear she's back at her trumpet. And they say kids learn structure and discipline. Teamwork, too. I think she can benefit from, from--"

"Sure, Dad."

Will sensed that he had said too much. He remembered that he was there to listen. "So, how are you, James?"

"I'm doing better. Had to shut myself down for a while. The voices were crowding me . . . I mean, between my daughter and my girlfriend and my own, uh, inner turmoil, I had to slow down and sort things out. And I had to have some serious talks with Deb."

"Your lady friend? I didn't know," Will said, but he did have secondhand knowledge of Deb from Hazel.

"We aren't exactly sure about our relationship right now because I need to be in California by the end of the . . .."

"You're going?"

"Hazel and me."

"Congratulations! But . . .," Will stopped, overcome with the conflicting emotions that accompanied the news. Yes, he had wanted Stanford for his son all along. But now he would have families on both coasts, while stuck in the Midwest. He disliked flying. He also disliked long road trips and long phone conversations. And he hated those popular internet Zoom-type platforms for video calling.

"But I'm gonna hate . . . to see you go, son," he said, struggling to get the words out.

James stopped as they walk to his car and turned to his father. "Look at me, Dad." He waited for Will to raise his head. "I could not communicate with you because I didn't want to make a decision for the wrong reasons."

"I'm sorry, James. I understand."

"And we don't always agree on things, but that's okay. I hope we can agree to disagree. But Hazel and I are always gonna be in your life. No matter where we are. Okay?"

"I wanted the best for you. And I know you have talents . . .."

"Wait, Dad. You said you understood. This had to be my decision."

"Sorry." *What had James responded to? "I wanted," must have been it*, Will thought. James had drawn the line.

"What about Deb?" Will asked, as they drove through James's working-class neighborhood. He had never met Deb. The name sounded strange on his tongue.

"Deb and I are trying to work it out, but she has two kids in school here, and an ex with visitation rights, and a good job. It won't be easy for her to pick up and leave. So we'll see. But she is very special to me."

"I'm glad you have someone in your life, son. I hope it works out for both of you."

"Thanks, Dad."

Not having heard from Sheldon in weeks, Will reached out. Denise answered the phone.

"Shel's been meaning to call you. He had surgery last week, but he's feeling better."

She told him that Sheldon was suffering from congestive heart failure. He had been fitted with a pacemaker, along with an adjustment of his medications. His cardiologist said that a valve repair might be in order, pending the result of tests.

Will was alarmed. "I wish I had known," he said. "Is he well enough to speak on the phone?"

"He's sleeping now. Can I have him call you?"

"Please. I'd like that. Tell him I'm thinking about him."

"Okay. And Will . . . Sheldon tells me how much he enjoys his lunches with you. I'm glad you two have renewed your friendship."

It was not until Thanksgiving weekend that Will got the call. Because he was afraid to fly and afraid to drive all that way with his compromised eyesight, which was not all that compromised, he had cancelled his planned visit to New Haven to see his son's family.

Sheldon said he had been in the hospital again for a "procedure," and was feeling better, but still not well enough to leave the house.

"Sorry to hear that, Shel. Are you in pain?"

"Just tired. My breathing is off, and I haven't had much energy. The doctors changed my meds, and that helps, but they say I may need surgery."

"Well, hey, I miss our lunches. I'm gonna keep tabs on you."

Will brought up the ongoing war in Gaza. Sheldon was apologetic for Israel's continued attack on Gaza.

"Thousands of children are dying, you see. We need an end to it, a withdrawal from Gaza. This war is not heading toward a good outcome."

"And Hamas must release the hostages," Will added. He prioritized Israel's hostages, those who might still be alive, but he was beginning to see that neither Israel nor Hamas was serious about having all of them released.

"Yes, of course," Sheldon said. "So many victims!"

*****

They had ended the call with a promise to talk again soon, but a week went by with no word from Sheldon. Will initiated contact.

"I'm still weak," Sheldon reported, "but the doctor is saying no surgery. They have a monitor in me, though, so we will see."

"Sounds to me like your ticker will be working better soon, and you'll be good to go."

"I hope so. My wife is sick of looking at me."

"And I'm getting sick of keeping my own company," Will said. "You need to get over to the Coolidge."

"I'm not ready for the Coolidge. A call from my brother was the only connection I've had with the outside world."

"How is Mel?"

"As irresponsible as ever, but it was good to hear from him. The good news is that we got a roof on the old house a few weeks ago."

"Did he say anything about water damage?" Will asked. "I wouldn't be surprised if the attic and some ceilings were getting wet."

"I'm sure Mel is oblivious to all that, and I wouldn't be much help."

"You may want to get your roofer in there to inspect, if he hasn't yet. Or I could have a look if you'd like."

"I'd rather it was you, Will. Mel knows you, he once knew you, and he does not get many visitors. I need to know what it needs so we can sell that place someday."

They agreed to schedule a date and time for Will to visit the house. Sheldon also invited Will to his house in Southfield during the holidays.

"During the Christmas season would be okay," Will said.

"That's Hanukkah in this neighborhood," Sheldon reminded him. "The kids will be here, but you're welcome any time."

"I'd like that." At some point, he would join his daughter for their annual Christmas dinner. He had also committed to helping James with the weeding and packing project that was taking place in readiness for his move to California. That was the extent of his plan for Christmas.

"Hanukkah runs from the seventh through fifteenth this year," Sheldon said.

"That's early. Back on Cloverlawn, it always came during Christmas," Will said. "We goys called it the Jewish Christmas."

"And we Jews would snicker about that."

10

Waiting for someone to answer the bell, Will noticed a *mezuzah* hanging on Sheldon's front door. He had not seen one since his Cloverlawn days. The Jews would joke that the Christian crucifix was a "*mezuzah* with handlebars."

Sheldon, whose voice sounded stronger than ever, had called the previous day to remind Will of his invitation. "Come tomorrow night," he had said. "Denise and I want you to have dinner and meet our family," but Sheldon had not specified a time.

Penny, the Weiss's oldest daughter, opened the door to a warm house that smelled of garlic and onions. She and her husband Peter were first to shake Will's hand. Will guessed that Penny was named after Sheldon's aunt Pen, who lived in the Vilna ghetto with her mother until they were taken to the death camp.

"My father-in-law told us all about you," Peter said, to which Will smiled, but thought, *what could he have said about me?*

He was greeted next by the Weiss's daughter, Libby, in town from Minneapolis with her husband, Ari. Anna, the Bohemian granddaughter Shel had often vented about at some of their lunches, and who Will realized must be the daughter of Penny and Peter, was there with her boyfriend, Spencer. "Grandpa talks about you all the time," Anna said, to which, again, Will was surprised and flattered. Sheldon had complained about Spencer's dreadlocks, but Will later heard that the real issue was Spencer's family's membership in the Lutheran Church. Will chatted with Spencer about their mutual interest in the Lions, who were making a run for the Super Bowl for the first time.

After greetings with Sheldon and Denise, Will sat at the dinner table with Sheldon. The family had already eaten, but Denise fixed Will a plate and poured him and Sheldon glasses of

Manischewitz, a sweet Moscato wine. Will was reminded of his tenure as a stock boy at the kosher Dexter-Davison Market, where Mogen David and Manischewitz were the most popular wines.

"Man-oh-Manischewitz, what a wine!" Will said, taking a sip after he and Sheldon touched glasses.

"We heard that jingle often, didn't we, Will? I suspect many Jews drink it less for its taste than for the tradition."

"I'm a beer drinker, or was," Will said, "but I'm happy to have a glass with you."

Dinner was surprisingly healthy—salad, roasted veggies, baked fish, and gluten-free bread—no dessert--and unlike what Will had expected, having witnessed Sheldon's eating habits at several area diners. After dinner, Sheldon guided Will to a small room that he used as an office and library.

Sheldon appeared to lose his balance momentarily while settling in his desk chair. "Oops," he said, spilling a few drops of Moscato down his chin and onto his white shirt. "Maybe Denise can spray some of that stuff on it, like she does, you know . . . "

"'Spray-and-Wash' or, um, 'Easy Off.'"

"She needs both of them with a spouse like me," Sheldon said.

"So tell me," Will said, "why is your holy week so early this year?"

"The short answer is that Hanukkah is based on the lunar year, which is ten days shorter than the solar," Sheldon said. "But this is the earliest it gets."

"The short answer works for me," Will said. "I don't think any of us goys on Cloverlawn had an inkling of what Hanukkah stands for."

"I'll tell you. In the second century before Christ, Israel had been dominated by Syria. The Syrians, you see, tried to wipe out our culture and religion. Some of the Syrian rulers were repressive, to say the least. During Hanukkah, we celebrate the liberation of Jerusalem and the restoration of the temple."

"Thanks for the invite, Shel. I'm grateful that you would share some of your Hanukkah with me."

Sheldon wasted no time putting away his wine. As he emptied his glass, he said, "Are you still willing to inspect the Cloverlawn house for water damage? I can pay you for your trouble, Will."

"Sure, and no payment necessary, but can Melvin help with any of this? I'm not asking for myself, but he seems to be the respon—"

"My brother is a seventy-four-year-old child. He seems to have a roommate, temporarily at least. I met the guy, Sam, a surly character, back when the roofer did the estimate. I don't know what Mel told Sam about me, but he looks to be twenty-five years younger than Mel, and he was not friendly to me, to say the least. I do not think Sam is paying rent."

"It would be no trouble to look the place over," Will said. "I would need to get into the attic, and take a close look at roof trusses, ceilings, window casings, doorways. It might not take more than half an hour. There could be drywall damage, and mold is very possible. But I can't do the repairs, if any are needed. Do you have a ladder over there?"

"In the garage."

"Sorry to hear Mel is struggling."

"Or lazy," Shel suggested. "I took him out to lunch the day we got the roof replaced. That was the last time I saw the Cloverlawn place. It stank, Will, and I wanted to get him out of there. I wanted to get *myself* out of there. He had lost his phone. Maybe it was foolish of me to get him a replacement. And he looked like he could use a meal, so I took him to Lou's."

"Lou's Deli? It's still there?"

"It's in three locations now. Mel wanted to go to the original Lou's, the one on Seven Mile Road."

"I used to love their corned beef. And their fries!"

"The fries are still the best, even though old Lou is long dead."

"So what did Mel have to say for himself?"

"He doesn't have a car, or much money to speak of, so he's on the edge. But he's okay. While we were eating, a friend of his, a Black woman, came in and sat down with us. That neighborhood is very multicultural now, of course, and she—her name was Ty—seemed to be very fond of Melvin. They hugged, and she kissed him on the cheek. They talked about people they knew in common. He laughed a lot."

"Did Mel ever stop laughing?"

"It's his default, eh? He's getting by. He acts like a *putz*, and I worry about him, but he seems happy. I cannot tell him how to live. He would never listen to me, anyway. But this woman, this Ty . . . she was sweet, and it was clear that she cares about him. And he has the roommate, though I would not call Sam an asset, or even an ally. I'm only saying Melvin seems to have people in his life."

"That's a good sign. I always thought he was a very social guy. He talked to everyone. You were more . . . selective?"

"How do you mean?"

"Well, you didn't have as many friends on Cloverlawn."

"And Melvin did?"

"Mel was a hotdog and a *putz*, for sure, but he was out on the street with the kids . . ."

"Wait, Will," Sheldon interrupted. "Do you know why I wasn't out on the street with the kids?"

Will answered carefully. "I didn't think your parents wanted either of you socializing with the Cloverlawn goyyum. And Mel rebelled . . ."

"I was Elena's English teacher, Will. She was isolated. And she had only something like a fourth-grade education in the Ukraine."

"What are you saying?"

"I'm saying every day, when I got home from *shul*, instead of hanging out on the block with the Cloverlawn kids, I worked with my mothe . . . with Elena. I'm sorry you never got to know her, Will. She was so . . . well, you knew she was in a constant state of terror. Very insecure. But she was brilliant in her own way. She taught me a bit of Yiddish and also Ukrainian, which is a Slavic mix of Polish and Russian. But I was the teacher. English at first, and later we learned Hebrew, studied the Torah, and did much of my other homework together, so she could learn along with me. And my father, when he returned from work at the end of the day, sat in on some of those lessons with us."

"My God!"

"And she practiced her English with the Gordons—do you remember them?"

The image came to Will of Elena running down the block like a frightened child—to the Gordons. "Of course, the old couple at the end of the block."

"The Gordons understood her wounds. They treated her like a daughter," Sheldon said.

"Wow, I had no idea," Will said. "But . . . but you said you didn't have much of a relationship with your mother."

"She stopped being a mom to me, Will. She was damaged. You remember. You always felt so much pity for her. But she became my *talmide*, my student. And she was a good student, hungry to learn."

"You were her professor, and then you *became* a professor."

"I was that, at eight and nine and until I got out of high school and moved to New York."

Will detected, understandably, resentment in Sheldon's tone. "Okay. I think I get it. But I'm sorry, that wasn't fair. You didn't have a choice, Shel."

"True. I did not have the freedom to play in the street as much as my brother, but I loved my mother. And I was not chained to the table we worked at. Besides, Melvin could not have been a help. He was not suited for it. I was a . . . a natural."

"Agreed. I always knew that." It was true. And here they were in Dr. Sheldon Weiss's home office, a room that smelled of old books that were full of big words, big ideas. Will could not begin to fathom it all. *No wonder Shel brought me in here.* Was he more comfortable in that room with those books than he was with his family?

Will looked around and said, "And you are still, even in retirement, a professor?"

"I still read and write, but I am free from office politics and publishing expectations and staff meetings. No *bubba maisa.*"

"No bullshit?"

"You remembered!" They laughed.

"Have you . . . made peace with that . . . that part of your childhood? You once said that the parents' wounds get passed down to generations, that you and Mel were victims, in a secondhand way." As Will asked the question, he wondered how, if asked, *he* would have answered it.

"I think so. You noticed during our talks at the Coolidge that I had mixed feelings about Elena. I think of her as Elena now, like Melvin and like you." He laughed, and finished his wine. "It's easy to conjure up rage about her neuroses, and those tiring after-*shul* hours studying with her, teaching her. My lost childhood, eh? But there was so much more. Elena had no choice but to grow. Our relationship became closer after those years on Cloverlawn. I do not claim to have mastered the art of living fully in the present, Will. I've had to work on myself. I was lucky to have a career and family that kept me involved and growing."

"I don't think of you as a victim, Sheldon. You're an accomplished guy. I'm impressed with this home and the beautiful family you've put together."

"Thank you. I'll pass that remark along to Denise, who wears the trousers around here."

Will nodded, as, on cue, Denise knocked and opened the door.

"Sorry to interrupt, guys." She looked at Will and said, "We need to leave. We're taking Libby and Ari to the airport tonight," before smiling and closing the door.

"Will," Sheldon said, almost tentatively. "I've told you many things about my family, not all of them happy things, yes?"

"Sure, and I'm humbled to know you, to learn about your parents. Thank you, Sheldon, for the sharing. And tonight, for inviting me to your home."

Sheldon hugged Will and said, "Shalom, my friend."

11

Since his kids had grown and his wife had died, Will got little joy out of Christmas. He was no *Grinch*, and he appreciated the *Christ* side of Christmas, but the holiday season was no longer appealing to him.

He was happy to get a Facebook Messenger call from his son Pat in New Haven. Pat put his wife and all three teenagers on the screen, but it had been so long that they were like strangers to Will. He asked questions of everyone, though. They were polite and willing to share. Then they shared news of family. James's job with Stanford University was a big topic, but, given James's reticence, no one knew any details about the position.

*****

A few days before Christmas, Will drove to Flint to help his son, who was in the middle of his move project. Done with his community college semester, James had plenty of time to pack, but he was getting in his own way. Will cleaned kitchen cabinets and wrapped and boxed some essentials, while seeking disposition advice on questionable items. James, hovering nearby, fretted over whether to discard or donate or bring to Sunnyvale a never-used toaster.

"But you have a toaster in the kitchen, don't you?" Will asked.

"Technically it's a toaster-oven."

"Is it in good shape?"

"Yes, but it belonged to Lily." Lily was James's ex-wife. "Maybe I should ask her if she wants it back."

"Dad?" Hazel was passing through the kitchen, just in time. "Let's donate the toaster and keep the toaster-oven. We don't need both." She picked up the toaster, which was still in its box, and set it on the donations pile. "Agreed?"

"Wholeheartedly," James said, relieved.

✳✳✳✳✳

On the night before Christmas Eve, Teresa arrived at Will's place for their annual Christmas dinner outing. This time was Will's favorite with his daughter, a rare meeting that did not involve tools or a lawn mower. He had not seen his daughter in months, but had been hoping for a new closeness with this woman who lived nearer than any of his relatives but who seemed most distant from him.

In recent years they had gone to the Oak, or First Watch, or Lucy and Ethel's, or other diners that featured eclectic or retro or vegetarian or ethnic. This year it was a Polish restaurant Teresa had heard about. It was in Hamtramck, the old Polish enclave completely encircled by Detroit's east side.

After Will invited her in, Teresa inspected his home with interest. She had not seen the place since Joan's funeral—five years before. He stood by, embarrassed, as she opened doors and peered into rooms.

"Place hasn't changed much," Will said sheepishly.

"She's everywhere in here," Teresa said, looking at photos of Joan and Will, or Joan alone, and other family photos hung everywhere she looked. It seemed that most of her mother's possessions, including her clothes, were still there.

"Her painting! Is that a new frame?" she asked, staring at a pastel based on a photograph Joan had taken at Yellowstone the same year as the Cloverlawn reunion. Everyone in the family agreed, and it was true, that it was an excellent painting, that it captured the otherworldliness that was Yellowstone. Joan had been an amateur, but she had talent.

"I never liked the old frame," said Will. "This one doesn't get in the way of the scene." Will borrowed that idea almost word for word from a neighbor who ran a framing business in his basement.

Teresa stopped again, this time at the kitchen window. "Mom's Viburnums. It looks like they've been trimmed recently."

62

"I've been taking care of them for her," Will said. It thrilled him that as different as they seemed, he and his daughter shared this one love for Joan. He came to the window and stood with her. "She loved to stand here, doing dishes or whatever, and looking out at the yard. And those bushes," he said, his voice cracking.

Teresa put a hand on Will's. "I know, Dad. She was all about nature and art, but she never . . . "

"She could have been a professional, but she was content to dabble. Family gets in the way." He spoke before—while--realizing that Teresa was quite aware of the sacrifices her mother and other women make, the compromises inherent in lifestyle choices. Terry was divorced after only a few years of marriage, and had remained single to pursue—what? He felt a pang of regret that he had never been interested enough to learn about his daughter's career, to know her in a meaningful way.

"You really did love her, didn't you, Dad?"

"Of course. She was my . . . my lifeline. If it weren't for your mother, I would be . . .. After the Army, I was headed in a bad direction, Terry."

"I'd like to hear that story, Dad. Mom saved my ass, too, back in my crazy days."

"Were you ever crazy? I don't think so."

"You wouldn't know, Dad."

Have we ever spoken with such frankness? Will thought. They stood staring at the bushes along the garage---the Viburnums.

"There are more berries on the ground than on the bushes," Teresa said.

"The birds like 'em."

*****

The Polish restaurant was the Ivanhoe Café, in a neighborhood Will had not seen in many years.

63

"I've had the Perch dinner here!" Will said as they parked near the building. "They called it The Polish Yacht Club back then," he said, laughing. The working-class Poles who gathered there were unlikely to have yachts.

"They still use that nickname, Dad. It's famous for Perch and Walleye, but it has traditional Polish entrees, too."

Seated near the bar, Will looked around at the crowd, a mix of crusty veterans and their wives, retired auto workers and their wives, a few geezers at the bar, and a few curious millennials. "Thank you for taking us here, Terry. You did it again. This is a treat!"

Terry ordered the standard pickles and slaw, with a bowl of hearty chicken noodle soup and a beer. Will asked for the Walleye dinner with a glass of water, no ice.

"You were saying Mom saved your ass," Will said. "Where was I during all this? I know you had a reckless youth, but you had some hard times?"

"Wait, Dad. I thought you were about to tell me your Joan of Arc story. How Mom rushed in when you hit bottom."

"I won't give you the gory details, but your mom and I were acquaintances in college before I got drafted."

"You actually went to college?" Teresa smiled at the thought of her father in academia.

"For a while. It wasn't my thing, as you know. When I got out of the service, your mom and I continued to be in the same loose circle of friends . . . but I was having trouble. Call it anxiety or PTSD or . . . I saw some war, Terry."

"Mom told me you were in the middle of some horrific stuff in Vietnam, but you never talked about it, so I never understood. I'm so sorry, Dad."

"The funny thing was, I didn't see nearly as much as so many others. But . . . I saw victims. On both sides. We evacuated dead and wounded kids out of combat zones. That was the worst of it for me, but it was enough to shake me up in a way that I'll never forget."

"Anyway, Joan must of seen something worthwhile in me, even though I had loads of anger and guilt. She was patient. We didn't even date for about a year and a half. But we'd get together, mostly with friends. She was always the smart one. And she was a good listener. We built a friendship. There were no expectations. I mean, I would go off and party with my Cloverlawn buddies, or friends from work. I had acquired a taste for weed and beer. Sometimes a hit of coke. But substances weren't the issue. I was lost in those days.

"Gradually, I didn't want so much of that reckless world, the confusion and the lost weekends. I began to settle down. And lucky for me, or we can call it divine guidance, I was still in Joan's orbit, and she was available. She didn't need me, but she had something I wanted. I think you know what it was."

"I do, Dad. I'm glad you found each other. She may have been good for you, but you were also good for her."

"I hope . . .," Will started, but did not finish his thought.

"And Dad, maybe it's time to donate and store some of Mom's things."

"I know, I know, but that stuff is all I have of your mother."

"That house has more of mom's stuff than your own. And you don't need a three-bedroom house with a full basement and two-car garage. Maybe if you were to unload some of the burden, the burden of all those relics from the past, it would help you adjust to this next stage of your life."

Will was surprised by his daughter's honesty. *Next stage? What did the poet say? "Why not get started?"* Yes, Terry spoke the truth.

"I ask myself why I'm hanging on to her. I had Joan, but I was never a good husband or father. I had trouble with those roles. And now I want them back."

"You were always good to me, Dad, and good to Mom and my brothers. I needed that. But Mom was present for me in a different way. She listened. I needed that, too: someone to listen without judgment. Someone to *get* me."

"I hope it's not too late for *me* to get you, Terry."

"You had the boys. It was all guy sports and guy stuff. It got lonely for me, Dad. Sometimes I think our house was not such a great place for a girl to grow up. And it wasn't only our family. There just were not many girls in our neighborhood. And most of them were beauty queens. I didn't know how to fit in. What I really needed was to be heard, because not only was I a girl, but I was also a girl without boyfriends as a teenager, without much validation as a person, Dad.

"But I had Mom. Not at first. I don't think Mom got me at first, either." She reached across and patted her father's hand. "Maybe, at times, she tried to treat me the way *she* thought I should be. Eventually I had to *teach* her how to treat me. And she got it, Daddy! But sometimes I think you don't really see me, that you don't take me as I am." Terry's voice faltered. She wiped away tears with a hand and took a breath to compose herself.

Will turned his head away. It killed him to see her cry.

"Why can't you see that I'm somebody special, Dad?"

His daughter was forty-nine years old to his seventy-seven. It hit him hard that she never thought him safe enough to talk with. When she tried to speak to him, if ever, he did not *see* or *hear* her.

His first reaction was defensiveness. *I fed and clothed you, put you through college. I'm your personal handyman, by God. Look at the scar on my hand that I suffered while building your damn shed.* But that feeling passed quickly. It was followed by another: remorse.

"Will you," he began, as tears came to his eyes. "Will you teach me like you taught your mother? Will you let me try to be a father to you, one more time?"

There, at a table for two in the middle of The Ivanhoe, also known as the Polish Yacht Club, Will and Terry sat and held hands.

12

On a frigid morning between Christmas and New Years', Will had a big bowl of cereal and a walk to Kava Korner before driving to Oak Park. Sheldon had arranged the date and time for this visit with his brother Melvin, whom Will had not seen since the Cloverlawn reunion, thirteen years before. He drove past the Coolidge Café into the business district and saw delis and diners where he had, long ago, often met with friends and girlfriends. Hy Horenstein's Deli was gone. Davison Coney Island was also gone. He recognized a few other businesses, but most were new to him.

Instead of turning onto Cloverlawn, he pulled into the lot for the Oak Park Municipal Park of his childhood and got out of the car. The temperature was hovering around ten degrees above zero. A light snow was in the air; several inches of overnight powder covered the ground. A brightly colored playground of swings, slide, and monkey bars sat empty, not far from the lot. He thought it ironic that kids today might prefer those rubbery plastic fixtures to the natural wonders of the wooded area where he and his friends had played.

He walked on into the woods. Twin Ponds, as the kids had called it, an oasis amid the trees, had been filled in. A twenty-first century parent would never stand for a few inches of open water in the vicinity of children. But the tree from which he hung a rope to swing over the ponds was still there. He saw the scar on the limb that the rope had been tied to. He stood and looked around him. His were the only footprints in the snow.

Moments later, he was idling down Cloverlawn. A few homes had Christmas lights displayed. No bikes or toys were strewn about. No children making snowmen. The McPhail's old place looked strange without lights and the backlit nativity scene that never got taken down until March. The Cunningham place was barely recognizable—someone had invested in an expensive makeover. Coming upon obese, bullied Stephanie (Titanic) Katanick's old place, he regretted that he was too peer-dependent to protect her.

After identifying the rest of the family homes he had known on that end of the block, he parked and walked to the Weiss home, where a ladder leaned against one wall. The roof, he could tell, had recently been shingled. The white trim around the windows and doors was peeling badly. He climbed the crumbling cement steps to the porch.

Before he reached the bell, the door opened. A short, muscular younger man with a shaved head and a few days' growth of beard said, "What do you want, Sport?"

"Hi. I'm looking for Melvin Weiss."

"He's busy. So who are you?"

Sheldon would call this guy a *putz*, Will thought. "An old friend. I grew up next door." He pointed to his old house.

"I need a name, Sport. Mel is resting."

The attack-dog roommate, if he was a roommate, was less than welcoming. After Will told the guy his name, he stood shivering on the porch, hands stuffed in pockets, surveying the houses across the street. Some of them were now owned by Chaldeans, he knew.

The putz returned. "Get in and close the door behind you. Don't let the cold air in."

Will closed the door to the smell of mildew and dirty underwear. Turning from a small entryway, he looked upon a dark, overly warm living room of vintage furniture that had not withstood the test of time. A small, flat-screen television sat precariously on a cardboard box. A rerun of "Three's Company," was airing, the volume turned low.

Peering out from under blankets on the couch, holding a TV remote, was Melvin Weiss. He looked older, of course. A few strands of white hair lay over the top of an otherwise bald head. Most noticeable was Melvin's badly swollen jaw and discoloration under an eye.

"Remember me?" Will said. Mel's friend, whose name Will remembered was Sam, had taken a seat next to the couch. Will could tell by Mel's wide eyes that he recognized him.

"You look great, Will," Melvin said weakly. "But we got old, didn't we?"

"That, we did. Are you okay, Mel?"

"He had an accident," Sam said. "He's gonna be fine, just needs a little rest."

"Shel asked me to look around for water damage. I hope you were expecting me."

"He told me something, but I didn't know it was for today. He said you two been getting together or something," Melvin said. "I remember when you went to 'Nam." He looked at Sam, and said, "Will was, like, the only guy on Cloverlawn who had to go."

"Danny McPhail went, too," Will corrected. He had been friends with him, but Danny went to Catholic schools. Will got drafted several years before Danny, who was smart enough to stay in college for three years, thus keeping his student deferment that much longer.

"That's right. I remember Danny . . . down the block. His sister was a beauty," Melvin said.

"Thank you for your service," said Sam, unenthusiastically.

Mel lifted the blanket. His body was as skinny as ever. A twig-like forearm hung from a sling. Beginning at the wrist and extending along his thumb, his skin was blackened. As Will noticed the edge of an ugly bruise over the waistband of his sweatpants, Mel's friend replaced the blanket to cover his shoulders. Mel closed his eyes.

"What happened?"

"Watch your mouth, Mel," said the friend.

"Shut up, Sam," said Melvin. "I got jumped."

"Punks," Sam added.

You two would know, thought Will.

"Couple of *schvartzes*," Melvin said, referring to Blacks. "But Mafia was behind it."

"There's no Mafia, man," Sam said to Mel.

"Maybe not anymore, but I'm sayin' the Chaldie Mafia."

"Chaldie's are all in jail," Sam said.

"Okay, but some of 'em are still out there," Mel whined, referring to small-time Chaldean gangsters who mainly dealt drugs. Before the casinos hit Detroit and stole most of their market, they ran gambling rackets, too. "And they hire out the *schvartzes* to do their dirty work."

"But why were these Chaldeans out to get you?" Will asked, surmising that a skinny old guy like Melvin was more likely a random victim of muggers than the target of Chaldean or African-American gang members.

"I didn't do nothing, Will," Melvin said. "It's Thursday night and I'm leaving Lou's Deli."

"The one on Seven Mile? Tough neighborhood at night," Will said. It was the same Lou's where Sheldon said he had taken Melvin to lunch a few weeks previous.

"Tough, yeah. Don't I know. So I'm walkin' through the lot, eight o'clock at night, two guys drag me behind the dumpster, empty my pockets. They got about fifty bucks. Then one guy knocks me down and he's kickin' me. Other guy has a, looks like a night stick or a blackjack. I'm folded up, tryin' to protect my balls and my head. That's how I got this." He lifted the blanket to expose the wrist. "A car comes up and they jump in and take off."

Will looked at Sam, who stared at him like he might be a cop. Neither he nor Mel had offered Will a chair.

"Are you getting some attention for that wrist?" Will asked.

"I'll be okay. Doc Singer looked at me."

"Doc Singer is kind of a friend," Sam said.

"So, who sent this doctor?" Will asked.

"Another friend," Sam said, "Why the fuck do you care?"

Will looked at Sam. "Mel and I grew up together. Next door neighbors. And I'm a good friend of his brother. Is that reason enough?"

The place got quiet. "I need to get into your attic," Will said. "Can I use that ladder out there?"

"What ladder?" Mel asked, oblivious.

"The one leaning against the house."

"Oh, yeah. Sure."

He brought the ladder in with no help from Sam, who had followed him outside and back in. Will knew how to get to the attic because the Weiss home was identical to the house he had grown up in. He accessed the attic from a hatch in a hallway ceiling. Inspecting the roof was difficult, since he had to squeeze into areas where the roof met the walls. He noticed that the roof had been shingled over areas of rotting plywood, never a good idea. He also checked around the chimney, fans, and vents, and saw places where water had penetrated, and insulation that had once been wet. As far as he could tell, though, there were no current leaks.

Next, he came back down to the main floor to look at the ceiling and walls. Will was not the kind of man to be easily appalled, but this house needed some looking-after. He tried not to notice the general messiness around him, which reminded him of Sheldon's comment that Melvin lives like a teenager. The toilet in the bathroom was especially disgusting.

None of my business, he thought. As he moved through the house, he took notes and snapped photos with his phone. He noticed places where leaks had caused flaking or bubbling paint along several walls and on ceilings. He pounded on an area of drywall to test for damage.

"Hey!" yelled Sam. "Keep it down, will ya?"

Will ignored him. He identified damage by the feel and by the sound, and damage there was. He saw no visible mold, but he guessed by the smell that a good drywall man might find plenty.

When he finished, he asked Mel, who turned to him with a grimace, why the ladder had been at an outside wall. "Were you on the roof for any reason?"

"I don't know, Will," he said. "Maybe the roofer left it?" Melvin tried to sit up, but fell back on his pillow. *This poor guy is in pain*, Will thought.

"Okay, if your garage door works, I'll put it in there."

"Just be careful on the one side. The rail's bent."

"I noticed some water damage, Mel. How about if I tell Sheldon what I found?"

"How much is it gonna cost?" Melvin asked.

"I don't know, but your roofer cut some corners. We may need to bring him back here."

"Shel's gonna shit when he hears about this."

"I'll break it to him gently."

Sam, who had been pretending to be engrossed in the television, rose to his feet and turned to Will. "Can I see you to the door, Sport?"

Will stood his ground. "I can see you're hurting, Mel. Anything I can do to help? Should your brother know about this?"

"I'm taking care of Melvin, Sport," Sam said. "Pain meds, ice packs, and Doc Singer is coming back with a compression bandage, he says, for the wrist. Anything Melvin needs, he'll get."

"How about an X-ray?"

Sam shook his head and pointed to the door. "All right, inspection's over, time to hit the highway."

Will looked back to Mel.

"Don't say nothing to my brother," Mel said. "I'll call him."

Before Sam closed the door on him, Will smiled and said, "Merry Christmas, stud."

He fired up the truck, sat for a minute in the late morning chill. The next house on the left was his family home, looking abused by well-meaning attempts to upgrade it. He idled past homes once owned by the Colangelos, then the Brauns, the Kellers, the Elkins, and on the other side of Cloverland the Derrys's house, the Farley's. He named them on down the block, all the gone old families, to the Cassidy place and then the old Jewish couple, the Gordons', at the corner. He could almost see Elena Weiss in her housedress, wild hair, and clunky shoes, looking frantic, running.

13

Will gave Sheldon the news in a phone call. First, someone would need to speak to the roofer about replacing plywood that should have been replaced earlier. Next, Will said, the home needed remediation--someone who specialized in water damage to get in there, inspect for mold, and determine whether insulation, plaster, drywall, and other materials needed patching or replacement or nothing at all. Will told Sheldon about a guy he knew, a recent retiree who often took on projects like this one.

"His name is McGuinness. I can send him my photos and my notes."

"Can you put me in touch with this man?" Sheldon asked.

Will told Sheldon about Mevin's injuries, while downplaying their severity. He also revealed what he knew about the care Mel had been given. He had deliberated about bringing up this subject, given Sheldon's heart condition and Melvin's request that he keep it private, but he felt the communication was necessary.

"My son-in-law, Peter—did you meet him?"

"Briefly at Hanukkah," Will said. "He and your daughter didn't stay long after I got there."

"I'll talk to him about this. It's best that someone in the family finds out if Mel needs help."

"I'm not sure why," Will said, "but Melvin wanted me to keep this from you."

"Peter knows Melvin. He'll make it look like a social call."

"Good. Maybe Peter ought to check out this Sam character. I don't know anything about his friendship with Mel, but I don't like him, and I think he's hiding something."

"I think of Sam as another of my brother's poor choices. Maybe we need to look more closely at him. I'll approach Peter about this."

"One more thing. Your brother had this wild idea that a Chaldean gang, or Chaldean thugs, were behind his mugging. That they had hired Blacks to rough him up. Is he delusional, or what?"

"Or senile? It would be funny to think that my Melvin is on the radar of a Chaldean gang, but his idea of Chaldeans goes back to the eighties, when they began populating Oak Park and the north side of Detroit."

"My father sold our family home to Chaldeans in around '83," Will said. "They paid cash. Strange that they would choose to settle in a Jewish neighborhood, though. Isn't there animosity between the two groups?"

"Jews and Chaldeans have been in competition with each other historically. It is true that Chaldean gangs were once active in gambling and the drug trade, but the two cultures have common interests. Both have seen trouble in the Middle East. And both have strong small business values. I think Mel's ignorance is getting the best of him. And he is vulnerable to thugs."

"I hope he's on the mend. I'd like to see him strong enough to throw his roommate out the door. Now, what's going on with you? How goes your rehab?"

"My doctor has cleared me for a visit to the Coolidge, but my wife is another story. I'll work on her."

"Please do, Shel. You need an outing."

*****

Since his reconnection with Sheldon, Will had discovered not only a need to hear about Elena Weiss, but also a need to talk to Sheldon about something that took place when they were kids. He was becoming aware, too, that he had been giving everyone, including Sheldon, the impression that his childhood, family life, and personal

76

life were one long success story, that his father's hankering for the bottle was no big deal, and that Vietnam was nothing but an interesting place where he made lots of friends.

Will had always been a glass-half-full kind of man. He was never one to dwell on personal issues. He downplayed his failures, his wounds, and his sadnesses. But the recent past had shown him a different side of himself, the half-empty side that he was forced, somehow, to consider. And recently, he had experienced that it felt good to tell his truth. Not only did it feel good, it seemed to be the only way forward.

His dinner with Teresa had hit him hard. He wanted to begin a new relationship with her. He hoped to begin by listening, speaking from his heart, and treating her like the capable woman she truly was. Her remark about letting go of some of Joan's things had stunned him, yet it rang true. His home, the home he had shared with Joan for thirty-eight years, a place where he rarely had guests, was a shrine to Joan. He resolved to keep a few special things, and he would keep the Viburnums along the garage trimmed for her. And he would never part with her Yellowstone painting. But the knick-knacks, the clothes, the mounds of photos? He could donate things, gift them to family and friends, and maybe even trash some items that no one wanted.

*****

Will drove to Flint on the morning before New Years Eve. A small U-Haul trailer stood in the driveway near the side door, looking precarious with its load. James and Hazel were almost packed and ready for their trip, but James had asked his father to dispose of numerous items that they would need to leave behind. Will was glad to help, but the task would take another trip, a half-day's work. He would also need to finish cleaning so that he might help his son retrieve his security deposit.

He swept and mopped the kitchen and bathroom floors. He removed assorted trash and shopping flyers from the front porch and shoveled the snow. Then he went to Hazel's favorite pizzeria, Jets, and picked up an eight-piece square with pepperoni and mushrooms.

They sat on boxes with pizza on paper plates and soft drinks and toilet paper napkins. The mood was somber. Hazel would miss her friends, she said. She seemed less excited than before about California and a new school, new friends. James had seemed nervous as he labeled and taped boxes. As they ate, Will resisted the urge to try to save the day. He did not know how to help James, who was not one to take change easily. Will wanted to ask about Deb, but he feared that this was not a good time.

So they discussed the route James planned to take, the sights they might see, the work he would be engaged in at Stanford, and the apartment that was waiting for him and Hazel in Sunnyvale.

"You gotta show Hazel some of the sights," Will said. "Do you remember our trip to Yellowstone?"

"Hazel will get us there, Dad." James looked at his daughter.

"GPS," she said, holding up her cell phone. "I'm already on it, Gramps."

When Will was on his way out the door, he sobbed through the goodbye hugs.

"I don't think I've ever seen you cry," said James, his hands on his father's shoulders. "Not even when Mom died."

"I hope I'm not too late, son."

14

On January 14, a Sunday, Will was surprised and pleased to get a call from his son, Patrick, in New Haven.

"Are you okay, Dad?"

"I could bitch about aches and pains, but yeah, I'm fine. Why?"

"Jill mentioned a remark you made to her on Facebook. Something about a knife. She doesn't know what you were talking about."

"A knife? Oh yeah, the knife in her poem."

"Jill posted a poem about a knife?"

"Yeah. There was a line . . . here, let me find it. I wrote it down." Will rifled his desk drawer and produced the poem. "Here it is. The line goes, 'Let me be as urgent as a knife.'"

"You wrote that down? Are you okay, Dad?"

"Dammit, Pat, I copied the poem Jill sent me. And that line was important."

"So you're reading poetry now, Dad? What's up with that?"

Will tried, not very successfully, to explain the "knife" to his son, who feared that his father was preparing to stab someone, or himself.

Patrick called to Jill, who was in another room. "Hey honey, did you send a poem to Dad? Here, Dad, I'll put the phone on speaker."

"No, I don't remember sending you a poem, Will, but I may have 'liked' a poem," Jill said. "I mean, maybe I clicked on the 'like.' My sister is always posting poetry online, but I don't read much of it."

"Okay, I get it," Will said. "Jill, you couldn't have known what I meant."

"So what were you saying, Dad?" Patrick asked.

"Here, I'll read it. Are you still listening, Jill?" Will read the poem to them. Neither were readers of poetry, nor was Will, who only wanted to ease their suspicions about his state of mind. After he finished, he read the poem again.

"Who is Keats?" Pat asked.

"Keats was a guy who thought he had a lifetime."

"Wasn't he a poet, too?" Jill asked.

"It doesn't matter!" Will almost shouted.

"But he didn't—have a lifetime?" Jill asked.

"Apparently not," Will said.

"But you've had a lifetime, Dad," Pat said.

"Not yet I haven't."

Will was embarrassed. He was not in the habit of explaining poetry. And he had little experience in the kind of self-disclosure that would explain why it had a profound meaning for him, but he struggled to articulate that meaning anyway.

"I want you both to know that it's as urgent to me as a knife that I need to move on with my life."

"That rhymes, Dad."

"Screw that."

Pat and Jill *got* the poem. They *got* Will. They wanted to hear what he had planned for this new chapter of his life. So he talked about Joan's things and the house that no longer served his needs.

"But first," he said, "I need to behold."

"Like in the poem, 'To bless the feet that take you to and fro,'" Jill said.

"Exactly. And it's more than that. I want to 'bless touching.'"

"Touching."

"Yes. I want to touch you two, and all the people in my life, and I don't know what-all else."

"Oh, that's sweet," Jill said.

15

On one of those January thaw days that were once winter rarities but with climate change had become common in Michigan, Will agreed to transport Sheldon for lunch at the Coolidge. The two had spoken by phone several times since Hanukkah, but Will found their calls to be less satisfying than face-to-face confabs over lunch.

Sheldon seemed weak and slow of foot. Will helped him from the condo to the pickup and from the truck to his seat at the Coolidge. Sheldon reported that he was feeling stronger, but his recovery was slower than he had hoped.

He ordered one of those bacon-topped hamburgers that had become popular in pubs and diners everywhere. Will waited until after the waitress had left, and said, "Sheldon, are you sure, with your heart . . .?"

"If you knew what my wife feeds me, you would understand that the only times I get to choose my meals are at these lunches."

"Really! I had the idea that . . . um . . .," Will stopped, realizing that anything he said might take him into offensive territory.

"That I have a lousy diet?"

"Well . . . .."

"Denise is a foodie, Will. And she has learned that the only way to keep me out of the grave is to give me a Mediterranean diet—meatless, except for a few morsels of fowl and fish. I eat more yogurt, hummus, lentils, mushrooms, pita bread, kale salads, and veggies than humanly possible. I am very grateful for Denise, but yes, I fall back into old habits. And I hope you will keep my little secret."

Will nodded. He shared, with more candor, less bravado than previously, about James' and Hazel's California journey, his Christmas lunch with Teresa, and his calls with Pat's family out East.

"I donated almost all of Joan's clothes, Shel. I found a group that provides help for single moms in need, and they were happy to pick up everything I'd set aside for them. Now I'm sorting out her books and papers."

"That's a tough job, but it sounds like you are doing the right thing," Sheldon said.

"Yeah. I had to start realizing that her *stuff* is not her. It's just *things*. That has made it easier, but it isn't easy."

"You don't want to part with her," Sheldon said.

"Sometimes I think I've held on to those things because I— we weren't finished. I mean, I wasn't ready to let her go when she died."

"But *she* was ready?"

"Yes. She told me so. But I held on, as if for her, you see? And I've been in some weird kind of denial ever since. I knew, but . . . I have regrets, things I wish I'd said and done. You see, I could have loved her better."

"Regret is a good thing. It's best If it is followed by resolve."

"Lately I have come face to face with my shortcomings with the people in my life. Joan, the kids. And you, too, Sheldon. There is something about me . . .."

"What are you saying, Will?"

"I need to tell you something true about myself."

"I'm sorry if I haven't given you the opportunity to speak."

"Oh, you have. You have. But the time was never right, and I've been afraid to . . . cause harm."

Sheldon sat up straighter. "I want to say the truth never causes harm, but I'm not sure of that."

"My father was anti-Semitic," Will said, "and he passed some of that along to his children."

"Really? You said he was in on the liberation of Buchenwald."

"Dad told us he was part of that liberation, and in a way he was. His Third Army freed the camp, but I found out from my mother that Dad's unit was sent to a sub-camp, a small factory, fifty miles away. The forced labor from that camp had been set free days before Dad got there. He never set foot in Buchenwald, but I think Dad's hatred of Jews began long before the war."

Sheldon sat forward. "This is . . . news, Will."

"I told you my family, going back, were farmers, like yours. Anti-Semitism was common among farmers in this country. My grandfather lost his farm after the First World War because many people believed that rich Jews controlled the markets, and they set prices at unsustainable levels.

Sheldon sat forward. "I've heard about these claims."

"So my grandfather, who I never knew, passed that idea down to Dad, who grew up buying into rumors and conspiracy theories . . . about the Jews," Will said.

"Anti-Semitism based on economic and financial myths has been around for a long time," Sheldon said. "Many believe that Jews were behind the Recession of 2008. During the Great Depression of the '30s, people were saying all kinds of crazy things, for example that Jews purposely caused it."

"I haven't heard that one," Will said. "But before the war, Dad worked for Ford. And I know you've heard about Henry."

"Yes, Ford was famously anti-Semitic," said Sheldon. "No Jews were climbing the corporate ladder there. They were not even *on* the ladder. I read that Henry Ford put out a newspaper that propagandized about Jews. His ideas were said to be like Hitler's, in *Mein Kampf*. Ford believed that Jews wanted to control the world."

"I hate to admit it," Will said, "but my father was small-minded enough to think that Jews *caused* World War II."

"Did you ever confront him about that stuff, Will?"

"Not until I was an adult. He was not an easy man to argue with. He was a closet alcoholic. In fact, it was alcohol that killed him. But he was a secretive drunk and a functional drunk. Once, you mentioned the many times you saw Dad in our garage? Well, he kept his booze out there. We couldn't always tell when he'd been drinking, because, as Mom said, he would quit, but then he would begin slowly until it got to the point where she would confront him again about quitting."

Sheldon crossed his arms and placed his elbows on the table. "You said that he passed his . . . ideas . . . down to his children."

"That's true. We idolized Dad, of course, even though we were afraid of him at times. He would make hateful remarks—'goddamn Jews own all the banks'—stuff like that. And we caught on. Well, I'll speak for myself. I caught on, and I'm coming to the reason I brought this up."

"But you were a child. You could not have known better."

Will paused, readjusted himself in his chair. "I never told anyone, but I'm telling you now. Devil's Night? It was me who soaped your window that night."

"You mean the swastikas and the . . .? Your mother sent your *brother* to clean it up."

"Al and Danny didn't do it, though. And only one person knew that it was me."

Sheldon turned his head. Then he looked Will in the eye. "But you were my friend."

"That came later, Sheldon. And that friendship, despite our different personalities, our separate paths, has always been important to me."

"So you're saying you soaped swastikas and 'Jew go home' on my family's window when you were, what, ten or eleven years old?"

Will nodded. "I had to stand on a milk crate to reach that window, Sheldon."

"But you changed, after that night? You *did* change, Will?"

"I believe I changed *that night*."

"Do you remember how that came about? I'm just trying to understand."

"It was your mother, Sheldon. Elena."

"My mother, again?" Sheldon looked at Will with disbelief.

"She saw me that night. I told you I was standing on a wooden milk carton."

"Yes."

"It tipped over. When the wood hit the cement walk, it made a clapping noise. I lost my balance, fell into the shrubbery. By the time I got myself together and ran up your driveway toward the gate to our yard, Elena was standing there."

"Did she see you at the window?"

"I don't know. She must have heard the noise from inside, then came out to investigate. But she saw the window, saw the bar of soap in my hand."

"What did she do?"

"She was blocking my way to our backyard. I wanted to go around her, but then I saw her face and stopped. She looked at the window and back at me. She looked sad at first, but then she reached out and touched my arm. I couldn't take my eyes off her. She had a kind face, Shel. She smiled and said 'I know you are a good boy.' Then she turned and walked away."

"She forgave you."

"I believe she did. I was relieved when I heard that Mom told Al and Dan to clean off that soap. And I never soaped another window again. I think now that I never felt the same way my father did about Jews, about Blacks, about the rich, or politicians, about any of his rants. But I wanted, in some twisted way, to honor him."

"I can understand that kind of loyalty, Will."

"Please accept my apology, Shel."

"Absolutely. And after we finish our meals and get refills on our coffee, you can make amends by giving me a ride home."

16

After breakfast the next day, Will Miller's morning walk and coffee at Kava Korner was more wide-eyed, more conscious than usual. At the café, he had a conversation with a grad student sitting nearby, and was amazed at the large snowflakes that floated outside the café's picture window.

Later, he assessed the mess in his garage. He had two more bicycles to fix. One was for a girl whose single mom had heard about him through a neighbor. The other was long-ago-abandoned, stripped of most everything useful. *I bet there are lots of kids out there who could use a bike,* he thought.

The abandoned bike seemed to be calling for his immediate attention. He dismantled what was left of the bike, prepared the frame for repainting, and ordered paint.

Then he went to his bedroom, the one he had shared with Joan. He was surrounded by her there: photos, notes, letters, drawings, trivia. Memorabilia of all sorts, some of which he had never paused to inspect. He sat on the bed and immersed himself in decisions about what to do with it.

He found money. Coins. A five or a ten stashed in an envelope or among papers. Over two hundred dollars in all.

He found poems and articles Joan had saved. In each, he was reminded of her sensitivity, her spirituality, her compassion.

He went through drawing tablets, sketch pads, and finished pieces that had never been framed. He saw how her rough sketches grew into something fine and compelling.

He found old photos and birthday and Christmas cards from himself, and from the kids. On some of them, he saw the few words he was able to put together, and he whispered regrets.

He beheld each piece in each drawer and in each box. It was a long, sad, time, but his tears were also of amusement and irony and reminiscence. It was getting on late afternoon, and he was tired. Will was nowhere near the end of all he had set out to do, but he had felt the knifeblade of urgency.

He had begun.

LATE BLOOMER

It was 2013. I was sixty-six and recently laid off. I took a parttime volunteer gig at a library a few blocks from home. I spent my time in contemplative bliss, browsing through returned items as I returned them to the shelves.

I often spent my twenty-minute break on an outdoor patio near the library entrance. I would bring a novel or biography or a newspaper and a coffee. Or I would rest my eyes from the strain of reading Dewey Decimal codes on the spines of all those books.

That was eleven years ago. I was not ready, financially or otherwise, to retire, but I enjoyed that job. People, even kids, seem to be on their best behavior in libraries. I did not seem to need or want anything. The mortgage on my bungalow was paid off. I had filed for Social Security. My life was not finished, and it is still not finished, but then? It seemed settled.

It was during one of those coffee breaks that an unsettling came my way, the return of something I thought I had put behind me.

2

I attended high school at Detroit Catholic Central, about five miles from my home. My parish, Our Lady of Fatima, had only a grade school, so the kids were scattered between the local public school and several more remote Catholic schools. I and a handful of other guys from my parish went to CC.

I was skinny and uncoordinated, with horn-rimmed glasses and major social deficits, including a hesitant way of speaking. Of yet to blossom, invisibility was my game. From freshman year, I shied away from the boys of CC. I had friends in the comfort zone of my own neighborhood. On my street, Cloverlawn, there were kids I'd known all my young life. Most of them were public school kids, but at CC I was a small fish in a pond replete with bigger and classier boys. Many of those boys were being groomed for success.

One of them was Tom Dolak. Tom and I eventually became friends, but that friendship was not, at first, by choice.

Tom was from Precious Blood Parish. He lived a mile and a half from CC. He was a big boy, likeable, a natural athlete. Funny and fearless, he was confident enough to enjoy being the butt of a joke in front of the class. And he seemed to like everyone, including me.

I loved baseball, still do, and in freshman year I went out for the reserve baseball team as a first baseman. I owned a lefty first baseman's glove, a Wilson "Ted Kluszewski" model. My dad showed me how to treat the glove's pocket with neat's-foot oil. Like most kids, I burned my name, "Dan M," into the leather while sitting on the porch steps, using the sun and a magnifying glass.

That glove was everything I brought to the CC Shamrocks. I was too short to leap or stretch for the high or wide throws that came across the diamond, and a pop-up in a high sky was trouble for my troublesome eyesight. At bat, I had no power and could not connect with the faster pitches that came my way.

Tom Dolak, my competition at first base, won the job hands down. The team's best hitter, he had a bona-fide power stroke and batted clean-up all through high school. That spring, I once saw him hit a ball so far over the center field fence of our practice field that it crossed Six Mile Road in the air, bounced once, and put a ding on the roof of a car parked next to the Toddle House Restaurant. In the field, he was not fast but was quick. He could catch the grounders, liners, and pop-ups that came his way. Taller than most, he could reach the errant throws that came across the diamond.

Tom didn't run the bases all that well, but no matter, his purpose was not to stretch singles into doubles or steal bases. His lack of speed, I realized later, was due in part to chronic congestion caused by asthma or hay fever. He carried a big handkerchief in his back pocket, and he often used it to blow his nose or wipe his mouth and chin.

In the short time I attended practices before I was cut from the team, Tom gave me lots of encouragement. In fact, he taught me how to maximize my swing. He saw that I was not getting the bat around quickly enough to make contact.

"Do you know Nellie Fox?" he asked me one day at batting practice.

"Yeah. He, um, plays s-second base for the Sox," I answered. The Chicago White Sox were my favorite team after the Detroit Tigers. Their nickname in the press in those days was the Go-Go Sox because, despite their lack of power, they had speed, defense, and pitching, and they won most of their games.

"Yep, and what else do you know about Nellie?"

"Well," I said, "he's not a big guy but he's fast, and he . . . g-gets on base a lot."

"Yep, and he's played on All-Star teams and is probably gonna be a Hall of Famer, right?"

"He's a sh-shoo-in for the Hall."

"So, you're a small guy, too, and you're not a power hitter. You bat lefty, just like Nellie. If you stand like Nellie and swing the bat like him, you could probably get your share of hits and be a table-setter like Nellie, too."

Tom showed me how to stand, bent at the waist, out over the plate like Nellie. He got me a short, thick-handle bat from the big canvas bat bag. It was an autographed "Nelson Fox" bat that no one else on the team was using. Tom wrapped a single strip of tape about four inches from the knob. Then he wrapped the little finger of my right hand around that tape.

"Here," he said, coming around behind me, showing me a hitter's stance, widening my feet and, placing his hand over mine on the bat, holding it higher over my shoulder.

"Practice your swing with your hands choked up above that tape. When the ball leaves the pitcher's hand, be ready. Don't try to swing for the fences. Put the bat on it. Make contact. You'll get your share of hits."

I wasn't so sure then that I wanted what I thought was the lowly job of a table-setter—hitting singles so the big bats could drive me in. At any rate, I didn't make the team. But later, thanks to my speed and Tom's encouragement, in recreation leagues and in slow-pitch softball, I had some fun with the "Nellie-ball" batting style.

While I could credit Tom Dolak for noticing me and for treating me like a human being, I resented his height, his talent and coordination. He was the star of a team that rejected me. I was envious of his relaxed fun-loving attitude and even of his cheerful goodwill. I don't know if I ever let on that I felt that way, but for a long time after that freshman year, I didn't give Tom more than a hello.

Tom would not have felt slighted. He didn't seem to be the kind of kid to let petty feelings bother him. He seemed to like me, just as he liked everyone else.

*****

During freshman and sophomore years at CC, we had a fellow classmate named Ray Frentz. Ray was a sweet, simple soul, "retarded" as his type were called then, with an overly large head and ears, a small plump body, and a speech defect. In the early '60s, such a condition was often greeted with revulsion and fear rather than compassion. Ray was considered a freak, a retard.

I was in a first period Latin class with Ray. I saw how some of the boys taunted and teased him, while teachers, most of them Catholic priests, often ignored the abuse. My heart ached for Ray, but I wasn't the type to risk my neck to protect him.

One morning before class, a red-faced punk with the nickname of Big O, short for O'Shaughnessy or O'Something-or-Other, started in on Ray, snatching his lunch, then giving it back, then taking Ray's cap or yanking at his tie—yes, we wore ties at Catholic Central. Tom wasn't in that class, but on his way down the hall, he often stopped in and said hello to Ray, who loved Tom's attention. When Tom saw Big O toying with Ray, he warned him not to bother Ray again. A few days later, when Tom again saw Big O messing with Ray, he grabbed him under the armpits and pinned him against a wall. Tom spoke softly to him, his face in O's face, but no one present could have missed his sincerity.

I admired Tom for his defense of Ray, a defense I would not have attempted. I was a good enough kid, but that goodness came from fear. I often distrusted the goodness I saw in others, and I resented Tom for beating me out at first base. Besides, I had privately declared that gifted, confident, popular kids, and kids who came from money, were the enemy.

*****

After I washed out as a high school baseball player, I turned my attention to running. In September of my sophomore year, I went out for the cross-country team. As in baseball, I was up against taller, stronger, more athletic boys. My times were barely good enough to make the team. I believe now that I suffered from performance anxiety, a condition that hadn't yet been discovered in 1961. But I found out that I liked running and was comfortable running alone or in non-competitive situations. Getting started on a cold Detroit morning involved working the kinks out of my legs, allowing my arms to swing freely, transferring my breath from nose to mouth and from chest to diaphragm, finding a total-body rhythm. After a few minutes on the street, everything fell into place. Running, alone or not, became the highlight of my day.

Cross-country races, on the other hand, were not fun. The last half of races found me tiring out, falling back, giving up. I considered dropping out, even though I knew I was better than the times I posted that sophomore season.

Toward the end of that school year and into the next, I began to grow and fill out. The awkwardness of puberty was offset by a new comfort I was taking in my own skin and bones. My brothers and sisters kidded me about outgrown shirts and pants and the newfound depth of my voice.

My physical maturity came just in time. Early in that summer after tenth grade, that pre-Beatles summer of the Locomotion, the Twist, and the Mashed Potatoes, of "Venus in Blue Jeans," and "Roses are Red, My Love," a new family moved into the neighborhood. The Cassidys.

3

First time I saw Clare Cassidy, Cloverlawn was full of kids and after-dinner games. I was playing the old sidewalk standby, Monkey-in-the-Middle, with Chuck and Will, neighbors and baseball lovers like myself. The game was two guys playing catch with ball and glove, and one guy trying to cross the gap without getting tagged.

We stopped and stared when two girls in shorts and T-shirts approached and walked past us enroute to the corner park. While we gawked, the girls acted like we were not there. One of them looked vaguely familiar. I'd seen her at the library or the five-and-dime, but I did not know at that point that she was the same girl whose family had moved into the neighborhood. Both girls were pretty, but my eye was drawn to the familiar one. She had long black wavy hair and a good tan set off by white Bermuda shorts.

Not long afterwards, while riding my bike, I spotted the same girl walking the block with a book. I wondered if she was coming from the library. She had an eyes-wide-open look, curious but not confused, confident but not cocky. I didn't dare get close enough to speak to her. Those were the days when the closer I got to a female, the greater was the fear. Respect, too, but fear was my default.

I learned that the Cassidys were a family of four, and that the girl who so piqued my interest was Clare. Her dad was a tool maker in a shop that had contracts with auto companies. The family had moved to our side of town, to Cloverlawn, to be closer to his place of work. Clare had a freckle-faced younger sister, Margaret, who was still in grade school.

My dad had rigged a basketball backboard and hoop above the garage door for my brother, Frank, who was four years older than me. Frank had played on the JV team at Shrine of the Little Flower High before he gave up the game for music.

One afternoon toward the end of that summer, I was shooting hoops alone at the garage when Clare came walking up the driveway toward me. I was flustered, stunned by her boldness. When a rebound came her way, she tossed her book to the grass, caught the ball, bounced it once, and sank an eighteen-foot set shot. At some point after taking turns shooting, we introduced ourselves.

"I play Horse with the kids at my girlfriend's house. Do you know it?" Clare asked.

"Sure. We play Pig, too, or, um, we p-pick a longer name."

"Want to play some Horse?"

I remember how strange and awkward and exciting it felt to have this gangly girl in my yard. Clare put a clasp on her hair to hold it back, while I clanged my first shot off the rim. She was wearing shorts, tennis shoes, and a dark blouse that showed the outline of her white bra.

After a lame game of Horse, I suggested some one-on-one.

"Ok, let's play to twenty-one."

It was a thrill to see her exerting herself, in a sweat, as we drove for layups and chased down rebounds. Each point of contact sent a shockwave through my body.

We didn't talk much until, game over, I asked about the book she was carrying. *The Diary of a Young Girl* was written by a Jewish teen who hid from the Nazis in an attic in Amsterdam until she was found out and sent to an extermination camp. Clare was moved by Anne's story, which led to conversations that summer about things we both had begun to feel and think about. I told her that one of our neighbors, Mrs. Weiss, had been in a concentration camp when she was around the same age as Anne Frank. Clare soon became aware of other families in our mostly Jewish neighborhood, some of whom lost family or friends in Europe during the war.

Clare and I did not become immediate friends, but our concern for victims of the Holocaust led to shared feelings for victims in general. She led the way, but we both had a yearning for justice. We had concerns about weapons and war that not many of our friends were talking about at our age.

Her father, who I came to know as soft-spoken and good-hearted, was always kind to me. He was an Army infantry veteran of the war in the Philippines, and Clare relayed things he had told her about such places as Luzon and Mindoro. Sometimes Mr. Cassidy spoke of atrocities that the Japanese had inflicted on American soldiers and Filipino civilians.

My father was also in the Pacific as a Marine, and while he didn't speak much about the war, my brother Frank and I had access to a tattered, cloth-bound book with many photos, a commemoration of Dad's Fifth Marine Division in the Pacific. I have the book to this day. I remember sitting on our front porch with Clare one day after dinner, flipping through the pages with her while I tried not to stare at her knees. The book explains the battle for the strategic island of Iwo Jima. Dad was a gunnery sergeant in a tank with the Marines on that island. The battle that ensued was one of the bloodiest of the war.

While we both loved our fathers and admired their service, and we agreed that war was necessary to defeat Nazi totalitarianism, Clare shared her reservations about the bombings of Hiroshima and Nagasaki.

"Those were civilians, Danny," she said. "Eighty thousand dead in Hiroshima. Forty thousand in Nagasaki."

"But my dad said—"

"Did you know that tens of thousands died from radiation exposure? And that many thousands more were maimed and disfigured by those bombings?"

"But, you know, s-surrender was not an option for the Japs."

"Japanese people are offended by that term, Danny."

"Okay, but, um, they refused to surrender, d-d-didn't they?"

"Yes," she admitted, "but can you imagine the horror of those deaths? The victims of the bomb weren't soldiers. They were old people and women and kids."

I could imagine that horror, but when I sometimes discussed my concerns with my father, he was always indignant.

"If not for those bombs," he'd say, "my division would have invaded Japan. We were preparing for the invasion when the bombs were dropped. Can you imagine the Americans we'd have lost if we had fought the Japs on their own soil?"

"D-did you know Japanese people are off-offended by that term, Dad?"

"Don't tell me about 'offended,' Dan. Tell the seven thousand who died on Iwo Jima. Those A-bombs killed lots of Japs, but they saved American lives. They saved my life. And yours, too. You might not be here today, if not for those bombs."

Thus began my reputation, launched by those discussion with my father, as a dissident, a bleeding heart, a do-gooder. I was born with the attitude, but it was Clare Cassidy who dug it out of me.

*****

Clare taught me to lighten up about puns on my last name, McPhail. I took the "McFail" jabs from CC boys seriously because I had the debilitating idea that any kind of success was beyond me. But Clare was a validator. She could harass me about personal frailties and foibles while assuring me in her way that it was all in fun.

She might enjoy shooting hoops or trading barbs with guys, but she was no less a girl than any girl I knew, or knew of, in my limited experience. Still, there was no romance between Clare and me. I was all in for her from the beginning, but I knew not how to be a boyfriend. And while I was always aware that Clare cared for me, I could never figure out why. I was discovering that I could talk with

100

her as a friend, but I didn't believe myself capable of the next step. I don't think either of us was ready for that step. Not yet.

As my friendship with Clare continued and I struggled through my journey to mature, I sometimes hoped that she would become my girl, my lover, all of it. Back in eighth grade, Bobby Darin recorded "Dream Lover." "Every night I hope and pray / a Dream lover will come my way." "A girl to call my own, yeah-yeah." I saw the others, but Clare was the only girl in my world. Still, I did not see as much of her once junior year began and we went back to our separate high schools, she to Shrine, me to CC.

My Clare sightings were rare and of short duration, but friendly. She might show up at the skating rink or the library, at Sunday Mass with her family or walking along Cloverland's sidewalk to the park. I called her Hoppy or Hopalong, in reference to a television cowboy and a Detroit Lions football player. To her, I was either Dan, Daniel, Danny, McPhail, or "Flash," once she learned that I was on the cross-country team.

Clare and I were obedient kids, products of strict families and Catholic schools. We were taught to respect our parents, our teachers, and authority figures. If I complained to my parents about perceived abuse from one of nuns in grade school or one of the Basilian priests in high school, they wanted to know what I did to deserve it. Clare and I took religion classes and attended Mass on Sunday. Despite our roots, Clare was able to articulate personal ideas questioning the Catholic Church, while I had little experience with impiety.

I found her skepticism confusing, at first. But I was a quick study.

One day she asked me, out of the blue, "Do you believe in the infallibility of the Pope?"

I did not want to admit that I had never questioned it. "Well, the Ch-Church says the Pope, uh, speaks for God on m-m-matters of faith and morals."

"That's what the Church says. What does Danny say?"

I stalled for time, trying to think. Finally, I said, "Well, I don't know, but um, I believe J-John the Twenty-third is a good man. I f-feel like I can trust him."

"Yeah," she said, "I agree he is a good pope. But how can a man, even the pope, be incapable of error? What if he gets senile and tells us all to piss up a rope?"

I looked at her and laughed. Clare got me thinking about things. Eventually I got brave enough to think my thoughts, and later to speak them.

*****

I have regretted those days at an all-boys high school. Instead of guys with ties, I could have been matriculating with uniformed girls in skirts at co-ed Shrine of the Little Flower or in jeans at a public school. Most of my neighbors were at Oak Park High. Some other Catholic kids, like Clare, were at Shrine. At an ordinary school, I might have made the baseball team. And maybe I'd have moved through my debilitating shyness sooner.

4

Junior year, my second in cross-country, I barely made the team but improved as the year progressed. I'd been running in a ragged pair of hand-me-down tennies from brother Frank, but early in the season my mother took me to a sporting goods store in Royal Oak and bought me a pair of proper running shoes. The brand was New Balance, and they were black—all track shoes were black in 1963. They cost $18.00, a lot of money in those days. I loved them, and as I practiced and ran in meets with the team, my times for the two-mile began to get better and better.

CC's cross-country coach was the only African-American, students included, that I knew to be associated with the school. His name was Ernie Smith. A World War II veteran, Mr. Smith had run cross-country for the University of Detroit in the late '40's while attending with the help of the GI Bill. Coach Smith often used military training strictness on us, pushing us through high knee walks and lunges and sprints like a drill sergeant. He would see me walking, too slowly for his taste.

"Hustle up, Mr. McPhail!" he would yell. I was afraid of him at first and tried to stay out of his way, but I soon came to realize that I could learn from him.

That junior season, I began to feel accepted by the other runners. I had no real friends on the team, and I had not earned a varsity letter yet, but I was growing and getting stronger, and the guys noticed. The performance anxiety, if that was what it was, that had worn me down in earlier competition was no longer a factor. The previous spring and summer, I'd trained off-season, propelled by thoughts of my new friend Clare Cassidy. I ran at the park at the end of the block, or at Oak Park High's track. I ran or walked to my stock boy duties at Dexter-Davison Market. I hoofed it everywhere else, too, including all or part of the five miles to or from school.

*****

Training for my senior year began in August. We ran drills on a dirt-and-gravel track around CC's practice football field or along nearby city streets most mornings, ending at the school gym where we could shower and change.

One morning during our first week of practice before my senior season, a teammate came by my locker and said Coach wanted to see me in his office. I thought sure he was about to kick me off the team or get on my case for something, but I couldn't guess what I'd done wrong. A vague sense of guilt, that uniquely Catholic emotion, lasted until I walked into his "office," a cubbyhole in the gym basement that contained a student desk, two folding chairs, and a small blackboard. The coach pointed me to one of the chairs.

"How you doing, Mr. McPhail?" he asked, without looking up at me.

"OK, C-Coach. Something wrong?"

"No, we're good, we're good, but I got a job for you. You can say no, but you can do this, and I think you'd be good at it."

"Yes, sir," I said, but I had no idea what he was talking about.

"Do you know Tom Dolak?"

"Kind of . . .. Well, I've been in classes with him."

"Ok, I had a conversation with Father Miller the other day."

"The b-baseball coach?"

"He thinks Dolak could be a special ballplayer."

"He can hit it a m-mile," I said.

"But he has a problem."

"He does?"

"He can't run. He's quick to the ball if it's a few steps, but he's slow on the bases. Coach thinks he needs to get in better shape and work on his overall speed. He wants Dolak to run with us this fall."

104

I had watched Tom play enough to know about his speed, or lack thereof. "It c-could help him. I don't know . . . um, I don't think he can run our d-distances."

"Not at first. And he won't have to run meets. But if you run with him, start him out slow and bring him along. Push him, McPhail . . . but not too hard. We don't want to lose him."

"You should know, sir, that Tom gets, uh, c-congested. I think . . . maybe he has asthma . . . or something."

"I'll tell Father Miller you mentioned that."

I wondered who picked me, and why. I suspected that Coach Smith was sacrificing me for a greater cause, because by working with Tom, helping his baseball career and helping CC's baseball team, I might miss out on my own training. But I was also becoming aware that I *owed* Tom Dolak. Back in ninth grade, he had taken the time to work with me while he was competing with me for the spot at first base.

I was slow to rise from my chair.

"All I want is for you to give it a try. If it doesn't work out, we'll put Dolak on his own program. But your name came up, and I'm thinking you're the guy for this."

My name came up? I wondered who brought it up, but I couldn't say no. "OK, Coach. I'll try."

I turned to leave. Coach said, "Are you ready for senior year in a few weeks, Dan?" Until then, he had never called me by my first name.

"No, sir. Summer vacation s-suits me just fine."

He laughed. "Well, you enjoy it while you can. I'm looking forward to seeing you compete this year, but keep up the grades, hey? And will you stop in to let me know how Mr. Dolak is getting along?"

My parents were surprised when the phone rang that night, and it was for me. I did not get many phone calls. It was Tom, and he was very matter of fact. He wanted a training schedule right away, so I suggested a Monday-Wednesday-Friday routine to start. I did not want us running with the team. We'd never keep up, anyway. Tom lived a few blocks from a bus stop on the Schaefer route, which was my way into the city from Oak Park, so we planned to meet under the marquee of the Mercury Theater, near that stop, at 7 am. Eventually I created a routine for him to follow by himself on our off-days.

Our first morning did not go well. Tom was late, but I didn't say anything. He was fighting the idea of being made to do something he really didn't want to do, especially not at this hour of the morning. We mostly walked. He huffed and puffed and stopped and started. At 6'2" and 240 pounds, he was easily twenty-five pounds overweight.

It was also evident that he had allergies or asthma or some condition that affected his breathing. I'd noticed it before, but he told me later that he'd been using an inhaler and taking prescribed medication since he was ten years old. His nose ran steadily that morning. Sometimes he would pull out that nasty wet hankie and blow into it.

Our first session went for a half-hour.

"You can q-quit anytime," I told him. "If you start slow and get past the um, d-discomfort, it gets easier."

I admit it felt good at first to see him struggling, to know I had something over Tom Dolak, the guy who ended my baseball career and was now jeopardizing my cross-country success. He was out of his element and out of shape. "Do you realize how ridiculous this is?" he would say. "I have a car at home. This is pointless!"

He had a point. It was the way most people felt about distance running in those days. Cross-country was the least popular sport at CC by far, and not many schools offered it. The other CC students would kid us, too. "You guys are nuts!" they'd say. They understood "track" as a sport: sprinters, hurdlers, pole vaulters, discus throwers. But distance runners were a strange lot. Outsiders associated distance running with agony, boredom, and wasted time. But for many of us who ran, there was a kind of freedom in it.

Sometimes during my sessions with Tom, I would take off by myself, sprint ahead, then around a block, or two blocks, and catch up from behind. It wasn't hard to find him. He never got too far away from me.

"Hey, you g-got some shoes," I said one morning. It was a good sign. His old shoes were worthless, too small, and I'd suggested he invest in a good pair as a cushion against the concrete of city streets. "You made the commitment."

"Just like yours," he said, "but yours are looking ragged."

True, my shoes were a year old. I wore them only for running, but the soles were worn and peeling, and the seams fraying. They were all but shredded by season's end.

It was not long before Tom began to accept the challenge of our workouts and resemble the kid I often saw at the center of things in the hallways, between classes, or after school. But because our runs were only Tom and me, he had no crowd to play to. I was getting the real Dolak. We were on equal footing now, and I was beginning to realize that he was just another kid.

5

Sometime during the summer after junior year, I noticed a brand-new Oldsmobile Starfire sitting in Clare Cassidy's driveway. It was a convertible, white, with white sidewall tires. The car stood out amid the older Ford and Chevy sedans and station wagons of our street. My fear that Clare might be dating a guy was confirmed one day when I saw her with a kid wearing a Shrine High varsity jacket, getting into that car.

Once, the Olds passed by with Clare inside when I was walking down the street.

Clare waved.

I acted like I didn't see her.

Most of my Clare sightings during those days were occasions when she was with family or girlfriends, or with that jock in the Starfire. But I discovered the previous winter that Clare liked going to the public library on Saturdays. That library had always been a refuge for me. Most Saturday afternoons, I would walk through the woods and across the outfield grass of the baseball diamond, Diamond #1, past the municipal ice rink and swimming pool to the library for a few quiet hours before returning home for supper.

I did my homework or browsed the stacks, finding teen novels or biographies to poke through. I would often see her sitting at a table with her books spread before her. I always said hello, calling her "Hoppy," or "Hops," which made her laugh, or groan.

But I was afraid—of rejection, of displaying my abysmal facility with friendly conversation. I was afraid to intrude on her. Then one Saturday she came to my table and sat down across from me. I imagined that Clare was a serious student, and, not wanting to dare to be different, I put away my Sports Illustrated or Reader's Digest and turned to my geometry or history textbook.

I became a Saturday afternoon regular, and Clare often joined me at my table, the one farthest from the librarian at the circulation desk. As we got more comfortable, we would complain about homework or help each other with the turgid matters of high school academia. In a library, communication demanded closeness, and so we would often sit alongside and lean into one another to show our texts or notes. I remember how good it felt to be in her space, to smell her smell, to look into those brown eyes. Eventually we began to whisper and giggle like the not-so-serious sixteen-year-olds we were. These were the days when librarians shushed teenagers who dared to break the unwritten rules of library civility.

At closing time one evening in September, I walked her through the park toward home. We stopped at a picnic table under a big oak tree, in a wooded area between the outfield fence of the ball diamond and the service road that wound through the park. Clare had recently taken up smoking. I watched her light up, watched the smoke issuing through her lips. As we talked quietly, she hugged herself through a knit sweater to ward off the cool of a late summer day. I fought off the urge to warm her with a hug of my own.

She dropped the cigarette butt and mashed it into the dirt, then popped a mint to mask her breath from her parents.

"This park is why I love living here," she said.

"Huh? Here?"

"Yeah. These big old trees. And . . . see the white flowers? Bloodroot. This park is special. This city is okay, but by God it's boring," she said. "The identical homes, no hills or trees, and every TV is tuned to The Dick Van Dyke Show or Andy Griffith."

I had never thought of it that way, but I'd been living it, lost in the sameness and the colorlessness. I kidded her. "You-you don't like Andy and Opie and, uh, Barney? You c-can't not like Aunt Bea."

"Sur-prise, sur-prise, sur-prise!" she said, imitating Andy's drawl. "Oh, they're cute and funny, Dan, but . . . I want something else, too."

"S-same here, but I'm not sure w-what it is."

As we neared my house, she said, "Hey, I have something for you." She pulled a bookmark out of her bag and handed it to me. It was embroidered, with a little tassel attached. A prayer was stitched onto the cloth. It read:

God, grant me the serenity to accept the things I cannot change,

The courage to change the things I can,

And the wisdom to know the difference.

"I like it," I said, though I did not fully understand it at the time. "Thank you!"

"My aunt gave it to me. It's a prayer for alcoholics, but she says everyone can learn from it. Aunt Pat is a recovering alcoholic, meaning she doesn't drink anymore."

"I'll use it right now." I opened my history book to the spot where I'd bent a page corner, and inserted the bookmark. I promised myself never to lose it.

When we got to my house, I offered to walk her the rest of the way down the block, but she waved me off, saying, "I'm perfectly capable of managing the next few hundred feet to my door, but thanks, Flash."

*****

We were fifteen, sixteen. We watched each other grow. Clare had a way of bringing out dimensions of me that I didn't know I had. I was getting better at small talk, thanks to Tom, but with Clare we went beyond light conversation, from the relaxed to the intense, from goofy put-ons to sincere and self-revelatory confessions. We were teenagers, sure. The range of our experiences was limited to school, family, friends, and the pain of adjusting to the demands of growing up.

But hurt is hurt at any age, and Clare was willing to share. Something had happened between her and the jockstrap who picked her up in Daddy's car. One early summer Saturday, she sat across from me on the same picnic table bench near the outfield fence with a cigarette between her fingers, looking like she might cry. A few weeks before, she said, her date had taken her to a drive-in movie theater on Eight Mile Road. Clare's details were vague, but the two were—I believe she said snuggling—when the kid came on too strong with her. She fought him off and he took her home, but it upset her enough that, weeks later, she was still sensitive about it. After I got over wanting to kill the kid in the Starfire, I was honored that Clare felt safe enough to share her feelings with me.

Up to then I'd been socially challenged, with a barely existent voice. I had feelings and needs that I knew not how to interpret or express. But Clare showed me how to disclose, if only by disclosing herself. In her patient, non-judging way, she gave me permission to be candid.

*****

Clare alerted me to the emergence of the Beatles. She was a fan of Paul, the cutest Beatle, she would say. I began to tune in to local pop music stations and learn about this strange new British band. My brother Frank saw their subject matter as juvenile at first, but he liked their freshness as well as their musical chops. His Beatle was John. I decided that I would adopt George. I had recognized him as "the quiet Beatle." George made it okay to be quiet. I listened for George's lead guitar and confirmed him as my favorite. Tom Dolak, who was catching on to the raging Beatlemania, declared the lovable Ringo as his guy. Everyone had a favorite Beatle.

*****

On November 22, 1963, John F. Kennedy was assassinated. Clare and I were naïve about politics, but we fawned over the Kennedys like we thought everyone else did. They were filthy rich, but we forgave them for it. We saw JFK as witty and charismatic, the doting father of a beautiful young family. He was also courageous, a war veteran like our fathers. He had stood up to Nikita Khrushchev during the Cuban Missile Crisis, too.

My mother loved JFK. She and brother Frank saw him speak in downtown Detroit on Labor Day, 1960, when he was campaigning for president. Kennedy's Catholicism was a big part of his appeal.

Everyone remembers where they were when they heard Kennedy was shot. I was at school. In 1963, snow days and other dubious school holidays were far from common, but the Basilian Fathers of CC sent us home early that sad Friday. That night, I left the house on foot for Katz's Deli to pick up a carryout order. My father wanted Katz's hot pastrami on rye with Russian dressing. Frank and I always went for the corned beef on an onion roll. Katz's kosher dill pickles were the best.

As I neared the end of Cloverlawn, I came upon Clare, looking distraught. We shared our shock and disbelief over the assassination.

"Let me come with you," she said.

The atmosphere at Katz's was somber. Everyone seemed to be lost in thought. Clare and I, who may have been the only non-Jews present, found a table and waited for my order. We overheard a man at a nearby table ranting against Kennedy, who was a supporter of Israel. This guy saw any US overtures toward Israel's enemy, Egypt, to be anti-Israeli—a threat to Israel. At one point his anti-JFK comments became audible throughout the deli. "Kennedy was a bum!" he proclaimed.

Another man said, even louder, "*Shtilkayt!* Shut up, fool! Kennedy was a friend of Israel." After that short exchange, the deli went back to its previous mood of hushed whispers and shaking heads.

We walked home, not speaking much. I hugged Clare at her door, our first close, meaningful hug. Our grief notwithstanding, it was a thrill to hold close the one I cared about, to share in her pain, to feel her body through her clothes.

The next day, a Saturday, both Clare and I tore ourselves away from our respective family TVs, where news of the assassination was broadcast on all three Detroit networks. We met at the library but barely spoke. Later, we sloshed through fallen leaves to our picnic table and sat, shivering. Words did not work, but I felt close to her that day.

"I'm sorry," she said, lighting a cigarette. "If you want to go home . . ."

"I'll go w-when you go," I said.

I write about those times with some regret. Why hadn't I tried to initiate a formal relationship with the girl I cared about? Guys talked about "making it" with a girl, "making her mine," "putting a move on," "getting to first base." But the fact was that I was not alone. Most of that guy-talk was wishful bragging. Few of the guys in my orbit had girlfriends.

But most were not so confused, afraid, awkward, inhibited, immature, and reticent, like I was.

6

The Tom Dolak Project was picking up speed, as was Tom. He did not enjoy those early morning runs, but he showed up and he put in the work. For all his blather, I noticed that he was the same nice guy from freshman year who taught me how to hold a baseball bat like Nellie Fox. Because I wasn't much of a talker, he asked a lot of questions on our morning runs. And because my answers were often short, he talked. He told stories about the baseball team, about his older brother and his parents, and about girls he knew, or would like to know.

I almost laughed out loud when Tom said he told his baseball coach we had been "friends" since ninth grade.

"I didn't know they would pair us up this way," he claimed, "but I'm glad they did. I couldn't run with those other guys on the team, especially not at first. I had a feeling it'd be cool running with you, Dan."

I wondered if he meant that the other runners might heckle him for his lack of speed or wind, while I would quietly give him a pass. Or maybe he was saying that I was not as good a runner as the others? He knew I was that quiet kid who didn't make the baseball team back in freshman year. So why did he recommend me on such little experience as his friend?

All along, I thought Coach Smith had picked me only because I had less to lose than his top-tier runners. Or because I was less likely to object to the inconvenience of baby-sitting the slugger. I saw myself as a pushover, too unsure of my own voice to object.

Tom's voice, though, was always loud and clear. I learned that he was very fond of his mother. "A saint," or "My guiding light," he would say. He seemed afraid, or less admiring, of his father and brother. His dad, Ed, seemed to want to control his life. His older brother, Wes, had been a popular frat-boy at Ferris State University, considered in those days to be the biggest party school in Michigan. Tom felt that his dad was grooming Wes to eventually take over the family business.

Tom said that he was being trained in the business by both his father and brother. It sounded to me that their methods were harsh and punitive. He was the company's janitor and a crew laborer, and brother Wes, his direct supervisor, was riding him hard. But Tom resisted, and he found a humble ally in his mom. He was uncomfortable talking specifically about this, and would change the subject if I questioned him.

"Dammit, McPhail, how do you survive running alone before the sun comes up?" he asked me one morning as we stopped to catch his breath.

"Oh, it's not bad," I said. "Sometimes I count the street-lights or p-play little mind games, like, um, telling the year and m-m-model of parked cars. And I like running through the park near my house. It's nice there."

"Nice! At 6 am! Oh, you're too much!" he said, laughing.

"Really, Tom. I n-notice things in a different way when I'm running. Like trees, birds, stuff like that." I told him about a group of trees in the park that seemed to be opening their arms to me in welcome as I ran past them.

"I knew you were nutty. All you cross-country guys are nutty . . . but that's really cool, McPhail."

My awareness of trees came from conversations with Clare, whose reverence for them was rubbing off on me. Trees were elegant or majestic or forlorn, or even holy, to her. "The body of Christ on earth," she would say. I would listen to her, and running through the park to the birdsong of morning, I would consider, and later I would sound out my ideas to her.

Tom, though, would often look at me sidelong, with a raised eyebrow. "It's just a tree, dammit," he would insist. But his insistence was half-hearted, as if he soon might change his mind and admit the possibility of a spirit-life in that tree. Tom made it okay for me to, little by little, reveal myself.

He also sang, not very well and without an ounce of shame. "Candy Girl," by the Four Seasons, was popular that summer. It was a doo-wop tune that was sung by Frankie Valli in his trademark falsetto, and Tom murdered it. I got some of my musical taste from my brother, Frank, a guitarist who sings well to this day. Frank enjoyed poking fun at the teeny-bopper music that was popular with my friends. And in the summer of 1963, the British Invasion, featuring the Beatles and Rolling Stones, had only recently washed up on American shores.

So when I heard Tom singing, "I-I-I-I found me a gir-r-r-l / she-e-e-e- sets my heart a whir-r-r-l," in imitation Frankie Valli style, I wanted to hide. But where do you hide on a summer morning, house windows open, with only the hissing of lawn sprinklers or an occasional passing car to dampen the sound?

Tom was undaunted. "OK McPhail, I'm Frankie Valli and you're the Four Seasons. When I sing, "She_loves me," you come in like an echo with "loves me," and then finally after I go, "She's mi-yine," you come in with "'mi-yine.' OK? But wait . . . I gotta slow down and get my breath . . . let's try it again."

I didn't want to try it again, but Tom was hard to resist. After "Candy Girl," we did Frankie's other hit, "Marlena," and then Sam Cooke's, "Another Saturday night, and I ain't got nobody, I got some money 'cuz I just got paid," and then some Beach Boys, "Surfin' USA," yet another exercise in a high vocal register. To hear our Mutt and Jeff duo harmonizing the endless "wa-wah, wa wa-wah wa-wa wahs," in that song, in our running shorts at 7:15 a.m., both of us laughing our asses off, a family of five needed no alarm clock.

But one morning when he launched into Wayne Newton's version of "Danke Shoen," including the German verses, he was on his own.

*****

Tom's running improvement was slow, but I noticed it. By the time school began after Labor Day, I could see that he had more stamina than when we began in early August. His stride was becoming natural, longer and with less of a *whap* when his foot landed on pavement. He wasn't running in full stride yet, and he often needed to slow to a walk, but our sessions were going longer, to forty-five and sixty minutes.

During one of our workouts, he said, "Hey, I been watching you, Danny McPhail."

"Okay," I said. I was afraid of the criticism that might come.

"Do you remember the meet against U of D high last year?"

"I r-remember." I came in sixth on our squad, I think, and about thirteenth in the race.

"I was there," Tom said, "because the race took place before the football game, and your last lap was on the track around the field, right?"

"So you s-saw the finish."

"And I watched *you*. By the way, I always thought you were pissed at me for beating you out at first base."

"Oh n-no, I wasn't pissed," I lied. *Pissed* wasn't the half of it.

"Anyway, you looked like shit that night."

I had not the courage to argue with criticism. I could easily be crushed by it. Yet in that moment I sensed that Tom was not belittling me.

"Yeah, well, I ran like sh-shit, too."

"You seemed out-of-sync that night. I mean, I'm not even a runner, but I sensed it. Your posture, your step . . . you were not running free," he said, "but I'll bet you ten dollars you'd finish in the top five if you ran that race right now. You're a different runner."

"How so?"

"You have a lighter step. You're gliding, man. You're running with ease, and you don't wear out. I can tell. Have you lost weight?"

"No, I think I've gained a few pounds."

"Maybe, but you're bigger and taller, too. Something's changed."

A late puberty, I wanted to say. "I don't know," I finally said. But I did know that I felt more comfortable than ever. I felt good on my feet.

"Tell you what," he said. I'll time you on a two-mile course." He paused for a breath. "One of these weekends."

"Are you gonna run it with me?" I said, not seriously.

"I'll start with you, but I won't finish with you."

He wanted to prove his point, but I sensed he was correct. Something had changed.

That fall, Tom taught me something about being easy with others, being a teammate, being *the same* and yet different. I was loosening up, finding my voice. My stutter was less pronounced. I wanted to share myself with Tom much like he shared himself with everyone around him.

I began pushing him. I should say gently challenging him.

I would comment about his increasing distances, his breathing, the way he carried his arms, or his attitude. Then I would say, "Hey, you're breathing more from your belly . . . that's good," so that he would focus more on his breathing. I was asking about his diet and weight, his off-day training routine, his goals.

"My father wants me to devote my life to heavy equipment, clearing land for urban sprawl and laying down pavement, but I don't know," he said one morning. His father's construction company was keeping pace with the growth of the suburbs. Unlike Tom, the man was a morning person, a self-made man whose schedule showed no quarter for weekends or summer vacations. Tom worked for him summers and some weekends during the school year.

"What do *you* want to do?" I once asked him. I had picked up a new way of conversing—questioning--from Clare.

"Not sure, but the idea of working in a family business, with *my* family? It doesn't sound very appealing. My old man wants to remake the world in his own image. Everything's gotta be his way. My brother is going along for the ride."

"Are you along for the ride, too?"

"I'd rather play baseball, Dan, but I don't know if it's in my future. I dream about being free, living in California or Colorado. If I were to work in construction, I'd want to build a bridge in South America. I might want to coach, but not here in Detroit. I'd go somewhere."

"Whatever you do, you'll do it well, and you'll have fun."

Tom initiated me into the ways that boys talk about girls. I had heard this kind of talk from the guys on the block, but I hadn't participated much. Of course, we had little direct experience with girls, so most of our talk was uninformed, and looking back on it, we often got our facts wrong. But Tom was very open, and he encouraged that in me.

One morning as we approached a house, Tom said, "See the upstairs window on that green house?"

"That one . . . with the l-light on?"

"That's Mary Ellen Warren's bedroom."

"Who's she?" We were running between Tom's neighborhood and CC. I didn't know anyone outside of my own neighborhood besides Tom.

"She was in my grade at Precious Blood, and now she goes to Mercy High. She's a fox."

"How's that?"

"Well, I saw her in a bikini a few weeks ago at Cass Lake. She's got nice tits, and she's cool."

"Did you t-talk to her?"

"Yeah. She was friendly, but her girlfriends had to leave. I was getting a hard-on just standing there with her."

"Wow," I said, embarrassed. The last thing I wanted to picture was Tom Dolak's hard-on.

"Maybe if we ran by here more often, we could catch her getting out of the shower or putting on her bra, or something."

"Sure," I said, excited but afraid.

"Hang on a second." Tom stopped and caught his breath. He pulled the snot-rag out of his pocket and blew his nose. His upper lip was raw from the irritation of wiping and blowing. Then he popped a pill and gulped it down with a swig of water from a Coke bottle.

"Do you have h-hay fever, Tom?" I asked.

"Yeah, maybe, but we're talking about babes here. Do you have any girlfriends, Danny?" he asked, as we resumed our jog.

"Well, no, but I l-like this one girl, Clare. Sh-she'll be a senior at Shrine. We're kind of friends right now."

"So what is it about her? Nice ass, or are you a leg man, or big tits?"

I didn't know what to say. To me, Clare was beautiful in every way, but I was too much in awe of her to assess her body parts. Girls didn't display their cleavages back then. Halter tops and bikinis were not yet common with the masses, but, on a lucky day, I sometimes caught a glimpse of the creamy skin that suggested the possibility of a breast. I liked all the parts of the whole that was Clare, but I didn't yet know how to analyze them, or evaluate them, or verbalize my observations about them.

Finally, I said, "She has a great smile."

He laughed so hard, he had to use his inhaler to catch his breath.

7

Tom never got around to timing me on the two-mile run. It wasn't necessary because the first meet of our senior year came soon enough, and he was correct: something *had* changed in me. Before long, I'd moved into third place on the team; I came in second overall in one of our meets. I earned a letter but, despite Tom's objection, I never bought the letter jacket or sweater. It was more important to me that I'd earned it than it was to display it. I showed the letter to Tom, to my family, and to Clare. Not long ago, I found it in a box of old photos and comic books.

He made much progress over the four months that we ran together. We kept our sessions at three times a week, and by Halloween he was ten pounds lighter and jogging three to four miles nonstop. I clocked his times from the batter's box to first base and to second base. While his speed and conditioning were much improved, he was no speedster, and a full-out sprint from home plate to second base would leave him gassed.

His asthma, or allergies, seemed to give him trouble for days on end, but he would also go for other stretches where his symptoms were not apparent. He had pills and an inhaler, and was so adept and nonchalant at using them that a popped pill or a quick snort would go unnoticed. I noticed, but I rarely said anything unless his discomfort was obvious. He minimized his struggles with congestion so convincingly that only those who were close to him knew what he was experiencing or how he was self-medicating.

I began to realize over time that, for all his schmoozing and uninhibited interaction with kids of all ages and sizes, including girls, Tom did not have close friends. He had a multitude of friends, but I may have been his closest. One day that winter, Coach Smith revealed to me that I was chosen to run with Tom, not because Tom mentioned me, as he claimed, but because Tom *asked* for me. I found it strange because, other than our lopsided competition for first base during freshman year and our vague familiarity as classmates, I didn't know the kid.

But he was growing on me. At first, despite my resentment, I was in awe of his popularity and athletic ability. But that senior year our friendship became mutual. I was beginning to think that Tom thought more of me than I had previously suspected.

And although I wasn't his coach or caretaker, I was becoming concerned about a recklessness I sensed in him.

*****

In December, he called with good news. "Hey, I got a scholarship to play ball for U of D."

"Y-You're kidding. Really?" The University of Detroit is a Jesuit school, and just three miles from Tom's home. Several guys on U of D's baseball teams have made it to the big leagues.

"Tuition and books for one year. They said I gotta keep a 2.3 grade point and stay out of trouble. If my play improves, I can qualify for another year."

I had taken the entrance exam for Wayne State, near downtown Detroit, and was accepted. Wayne is a commuter school, so I would also be living at home and working part-time somewhere to pay tuition. Wayne didn't have the appeal of a U of D or UM or MSU, but it had an okay reputation for scholarship. And it satisfied my parents, who wanted to see me in college. At that time, I had no career goals and wasn't even sure I wanted to be in college.

*****

Tom continued to be at the center of things in CC's hallways and classrooms that year. He was ebullient, physical, and uninhibited. I was still the same quiet kid, if a bit less sullen than before. He continued to tease me at times. He also continued to be my friend. And he didn't care who knew it.

One night during Christmas break, he came by the house in his Chevy wagon.

"Want to go for a ride?" he asked.

It was a cold, snowy night, but I was glad to get out of the house. We went up to the Totem Pole, a drive-in restaurant on Woodward Avenue. Parking spaces at The Pole, as kids called it, had speakers with microphones mounted on a stand that also had a menu, so Tom backed in next to one, as was the custom, and we ordered from the car.

"This way we can see the babes cruising through," he said.

Sure enough, cars full of kids entered on the other side of the building and came around back and down our side, slowly, so they could check out the cars, and the kids in them, parked along the way. Sometimes they stopped to talk, or gawk.

"Don't order anything to drink," he said, as he pulled two bottles of Stroh's from under the seat. "They've been in the car for a few hours. Nice and cold, eh? But first, did you notice the rent-a-cop?"

"He's on the other side of the building now." I'd been watching.

"Just make sure he's not looking this way when you chug it."

I didn't know that I wanted a beer. The legal drinking age was twenty-one. I was seventeen and had never tasted alcohol. But Tom, practiced in the art, placed a bottle at a spot under the dash and popped the cap, and handed it to me. It was close to frozen, but after a few sips, the bitter taste was history.

Most of the items on the menu at the Pole had Native American names that had little or no relation to their ingredients. Or to Native Americans. Tom rolled down the window, grabbed the mike, and barked our order into it. He wanted a Big Chief Burger, a double hamburger that came with cheese, lettuce, and the Pole's special dressing. I asked for the Warrior, a single hamburger with dressing. We split an order of fries that cost thirty cents. Our total bill was $1.55, including tax.

We washed it all down with our Stroh's.

On the way home, Tom pulled out two more bottles of the cold stuff. I passed, but, like a seasoned barman, he popped the top on another longneck. It was gone by the time he pulled into my driveway.

It occurred to me, not then but on subsequent winter nights, that Tom's drinking wasn't good for him. And I had a notion, reinforced by Coach Smith, that I was responsible for Tom's conditioning. It wasn't exactly true, but I *felt* responsible. I did not want Tom's drinking to interfere with his athletic success, among other things. Even though track season was over and done with, baseball season was right around the corner. I wanted him to be ready.

When I arrived home that night, I tried to avoid my parents so they wouldn't notice my beer breath. But Frank caught on. He came into our room to get something out of the closet. I backed away from him, too late.

"Hey, you been to a party?"

"No."

"It's okay, man, I don't care, as long as you're careful. Where were you?"

"Tom and I went up to the Pole."

"Oh, cruisin' Woodward, eh?" he said, laughing. In those days, kids piled into cars and moved down Woodward from one fast-food restaurant to the next, and the Totem Pole was, for most, the southernmost joint on the strip. Drag-racing was a popular sport on Woodward, too. Kids with souped-up cars would line up, sometimes three or four across, at a stop light, revving engines. When the light turned green, they would pop the clutch, lay down rubber, and launch forward, hopefully avoiding the cops. Neither Tom nor I had the inclination to put money and energy into racing, but some of our friends dabbled in it.

*****

Before long I had a car. It might have been the ugliest and slowest car in the lot at CC, a faded green '59 Chevy Biscayne with a V6 engine. It was cheap and it got me through the rest of my senior year and beyond.

When spring baseball practice rolled around, Tom was ready, but he was not in as good a shape as he was in December. I watched a few of his games. He was putting on bulk and muscle and he looked good, crushing the ball and playing well in the field. If there were college scouts in the stands, they were not happy to learn that Tom was already committed to the University of Detroit.

He was a senior but not a team leader. His role was having fun and keeping his teammates loose. Tom was nothing if not loose.

8

When the Senior Prom came up, the only girl I could think about asking was Clare Cassidy. We did not have an official relationship, of course, but I cared for no one else. I was terrified that her response to me might be something like, "how dare you even *think* about asking me?" Or she might laugh in my face. I was torn about whether to skip the prom or ask her. It was Tom who goaded me into it.

"If she says no, you're free, Dan. You can ask someone else, or stay home. But at least you'll know where you stand."

Tom's advice only irked me. "I know where I stand. I told you. Clare and I are just friends."

"Fine. Take her as a friend. You never know where it might go from there."

I asked her. She was delighted to accept, she said, and I was thrilled. Tom asked a girl from his grade school days at Precious Blood. It was settled. I was happy to be taking Clare, and to be hooking up with Tom at the same time. My two best friends.

My dad took pictures on the lawn of Clare and me in our rented prom attire. Whole families up and down Cloverlawn poured out of their houses to see us off in Dad's Ford, a more acceptable option than my Biscayne, which had to be driven with the heater on to draw heat off the overly hot motor. Clare giggled while I struggled with the Ford's manual transmission—three gears on the steering column and a slipping clutch. I warned that she might have to kick off her heels and push, if necessary.

The prom was held at a ritzy banquet hall in Bloomfield Hills. After being served a big dinner at round tables, we were escorted to an elegant ballroom while the band played an old standard. It felt strangely uncomfortable to be in a tuxedo and in such plush surroundings, but Clare eased my anxiety. Early on, I understood that, for tonight, we were mutual supports. She was a source of my confidence, and I was her main man.

We didn't see much of Tom at first. He was busy being Tom, glad-handing the guys and flirting with their dates. At one point I brought Clare across the floor to meet him and his date. Later, we crossed paths on the dance floor and hung out at the punch bowl. It felt good knowing he was at hand.

The band was ready for a roomful of teenagers. Clare and I had practiced a few dance moves, like the Twist, the Locomotion, the Watusi, the Hully-Gully, and a slow box step, in her living room a few days earlier. She had some prior practice with these dances, but neither of us were as good as most of the kids out on the floor. Still, we got loose, laughed at ourselves, and took part in line dances to "Johnny B. Goode" and "Dancin' in the Street."

A slow dance came up. The band's lead singer did a respectable job with Ben E. King's "Stand by Me," a perennial ladies' choice, and Clare, shorter than me by now, stroked the back of my neck while I held her warm body closer than I knew possible.

Later, I introduced her to some of the guys on the cross-country team. Having Clare on my arm seemed to legitimize me and embolden me to reach out and say hello to guys, and smile.

And pretend that she was my girl.

*****

In the weeks following the prom, Tom let me know that he thought Clare was "choice." Even then, the suggestion that she was like a very select piece of meat *and* a quality human being was not lost on me. It was a common compliment among guys, and I admit I felt the same way. When I saw Tom that summer, he would ask, "How's Clare?" "Still seeing her?"

I didn't take her out on actual dates, but I saw her on the street, at church, or at the park, sometimes with a girlfriend. If it was convenient, we would talk. If we were both at the library on a

127

Saturday, we would meet afterward at our picnic table in the park. She had been accepted to the University of Michigan and would be leaving for Ann Arbor in September. I was working longer hours at the hardware store, saving for Wayne State's fall term. Our conversations tended to be about things bigger than ourselves—the book we were reading, the Church, the country, the world.

I had become more worldly since I met Clare. I did not have many opinions, but I wanted to learn, at first so that I could converse with her, and later so that I could satisfy my own developing curiosity. We were both very much in favor of the Civil Rights Act that President Lyndon Johnson had recently signed. She was concerned about the American naval operation in the Gulf of Tonkin, off the coast of North Vietnam.

And while Clare was very passionate about the issues, I was on the fence, but I, too, had been reading about Vietnam in the newspapers.

"A general said our military is trying to get information on the ships coming in and out of the harbor in that gulf. They say they want to protect South Vietnam from Communist aggression," I said, not strictly in defense of the US strategy, but in explanation of what I'd read in the Detroit Free Press.

"I know, but it's a military action and it could lead to something bigger. Our men on that ship are in danger," she argued.

"True, but the people of South Vietnam are being terrorized. They need protection, too. I'm confused, and I don't know if we're getting the whole story."

"And I'm afraid it could become a bigger war. They could draft you, Dan."

"That would be a dilemma for me," I said. "I'd have no choice but to serve my time."

"I'll be glad when you're a full-time college student. You'll have a deferment."

A few weeks later, the Tonkin Gulf Incident was the event that initiated the buildup of US ground troops in Vietnam. The war was becoming real to a growing number of Americans. For the next four years, an average of 300,000 men per year were drafted.

*****

One Saturday, not long after high school graduation, I came upon Clare at the library.

"Hey, it's Flash!" she said in a stage whisper.

"Say, Hops. W-what's that you're reading?"

She showed me the cover. *The Great Gatsby.*

"Fitzgerald. Another one of those p-patriots?"

"An EX-patriate," she said in a teacherly tone. "These American writers and artists were living in Paris after World War I. Hemingway, Pound, lots of others. Fitzgerald lived there with his wife. I read that we exported jazz to Paris during the 1920s."

"C-Can I borrow that book when you're d-done with it?" I asked. I had learned that, to Clare, borrowing a book was a high compliment.

"If you read it, we could talk about it."

I had told Tom I would come to see him play ball later that day. He was on an American Legion team that summer before college, and the game was at Jayne Field, on Detroit's east side. The game was at 6 pm because the field did not have lights back then.

"Want to come and watch Tom play baseball?" I asked, sensing that Clare might enjoy the ride and the game. It would be something like a date, our first since the prom back in May.

I picked her up later in my pea green Chevy. We got to the game in the second inning. There was a crowd. Amateur baseball in Detroit and in nearby Hamtramck was the best in Michigan in those days, and Tom was on a team with guys who had played on a Pony League National Championship team a few years earlier. Several players on the team had scholarships to play at various colleges.

In the field, Tom looked good, scooping a low throw at first and making a nice play on a foul popup down the line in right field. We saw him bat twice. The first time up, he banged one off the wall for a double. Next time, with runners on base, he hit another long ball that was caught. He looked like a pro at the plate, but I could tell he'd gained weight and lost a step or two since our workouts had ended a few months earlier. And it was plain to see that his allergies were bothering him. After a turn in the field, I saw him go to a spot behind the bench and pull out his nose rag. He dried his eyes and blew his nose.

We met him after the game. We joked about all of us going off to different colleges in a few weeks. Tom joined Clare and me at Buddy's Pizza on Six Mile Road. We squeezed into long tables with benches that sat 12 to 15 people. On Sundays, Buddy's was loud and busy. One might see three or four generations of a family at a table, and one might hear Polish or Italian or Greek as well as English. We ordered pizza.

*****

I look back on that night as the beginning of feelings that, as yet, I could not name. One of them, I know now, was *jealousy*. Another, *loss*. As I kept reminding myself, I never *had* Clare Cassidy. "When you got nothin', you got nothin' to lose," said Dylan. But as I sat there at Buddy's, a bright light shone on Tom, in his American Legion uniform, and Clare, in pedal pushers and a plain white blouse, her dark curls flowing past her shoulders. I watched myself fade out, a helpless bystander. Covetous and fearful, I looked on as Tom and Clare flirted with each other.

9

That fall, Tom, Clare, and I headed off to college. I saw Clare on some of those weekends when she was home from Ann Arbor. I would call or she would call, or we would see each other at the library on a weekend. We would sit our fannies on the cold pine of our familiar picnic table and watch the leaves fall, and then the snowfall, and then the rainfall. Sometimes, if one or both of us had money, we went for coffee to Hy's or Katz's Deli, or Stafford's, or the Coney Island.

Our talks were candid. Clare once mentioned a fellow on campus she had dated, discussing his weak and strong traits, debating whether she might see him again. I embellished a dalliance with a girl I met in a sociology class at Wayne State. While I did meet a girl, it didn't go anywhere. I remember being very ashamed of that lie. Was it pride? I wanted Clare to believe that I was enjoying myself and dating girls while she was connecting with guys.

The subject of Tom sometimes came up in the months after the good time they had at Buddy's Pizzeria. Clare seemed embarrassed about hitting it off with him that night. I acted dumb, but the chemistry I sensed between my two friends was unmistakable. Still, a relationship between Tom, the fun-loving jock, and the more serious, intelligent Clare did not seem likely. I understood that Tom had a great heart, a loving heart. He sometimes told me, flat out, that I was his best friend, that I should come to him if ever I needed anything. His playfulness was always contagious. He would sing out loud, off key, anywhere, without shame or embarrassment. Sometimes I would sing along. He helped me begin to break out.

But Tom was becoming more and more attached to his inhaler. He was drinking more and smoking more, too, and I suspected he might be smoking pot and taking more powerful drugs than those prescribed for him. At first, I saw his drug use as an attempt to open his airways and breathe easier. But as time passed, I sensed that he was escaping, avoiding. I worried he would flunk a class or lose his spot on the team at U of D. Several times, when his drug or alcohol use seemed excessive, I confronted him.

"I take stuff to open my lungs," he'd say. "And I like getting a kick now and then. I'm not hurting anyone."

I said nothing, but I was not convinced.

*****

One winter night Tom and I stopped at the Totem Pole for chili. The Pole had a great 65 cent bowl of chili with plenty of beef. We sat at a table in the dining area because the night was too frigid for the heater in my car. Despite my warnings (the Surgeon General did not require warnings on cigarette packs until 1970), Tom had lately been smoking. He went to a machine against the wall, inserted his coins, and when he pulled the lever to retrieve a pack, nothing came. He was certain he had put the correct amount of change in it. He jammed the coin return button; nothing came back. He began pounding on the machine and rocking it. Everyone in the diner was distracted and alarmed. It did not take long for the rent-a-cop to hear the clatter and come running.

Nothing came of this incident, but it revealed a side of Tom I'd never seen. I began to think he was under pressure on several fronts. To keep his scholarship, he needed a 2.3 grade-point average and steadily improving baseball skills, including foot speed. He also needed to blend in with his brother Wesley as a son in Ed Dolak's growing business, recently renamed Dolak and Sons, Contractors.

I fretted or fumed every time Tom Dolak reached for a cigarette, a joint, a drink, his inhaler, or the pills he kept in his pockets. But when Clare was present, he was his most charming self. Clare loved to laugh with him as well as at him.

132

*****

In the summer of 1965, with a year of college behind me, I was given an expanded work schedule at the neighborhood market. Clare had returned from Ann Arbor and was working at a day camp for kids at the corner park. Because we were both on Cloverlawn and our jobs were so close to home, I expected to see more of her than ever before, and I had an idea that maybe the time had come for me to expand our friendship. A few casual dates, I hoped, could lead to, who knew, a summer romance?

Tom had scraped through the year academically and would spend his summer playing ball for UD and working for Dolak and Sons. An opportunity for a date for Clare and me came up when Tom mentioned he would be starting at first base in a game against the University of Michigan in Ann Arbor. Both schools had good teams that year, so it promised to be a good matchup.

I hung up the phone after Clare consented to join me, and immediately began to worry. If I were truly jealous, I would have shielded Clare from Tom or anyone who might threaten my hopes for a steady relationship with her. But no, I reasoned, Tom could have any girl he wanted. Clare was not even his type.

I drove us out to Ann Arbor in the Biscayne, which was nearing the end of its usefulness. We talked in the car about the past school year's classes, books we were reading, our jobs, and our families. Clare and I shared an intimate friendship that seemed to me superior to most of the simple, scripted guy/girl dating games around us, and I was intent, without Clare's knowledge or consent, of course, on taking that friendship to the next level—whatever that meant.

Clare had become expert at getting around the campus and the city of Ann Arbor, which she had come to love during the school year. We drove past the "Big House," Michigan Stadium, where our state's best college football is played, and found a parking spot near downtown. We shared a sandwich at a deli she picked out. Then we trekked to the ballpark, Clare showing me points of interest along the way to Ferry Field, now called Ray Fisher Stadium.

Tom made a few clean plays at first base and looked good at the plate. In the second inning, we saw our boy smoke a line drive down the line into the left field corner. It should have been a standup double, but he barely beat the relay. When the next batter hit a long single, he was thrown out at the plate, not bothering to slide. He batted again a few innings later and grounded out on a ball to deep shortstop. I wondered if it was obvious to everyone that most of his teammates would have beat the throw. He sat on the bench for the rest of the game. His team eventually went deep into the AAU tournament that year, but Tom was used only sparingly as a pinch hitter and late-inning replacement when the outcome of the game was all but decided.

His scholarship had been renewed, but he was on probation.

It was evident to me, if not to Clare, that Tom was not in peak playing shape. I suggested more than once that he should be building speed and agility, but Tom preferred working almost exclusively with weights. He knew I would not push him or reject him. When it came to baseball, I could place no expectations on my friend, who needed no prompting on what his school expected of him. So, I worried.

After the game, we three walked to the stadium parking lot. His father had bought him a new car, a big black '64 Pontiac Bonneville with a leather interior and a V8 engine. I wondered if a condition had been attached to that gift. Ed Dolak was a shrewd businessman. Sometimes it seemed that Ed saw Tom as an asset, or as a business expense, more than as a son. I admired Ed for his success, but I didn't like the man. He often ignored me, and never asked about me or my family. I often felt he saw me as a slacker, a kid who would never amount to anything—at least not in the business world—and not an ideal friend for his son.

Tom took us for a ride, with Clare in the front seat pointing out local landmarks. When we arrived at my car, we stayed in the Bonneville and talked. I should say Tom and Clare talked. For an hour, with the windows down, they chatted in the front seat while I got a word in, edgewise, in the rear. It was Buddy's Pizzeria all over again. And again, Tom brought forth his most endearing self, and Clare responded.

*****

From that night forward, they were a couple, and I was thrust into a personal depression, a long dark night of my jealous soul. I withstood it quietly because I was ashamed of it, had no language for it, and the two people I trusted most outside of my family had inadvertently caused it. It was not lost on me that Tom had beat me out, once again, as in the game of baseball, the game of love. Marginalized and minimized, I had become a third wheel, the nerd who takes the jock's girl to the game.

10

Clare and Tom spent much time together that summer, and after school began in September, he would drive to Ann Arbor to see her. I spent my time trying to detach from my two friends, but they drew me in to their vortex. Ours was, for me, an unhappy triumvirate in which I was a reluctant member. For much of that time, Clare was away in Ann Arbor, and Tom was still living at home. It helped that the kids I had grown up with, my Cloverlawn friends—especially guys like Will Miller, Gary Braun, Chuck Farley—always had my back. I had also made a few acquaintances at Wayne State.

Sometimes I would see Tom's car in Clare's driveway and know that she was home for the weekend. After visiting Clare, Tom might come down to my house. Ever the charmer, my parents and my sisters, Kate and Mary, loved Tom. My younger brother Patrick saw him as an incarnation of sluggers like Mickey Mantle or Norm Cash. We would sit on my porch or he would take me in his Bonneville to the Totem Pole, where we'd sit in his car and listen to music or to the Tigers or Red Wings. He would often have beer or a pint of vodka under his seat.

"You feelin' a little down, Danny?" he asked one evening, while rolling a cigarette, which I assumed was marijuana, out of the view of the rent-a-cop.

I just shook my head. "I'm alright, it's just a mood."

"So talk to me, man."

Tom was the last person in the world I could open up to about my feelings for his girlfriend. He understood that I cared deeply for Clare, but I had always insisted that my feelings and intentions were not romantic. And until that spring and summer of 1965, I was telling the truth. Sort of.

He sealed the joint by rotating it through wet lips. "Want to catch a buzz, man?"

It was my first time. I had heard the Cloverlawn kids tell tales of euphoric adventures under the influence of pot, but I had always held back. I knew that my brother Frank had tried marijuana; I think it was connected to his music. Frank had got me listening to jazz and bluegrass and classical as well as rock and roll, and I noticed later the positive effect pot had on my experience of music. But in Tom's car we listened to Top 40 tunes, like "Wooly Bully" or "You've Lost That Lovin' Feeling" or the Turtles' version of Dylan's "It Ain't Me Babe" as we watched the kids cruising through the Pole or careening down Woodward Avenue. We'd reminisce about teachers and classmates at CC. We'd get silly over Father Enright's "slapshot to the ass" hockey stick punishments or the scene at Ernie's Pizza after a football game. I partook of Tom's brittle weed sparingly, but I loved the effect on my senses, as if seeing or hearing or feeling someone or something for the first time.

"Light's green," Tom would croak, as he exhaled from a toke on a quarter-inch roach. I had a way of falling deep into thoughts, from euphoric to panicky, at the most inopportune times while stoned. I resolved to be conservative—to enjoy the buzz when it came to me, but not to seek it out. By the following year, my third year of college, pot was everywhere.

But it was not long before Tom, with his problematic lungs, had moved on to the harder stuff.

And I continued to worry.

He spoke of his trips to Ann Arbor in his new car. He would take Clare to parties, games, and dinner, and he'd spend a night in a dorm or frat house. I heard about these visits from both Tom and Clare.

The better they got along, the more uncomfortable I was with them. I felt protective of Clare, sensing that Tom's wild side would eventually put her at risk. And I feared that if Tom screwed up and Clare dumped him, he'd fall apart.

*****

Rather than be influenced by Tom's erratic ways, Clare was becoming a curious and serious college student. This side of her seemed lost on Tom but familiar and welcome to me. She and I discussed the news of those revolutionary times, the books we were reading, and the happenings on campus, while Tom's focus was on doing just enough to keep his 2.3 average, being Clare's stud of an escort, and spreading joy at parties. Clare responded to his pure spirit, his openness, and even, perhaps, his vulnerability, including the possibility that his train would someday derail.

On several occasions, I rode along with him for a UM visit. Some of his friends on campus were CC grads. I knew them back in high school but, in the throes of shyness, rarely spoke to any of them. Tom would say, "Hey, they're assholes like everyone else. Just come along with me, it'll be okay." And it was okay, mostly. But I still saw myself as different. Not better, but not lesser, either. While I often took the bus downtown to Wayne State, worked various jobs to pay my way, and lived at Dad and Mom's house, most of Tom's friends had money. They got cars from their parents and lived in dorms or apartments near campus in one of the best college towns in the Midwest. The weekends brought parties, kegs of beer, women, and dope. It seemed to me that these kids were on the loose without restraints. I was not against it, but it was not my world.

One Saturday afternoon in Ann Arbor, while Tom was sleeping in or hanging out with the frats or the jocks, I ran into Clare at the UM library. We talked for a while and did homework together. I told her that I had finally read *The Great* Gatsby, the novel she had told me about back in high school.

"This young guy, Nick," I began, "was meeting people who were doing questionable things. Bad decisions. Reckless people. But

138

in Gatsby, Nick s-saw a pure love. For Daisy, I mean. He admired Gatsby, especially in comparison with Tom—I mean Daisy's husband Tom." I was struggling to make sense of the story.

"Yes," she said. "Nick admired Gatsby's passion. He saw something special in Gatsby's dream for Daisy."

"Yet Nick didn't approve of Gatsby," I added. As I said that, I could not help but be reminded of my friendship with Tom Dolak. Tom was special, I had always thought, and I feared for him like Nick for Gatsby. But more than that, I feared for Clare. I felt that Tom's love for Clare was not mature and not in her best interest. Was that because I was also jealous?

"Guess who I saw in Nick," she asked.

"No clue."

She pointed at me.

"Yeah?"

"Nick was smart, like you, Danny."

"You mean with my 2.5 GPA?"

"Your GPA means nothing, Dan. You can smell hypocrisy a mile away, like Nick."

"I don't know."

"Most times you don't say anything, but I can read your expressions."

I was flattered by the compliment, which led me to take the comparison further. Could Clare be Daisy? Daisy was married to a shallow, morally corrupt guy named Tom, while Clare was dating a Tom--one would not consider our Tom to have a sophisticated moral consciousness. But Daisy was loved and desired by the outsider, Gatsby. Wouldn't that make *me* Gatsby? A Gatsby without the money, charm, mystery, or courage of a Gatsby?

I walked her to her dorm, feeling closer than ever to her but unable to verbalize it, my reticence a function of my shyness and my reluctance to betray my best friend. On parting, we held each other for a longer time than usual.

As I turned away from her, she said, "I love you, Daniel."

I did not respond. Not that time. But I came to understand that I had a relationship with Clare.

A kind of love.

*****

During those two years while Clare was my best friend's girlfriend, I began dating. One girl, Sherry, was a quiet, sweet, sensitive wisp from the south side of town, Lincoln Park. We met in a World History class at Wayne. She liked me in a fragile way that was unsettling. Another Wayne contact was a lively blonde East Sider whose name escapes me. She laughed often and wore dresses and played Chopin's nocturnes on the piano. She lived far-enough away that we wrote each other off as geographic undesirables.

Another was Pat Cunningham. She was a grade behind me and a pal of my sister, Mary. I took her to a couple of Tigers baseball games, and once to a UM basketball game when Tom and Clare had extra tickets. I could never get past the "little sister" thing. It made no sense, but Pat was too close to home for me. Not only was she a friend of my younger sister, but her older sister was only a grade ahead of me. The Cunninghams lived only a few houses away.

For one reason or another, whether geographically, culturally, racially, or temperamentally, all these girls were unfit, unavailable, or undesirable.

That was the lie I told myself. They were, each and all, magnificent, but none of them were Clare. In hindsight, I realized I was refusing to allow relationships to develop beyond liaisons of convenience. Girls, and later, women, lost interest when they sensed that I was not serious.

I continued to admire Clare for her brilliance, her moral and spiritual consciousness, her good humor. And I was absolutely attracted to her. She was growing more beautiful as she left her teen years behind. She dressed simply and modestly and needed little to no makeup, yet she always had the glow.

Meanwhile, I had always appreciated Tom's natural charm, his openness, his sense of goodness, his playful nature. But these traits seemed to fade in the presence of new influences on his character.

*****

One night, fall semester of my second year at Wayne, I walked through the park to the library. There I saw Pat, the sweet neighbor kid. She had the keys to her mother's car and asked if I wanted to join her on a ride up to the Totem Pole. When we arrived, I saw a car that looked like Tom's new Bonneville. I took a few steps toward that car to verify that it was his, and to say hello. I saw Tom and a girl, a blonde—she was not Clare--making out in the front seat. I abruptly back-pedaled away, in the direction from which I'd come. I was almost certain that Tom did not see me.

"Can we go somewhere else?" I asked Pat, who was parking her car.

"Sure," she said, confused. "How about the Big Boy?"

I did not want Tom to see me see him, and as it turned out, I did not see him again that night. But I saw his little tryst as a betrayal of Clare. I didn't know to what extent Tom and Clare were committed, but it didn't matter. I considered him to be cheating. I could not and did not confront him; I couldn't and wouldn't say a word to Clare.

I had heard talk about what people in the '60s called the "double standard," a different code of behavior for guys than girls that was prevalent in those days. It was okay for men to be promiscuous, especially with loose women, but women were expected to stay virtuous and submissive and faithful. A guy wanted to marry a virgin, but he also wanted to sow his wild oats before and after marriage.

Tom never referred to this standard by name, but he walked the walk. Most men were honorable enough not to *act* on their desires. Was I honorable? I had never been tested. Was Tom? Not that night at Big Boy.

While I never mentioned that incident to Clare, we did discuss his asthma and his increasing reliance on the inhaler and other drugs, including recreational drugs, and his infrequent erratic behavior. Tom did a better job of hiding his behavior from Clare than he did from me, but she knew. On some level, she knew.

11

Freshman year was Tom's last with U of D's baseball team. He had been cut, a teammate told me, because of "performance *and* attitude." So, in 1966 he played American Legion ball. He was less serious and slower of foot than in previous years, but he carried a big stick and made some noise with it.

Then in December of the same year, he flunked out of school. Again, performance and attitude. He didn't show up, didn't do the work, and didn't seem to care all that much. Clare and I knew all along that Tom's heart wasn't in his studies. Eventually, he took his failures in stride. It was a relief to him to be out from under the pressure to perform.

But another kind of pressure awaited him. Without baseball and without school, Tom became a fulltime employee of Dolak and Sons, where the atmosphere was toxic. The old man put him on a labor crew or in the maintenance shop, depending on need, and brother Wes determined that need. As tough and as mean as the old man, Wes took it upon himself to break his brother down, which fueled Tom's appetite for drugs.

January and February of 1967 were slow months for Dolak and Sons. Tom spent most of his time in the shop, getting dozers, backhoes, graders, and other road-building accessories ready for the spring season. By April, projects had begun. He was doing hard labor in sixty-hour weeks with road crews all over the tri-county area.

On several occasions, I joined him in after-hours get-togethers with coworkers. These guys tended to be a few years older than Tom or me. One of them, Barney Phillips, or Barn, was a crusty roughneck, married and divorced. Barney lived in a trailer in Madison Heights with another guy, a factory rat named Red. Often, Tom would head for Barn's place after dinner. They would get stoned and go to a neighborhood pub or a strip joint. Tom was not yet twenty-one, but he looked it. He also had fake ID.

I enjoyed the times I spent with Tom and his work friends, but I was, as usual, concerned for him. I would partake in the pot, and on rare occasions I'd have a snort of coke. I had recently turned twenty-one and, because I was casually hitting on drugs provided by others, I would be the first to buy a pitcher of beer. Still, I was a working student with little room in my life for getting intoxicated.

Barn, on the other hand, could handle a few joints, a hit of speed or coke, several pitchers of beer, and something to help him sleep. Next morning, he would arise at 5:30 am for another shift with a pick and shovel.

Tom could party as hard as Barn, but he was not as resilient. Once, on the way home after dropping me off, he fell asleep at the wheel and ran off the road, knocked down a speed limit sign and tore up someone's lawn. And Tom had no cure for hangover mornings.

Barn and the boys on the crew at Dolak and Sons weren't the best choice of friends for Tom. They were uneducated, unskilled laborers, guys who worked long hours and partied just as long. Tom came from a different world. He'd gone to CC, a boys' Catholic prep school, and his father owned the company. But Tom had suffered two big setbacks, in school and in baseball. He got along well with the guys on the crews, but resented his brother, Wes, and believed his father, Ed, was a crook. Tom learned that Ed was involved in bribery and price fixing, and he didn't like the way Ed and Wes treated him. He often expressed his feelings to me.

"You won't be doing this forever, Tom," I'd tell him. "You're being groomed. You're learning the business. One of these days, you'll be a project manager. Someday you'll be part owner, if you are not already."

"I don't care, Dan," he'd say. "The thought of working with my asshole brother the rest of my life does not sound appealing. It's a cutthroat business. I'm hearing about how contracts are awarded. My father would be in jail if some people knew how he's operating. And I'm not cut out for running a big family business. I'm not respected there, Danny."

Compounding this issue was Tom's way, which was not a sustainable way, of dealing with it.

One night, as we sat in The Patio, a strip club on Eight Mile Road, Tom and Barn discussed a cocaine deal, an opportunity to invest in and turn over a sizable amount of powder. From what I heard, Tom and Barn stood to make about $5,000 apiece. It sounded to me like Barney was selling Tom on the idea. The stuff was coming from Chile into Florida. Barney's contact was a Detroiter, someone he had previously bought from, working with someone from Miami.

Tom didn't need the money, but he was intrigued by the idea of dealing drugs and being able to use coke at wholesale prices. This was 1967; the drug scene in the Detroit area was nowhere near as big as it was in '69 or '72, when drugs were becoming integral to the mainstream culture. Drug-dealing was more dangerous at that time than it was later.

"It sounds risky," I said, taking a risk to speak negatively of the deal. Only in the context of naked pole-dancers, cheap perfume, stale beer, and Pinesol-masked vomit did the deal make sense. I was sad for my friend.

"Barn knows his guy, Danny," Tom explained. "Barn says the guy is solid."

"What about the other end? Who are you selling to?"

"I know a half-dozen people at school who can take 10 to 15 grams off my hands, at $50 or more a pop. I'll bet I can drum up another dozen in Ann Arbor, and almost as many at MSU. Barn thinks I can get rid of most of my share on those three campuses alone."

Not only had I lost Tom to Clare Cassidy, and lost Clare to Tom, but I was losing Tom to Barney Phillips and a world I could not comfortably inhabit, a world I feared would destroy him.

I vacillated between seeing Tom as a hopeless fuckup or as a sick young man. When I got pissed at him, and I sometimes did, he got defensive. When I tried to help or suggest that he get help, he denied that he needed it.

That spring of 1967, I was working at a little machine shop on West Eight Mile Road in Detroit, running piecework on a drill press. It was mind-numbing work. I was also taking classes at Wayne, and still, at twenty-one, living at my parents' place. I had my 2-S student draft deferment, but the Vietnam War was heating up. Draft boards were going after kids who failed to maintain fulltime student status. If I couldn't earn the required number of credit hours by June, I'd need to take summer classes.

*****

Eight Mile, a long border between the suburbs and a rapidly changing city neighborhood, was considered tough. Whites were selling out and fleeing to the suburbs, and blacks were buying up homes in those city neighborhoods. A busy east-west thruway, Eight Mile was becoming a racial as well as a geographical borderland, rife with prostitution, studded with strip joints, cheap motels, and liquor stores.

But I'd discovered a quiet little Chinese restaurant on Eight Mile. It was near my workplace. I would stop there for lunch or after work, often lingering to read or do homework. Won Ton soup was served in a Jumbo Styrofoam cup with healthy portions of noodles and chicken. Brown rice, the healthy kind, loaded with steamed Asian veggies, was served on a paper plate. The food was good and inexpensive.

The diner was run by a cute young Chinese family. Dad was the cook, Mom worked the cash register, and their two teen children

146

waited tables and washed dishes. The teens, a boy and girl, sat at a table and did homework when not busy. Mom and Dad spoke very little English, so the kids sometimes practiced their limited language skills on me.

The establishment was on the bottom floor of a cheap motel frequented by prostitutes and transients, who used an elevator in the eatery dining room to come and go.

I would sit in a booth with my Won Ton while the hookers, who entertained their patrons upstairs, often took meals and breaks in the diner. They treated the family respectfully and tipped well.

One night in the throes of the munchies at Barney's trailer, I recommended my little Chinese discovery to Barn and Tom. I wondered if they would be struck, as I was, by the juxtaposition: this wholesome family and their cheap, good food amid the sleazy ambiance of the motel. I had junked my Chevy Biscayne and was now driving a '62 Plymouth Valiant. It wasn't much of an upgrade, but the Valiant, at least, did not burn or leak oil. Tom, with his bulk, sat shotgun. Skinny Barn sat in back.

The guys were not all that impressed at first, but the Chinese family grew on them. Barn got a charge out of the way Mom, at the counter, would bark customer orders in Chinese through a microphone mounted on the counter to Dad, who worked directly behind her on the other side of the serving window. The comings and goings of the motel's occupants were a sideshow for my friends, too. Tom, we soon realized, had snorted coke in the john and was flying high, and when two Black hookers in miniskirts and heels emerged from the elevator, he came on to them. He approached them at the counter, smiling and making small talk, but they were not buying. Or selling. One of the girls told him in no uncertain terms to fuck off.

Tom was undaunted. When he returned to our table, I was a few inches short of calling out his behavior. When the teenage Chinese waitress approached to take his order, he reached for her arm, but she pulled away from him and stood looking down at her order book, waiting nervously.

"What are you having, Tom?" I asked, hoping to spare the girl and myself any more embarrassment.

"I hear you have good 'Sweet and Sour.' Is that right, honey?"

She nodded awkwardly.

"Don't be sour, Miss. I'm trying to be sweet." His smile, intended to be friendly, was half-sinister.

"Just order, Tom, dammit," Barney hissed.

The ride home was quiet; I was angry. I finally looked over to Tom and said, "If I'd known you would act like a prick, I wouldn't have brought you."

He didn't say anything. He had embarrassed me, and I hoped he was aware of it.

Then Barney took a turn at him. "You need to learn how to act, Dolak. That waitress was just a kid, dammit!"

*****

Tom stopped by the house one night the following week. He was straight, but I was coming to understand he could change very quickly. He drove us to the Totem Pole, pulled a couple of Stroh's from under the seat, and, wanting to make amends, bought my Big Chief and fries.

"I'm sorry about the other night, Danny," he said. Even though he sounded sincere, I wasn't sure I could trust him.

"I don't want to be around you when you're messed up like that," I said.

"It won't happen again, Dan. You're the best friend I have."

"I care about you, too, Tom," I said, "but I want you to stay safe."

"I hear you, Dan. Look, I got a lot on me right now. Wes is riding me hard, scrutinizing every little thing I do, giving me tons of shit."

"Sorry to hear it, but I don't think you realize—"

"And Barn and I have another deal coming up . . ."

"You turned over that coke already?"

"Oh yeah, it was nothing. The next one'll be bigger, but we can cover the buy, and we'll make out very well when we get rid of it."

"Do you know the kind of people you're getting involved with, Tom?"

"No, but Barn knows how to handle these guys. It's cool, Dan."

This conversation took place before Clare and I "kidnapped" Tom. I suspected that he had crossed the line into addiction. And I would learn that stopping or cutting down his drug usage would be easier said than done. With a load of product in his possession, he would be the proverbial kid in the candy store.

<h1 style="text-align:center">12</h1>

During that Spring of '67, those days of panic over Tom, I had not seen much of Clare since the previous December when we found out that Tom had flunked out at UD. If Clare knew how badly he had been slipping, she would surely be troubled by Tom's drug use and its effect on his behavior. Still, I had no idea of the extent or seriousness of their relationship.

Lately, Tom and I had talked about her only in the abstract. If I asked about her, he'd say, "Oh, you know Clare. She's up to her ears in books, as usual."

"Have you been to Ann Arbor lately?"

"Yeah . . . but not so much."

Tom clearly was no longer comfortable discussing that relationship with me. Of late, he saw my interest like he had seen my concern—like that of a prying parent. And I believe I was more concerned about him than his parents or brother.

Clare took classes in Ann Arbor that summer, but she came home to Cloverlawn for a few days in early May, after winter finals. On the Saturday of her recess weekend, I spent the afternoon at the Oak Park Library. Clare might expect to see me there; I hoped she would want to see me. I wanted to find out what she knew. I hoped we could do something for Tom.

I also wanted to see her because I loved her, if quietly, like a thief in the night. I had reason to believe that, if they were still committed to each other, Tom had been cheating on her. I wanted to protect her. I wanted more than that. I was still playing out scenarios from old movies and hit records. A part of me wanted to save Clare for myself, but that desire was locked up in me. Guilt kept it there.

Working a full-time job and taking night classes at Wayne was another good reason for an afternoon at the library. I was lucky to be living at home, but I had turned twenty-one, and with three siblings and my parents at home, I would soon need to get my own place. My older brother, Frank, was sharing a big house in the city with a half-dozen friends. I was working toward some vague notion of an independent future, assuming I could keep myself out of the Vietnam War. I could keep my deferment by taking a full load of classes and passing them until I might graduate, by which time, I hoped, the war would be over.

I'd been sitting over my books with head down, eyes closed, when I awoke to a light tapping sound. Clare was sitting across the table from me, batting her eyelashes, mocking my sleepy gaze. She looked fresh and smelled like she had just washed her hair. We could always jump right back into something like an easy intimacy, and I hoped this time would be no different.

We made small talk and agreed to meet after the library closed at our picnic table under the oak tree, behind the left field fence. The Parks and Forestry Department had recently set out the tables for the season. A game of pickup baseball was under way on the field, but the shouts and chatter of spring didn't distract us; we looked only at each other.

While Clare knew about Tom's drug use, she did not know that he was dealing cocaine. In fact, she hadn't seen him since mid-March, almost two months before. Without giving all the details, I told her that Tom's behavior had been erratic lately. She was not surprised.

"Dan, he came to see me in Ann Arbor. It was a weekday night. I was in the middle of a research paper for my political science class. I had no idea he was on campus. I didn't want to push him away because he seemed desperate, so we went to the lounge in my dorm. He was acting . . . needy, I guess, repeating how much he missed me, and that he wanted us to get more serious about our relationship.

"I didn't want to be in that conversation with him, Danny. I mean, I love Tom, but he'd been scaring me with his moods, and it seems we've been moving in different directions. I'm sure he's aware of that. He was trying to fix things with me that night. He bought me a ring, Danny."

I looked down at her hand.

"I can't wear it, but it's beautiful! It's a gold band with an emerald. I'm afraid to think about how much it's worth. I told him it was too soon. He said it was just a friendship ring. He wouldn't take it back. And now lately we've been writing and talking on the phone. Something isn't right with him, I can tell. But we can't discuss the important things. Oh, he'll admit he likes to get high sometimes . . .."

"I don't think he realizes that 'sometimes' is more like 'all the time.'"

"I'm seeing him tonight, Dan. *Bonnie and Clyde* is playing at the Berkley." She paused, looked at the ground. "I think he's strung out on something. Where did he get the money to buy that ring? Is he selling the stuff?"

"He is. I don't know how much, but he's dealing." I had no choice but to admit the fact. To myself. To her.

"I won't tell him I know. He knows how upset I am about all this. I realize I need to support Tom right now, but my feelings for him are changing."

"I understand, but I think he needs both of us right now."

"Ok, he needs me. But the feeling is no longer mutual."

"Please," I said, surprising myself, "don't abandon him right now. And don't tell him I told you about the drug dealing. I want his trust."

"Okay," she said. "He's working 'til five, and picking me up at seven. I'll confront him about his behavior, and drugs in general. I *do* want to know where he got the money for that ring, though. Do you know what my father would do if he knew my so-called boyfriend got kicked off the team, flunked out of college, and is high on drugs?"

"Can we stay in touch, Clare? He has a work friend—"

"Barney? Tom has mentioned him."

"It may be foolish, but I want to have a talk with Barn. I'm running out of ideas here. I think you and I need to come up with something. God, he's been fucked up lately."

"You must be serious. I've never heard you use the 'f-word' before, Danny. Let's kidnap him. We'll keep him away from drugs until he's clean."

We laughed at the idea, at first, but it began to grow on us.

*****

I arrived at Barn's trailer that Sunday morning, late, hoping he'd be available. His roommate seemed to be gone. Barn had been sleeping, so I waited in the piss-and-beer smelling living area while he got himself together. A window air-conditioner was running, and the place was cold. A stack of 45s was loaded in the record changer. The song playing was "Can't Take My Eyes Off of You," another hit by Frankie Valli and the Four Seasons. At the top of the stack was a number by the Grass Roots. Ugh.

My brother Frank would have been disappointed if he knew I was associated, however loosely, with a fan of those two groups. They were popular Top 40 bands, and talented, but sweet Jesus, this was 1967, the Summer of Love! The Doors, Hendrix, Dylan, and Jefferson Airplane, not to mention Brit bands like the Stones, the Who, and, by God, the Beatles were in the record shops.

I wasn't comfortable enough with Barney to kid him about his musical preferences. I did summon the *cojones* to turn the volume down a bit so I could hear myself think.

Barn finally came out in his typical summer attire--bare-chested, in cut-off jeans, with a gaudy gold necklace and an oversized gold ring. He seemed glad to see me.

As we sat down, he began preparing lines of coke on the whitest side of a Monkees album cover. "No, thanks," I said to his invitation to partake, explaining that I had to be at work in an hour.

His phone rang, and a short chat with his ex-wife ensued. Barn said little and gave short answers. "Bitch. She'd fuck up a wet dream," he said after hanging up.

Tom had told me that Barn was angry with him because Tom had argued with their cocaine supplier about money. Tom had said he had enough to cover the buy at the quoted price, but he did not realize—I suspected he did not remember--that the price had gone up. He had to scramble to get cash and wanted more time. Barn had told Tom that he had gone against instructions on how to conduct himself with this supplier and that any screwups would jeopardize the deal.

Despite having heard about Tom's troubles with Barney, I presented my concerns about Tom's health, safety, and job security. I didn't mention drugs. Predictably, Barney did not want to talk about it.

"It's not my problem, man," he said. "I warned him about consequences. A guy can't get strung out on the product he's dealing."

"I thought you were his friend," I said.

"I *am* his friend, but we're in business," he said scratching his balls. "And it won't be for long if he doesn't get his shit together. What am I supposed to do?"

I had no answer for him. I got up to leave. I could blame Barn for his part in Tom's predicament but I couldn't count on him to be part of the solution.

*****

The "kidnapping" was a final, feeble, and foolish attempt to make a difference, to get Tom to wake up. It was futile, too, but we got his attention. We may not have inspired him to act, but he knew we cared.

Clare's family would be out of town for a few days, so we chose her bedroom—without Clare in it, of course—as the site where we hoped Tom would get clean. We stocked the room with treats and magazines. We promised to bring regular meals and anything else he might need. It seemed like a good idea, but the first night, while I fell asleep guarding the bedroom door, Tom removed a window screen and climbed to freedom.

Our intention was clear, but our plan was flawed, and Tom's will and cooperation were absent.

*****

A few days after the aborted intervention, I sat with Tom in his car at the Totem Pole with a burger and a beer, listening to Ernie Harwell's play-by-play of a Tigers' game, watching as carloads of girls cruised past us.

Out of the blue, he said, "I know you and Clare were trying to help me, Danny."

"Yes."

"I love you two more than anything. I'm gonna get myself together. For you, Dan, and for her. I'm losing you both, and it's my fault. I'm gonna try, man."

I was dumbstruck. Earlier that evening, I'd said nothing while watching Tom get a quick snort of powder from a fingertip. I'd been disgusted with him, and with myself for not confronting him, because I had asked him not to do his drugs in front of me.

But now, a confession. A profession of love. My own facility with love, including the *language* of love, was minimal. Yet here was

155

drug-addled Tom, wounded, struggling Tom. He knew where his heart lay.

"Clare and I . . . we want the best for you," I managed to say. "We want you to slow down, get some help." He looked at me, as if waiting for more. "Look," I said, "I don't want to be around you when you're high. It's not safe, Tom. Not for you or anyone near you. I gotta ask you, stay away from the hard stuff when Clare or I are with you. Please, Tom. Or . . . you'll lose her. Me, too."

"It's over, Danny. I'm done. Once we get this last batch off our hands, I swear to God, I'm getting out. And then I can clear up."

"Clear up" was druggie-speak for "get clean." A year later, in Vietnam, I came to know a few GIs who got addicted. But knowing Tom, I already had a feel for the hold the drug has on an addict, and how the lifestyle that accompanies addiction can change someone. How trust evaporates. How friendships fall apart.

But Tom was my first. That night, I hoped I could believe him.

13

I called Clare in Ann Arbor several times that month after the "kidnapping." Tom had gone to see her more than once, but she told me she was breaking up with him. Again I urged her, against a selfish idea of silence, to give him another chance to get clean, as he had promised. His twenty-first birthday was coming up, and I wanted us to take him someplace where we could all have a legal drink, even though he'd been drinking illegally since high school. Clare and I, both recently turned twenty-one, decided to take him out on the Friday night after his birthday.

We tossed out a few ideas: dinner, a ball game, a play, a club with dancing, a club with live music. Clare loved music and had become a jazz enthusiast in those days, and my brother Frank's interest in jazz was rubbing off on me. I'd told Clare about a club near the Wayne State campus that Frank had recommended. A respected trio with a brilliant young pianist had been the house band there, playing most weekends that summer. The place had a crowd that might be more sophisticated than the drunks and druggies at typical rock and roll barns.

"What's the name of that jazz spot you told me about, Dan?" she asked.

"Chuck's Corner. I think Tom would like it. Bobby McDonald's group is still playing there. It's an option, and the crowd might be a good influence on Tom."

"Sounds like a good idea," she said. "Let's see what he says." When she approached Tom, he was all in.

I picked up Clare, home for the weekend, in my father's Ford. Then we were off to pick up Tom. As evidence of Dolak and Sons success, the family had recently moved from Detroit to a new home in an upscale neighborhood in West Bloomfield. Tom's street could have been in a desert; it was flat, devoid of trees and grass, of children and their toys. The homes sat behind large attached garages ready to swallow up multiple cars so that residents would not need to suffer the elements on the trek into the house.

Tom was standing on the driveway in his best jeans, loafers, and a T-shirt with bold horizontal stripes. His black, straight hair was growing out, and he had the beginnings of a mustache. His face, when I got close enough to see it, was changing. The confidence and charm, the charisma that had been Tom, it had all become an affectation. He looked haggard.

Clare wondered if we would get a tour of the house, but Tom didn't offer. She got into the back seat so that he, with his bulk, could ride shotgun. He was in a quiet mood. He said he had an upset stomach but insisted he would be okay. Because he was usually at or near the center of the conversation when he was present, we were all subdued.

We took the Lodge Freeway to the inner city where we picked up my date, a tall, thin blonde classmate named Jill, who lived in an apartment near the New Center area, north of Wayne State's campus. Chuck's Corner was in the Cass Corridor, in those days an avenue of dive bars, diners, warehouses, and small apartment buildings that runs south between Wayne State and downtown Detroit. The Corridor, in those days, was becoming the home of many students and artists, lured by inexpensive housing and studio space and proximity to downtown, Wayne State, the Detroit Institute of Arts, and other landmarks. I found a parking space a long block away from the bar, not far from the Lodge Freeway.

"Are you sure about this neighborhood, Dan?" Clare asked, looking concerned as we walked past an abandoned house.

"Don't worry," I said. "This area is full of students. And my brother hangs out here."

Chuck's was crowded, but we found a table along a back wall near the bathrooms. Jill and I chatted while Tom and Clare sat quietly, resistant to our feeble attempts to involve them. After a time, I noticed them talking intently and seriously to each other, but I didn't catch much of it.

When the trio began playing, the crowd was attentive. I had once seen Bobby McDonald, at the piano, with another band. He was very good that night, but at one point he got visibly irritated over a noisy table. I was glad that tonight he had a respectful crowd, so far. He was in good form. His drummer and bass player were capable older guys, veterans of the local jazz scene.

While Jill and I appreciated the vibe, Clare looked upset, while Tom looked like he needed something stronger than the vodka and tonic in his hand. The two had not seen each other in weeks. I suspected they had relationship matters to discuss. I wanted it to come off well for the Birthday Boy.

When Tom went to the men's room, Clare and I shared helpless looks, afraid of what might be taking place.

"I gotta get in there with him," I said.

"Go," she agreed.

He was in a toilet stall with the door closed. I knocked.

"That you, Dan?"

"We talked about this, Tom," I said.

"It's cool, Danny. You know, when nature calls . . ."

"Yeah, I know." I got so I could tell when he was snorting. I suspected he was prepping a line on a paper towel, or perhaps a cigarette hard pack. As soon as he knew I was gone, he would snort it.

When he returned, it was obvious. The panic was gone. He was back in the zone. After he sat down, he leaned over to me and smiled.

"You were right, Danny."

"How so?"

"The physical work with the crew is good, but I need another outlet. What do you say? You want a running partner?"

"You're jacked," I whispered. "Be careful, will you?"

I was angry, but Tom was in heaven. When the band stopped playing and we could all talk more easily, Tom said he was enjoying the music. He thanked Clare and me for the outing. I smiled and gave him the stink-eye.

The jukebox came alive. People were up and about. Some were going outside to smoke, or to get away from the smoke inside. A guy approached our table. He was a white man, rather short, mid-thirties, black hair. I'd seen him standing at the bar with another man. He leaned toward Tom and they exchanged a few words. A minute or so later, Tom rose and told us he was going outside for a smoke.

I got on my feet, followed him for a few steps. "Wait up, man," I said. "Got an extra smoke for me?"

"No, Dan. Gotta talk to a guy. it's cool. I'll be back in a minute," he said.

Clare and I exchanged worried looks, curious as to what was happening. I assumed he was buying or selling—cutting a deal. It angered me that he would take advantage of his friends in this way, using the occasion of his birthday party to sell dope. Clare was shaking her head. Jill realized something was up.

We sat there nervously. A few minutes later, Clare elbowed me. "Will you check on him?" she said.

I went after him as if he were a wayward toddler. I looked left down Cass, saw nothing, and turned right, then turned the corner and headed down Willis, the side-street. When I got to the alley behind Chuck's, I saw a figure on the ground about two hundred feet away, curled on his side. Tom?

I shook off fear as I ran to him. Remembering his stomach ache, I wondered if that could be the problem. As I approached, he cried out, "I'm sorry, Danny. Tell Clare. I'm so sorry!"

"For what? What happened?"

He moved his hands slightly, and I saw the blood. I tried to help him hold his stomach, to stop the blood and guts from flowing out of him. I yelled for help as I ran back toward the street, where I saw two people crossing, probably on their way to Chuck's. They stopped.

"We need an ambulance! Tell the bartender to call for help!"

I ran back to him, afraid like never before. I tried to stop the bleeding with pressure. It helped, but Tom was quieter now, his lips moving. At one point he said he was cold. I held him, praying for help to come.

Clare and Jill and a crowd of others had heard the commotion and were soon running to the scene, followed by the police, but Tom was unconscious by the time the ambulance arrived. Eventually I made my way to Clare. We watched the attendants work on him shortly, then whisk him onto a stretcher and into the ambulance. I could see his big feet through a small rear window. As the ambulance sped away, a medic hovered over him.

We stood there, Tom's blood cooling on my arms up to my elbows, my shirt and pants soaked. In my attempts to comfort Clare, and later Jill, or in their attempts to comfort me, all of us in shock, I passed Tom's blood to them before driving us to the hospital, and later home, in bloody silence.

14

For the rest of that summer, I wallowed in a post-Dolak fog of grief, guilt, and horror. From the beginning, my family was supportive. My parents treated me like the sick puppy that I was, and my siblings were solicitous. Tom had made an impression on them and on my friends on Cloverlawn who, shocked and saddened, reached out with condolences and concern. They knew that Clare was Tom's girl, and that I was good friends with them both.

I did not know what the police told the Dolaks. I did not even know, at first, if the Dolaks were aware that Clare and I were with Tom that night. A cop had taken statements and contact information from Clare and me. I gave them a description of the guy who beckoned Tom to join him outside. I also gave him Barney Phillips's name as a possibility when he asked if Tom had "enemies." The cop said someone would be in touch, but I never got a visit or a phone call. Years later, when I inquired about the case, I was told that no arrests had been made "as yet."

I did not see or hear from Barney Phillips again after my visit to his trailer, but a few years later, one of the guys on Barn's crew told me he had moved to a small town in West Michigan. His wife and kids eventually joined him there. Was he laying low? Seeking greener, safer, pastures? I wondered.

No public laying-out or visitation of Tom's body was arranged, but a closed-casket Black Mass was held at Precious Blood, the parish church in Tom's old neighborhood.

I rode with my brother Frank and his girlfriend, later his wife, Ruth. My parents and the rest of my siblings arrived in my father's car. We saw Clare and her parents and sister in the parking lot. I had spoken to her, though little was said, on the phone several times in the few days after Tom died. Seeing her was awkward. We hugged.

Mrs. Dolak looked a wreck. She spoke through tears.

"Oh, Dan, Tommy loved you so. Thank you for standing by him."

"I'm so sorry. This is gonna take time, Mrs. D."

She did not reply. Her look suggested that for her, this was a wound that time would not heal.

Mr. Dolak did not look me in the eye or speak to me. I pitied him but gave him a hard look. I don't know if I ever really forgave him for his part, I know he played a part, in Tom's death.

The church was packed. The priest spoke about "Tommy" as if he knew him, but it was obvious that he did not.

After Mass, Frank, Ruth, and I, and many of the mourners followed the hearse in long procession to Holy Sepulcher Cemetery. As Tom's body was lowered into the ground, I remember thinking, *sad as I feel right now, Dolak, and as much as I will miss you, I never want to be like you. But I will always be sorry that I could not help you.*

As the mourners walked from the gravesite back to their cars, I saw Tom's brother Wes, and slowed. Frank and Ruth, unaware, kept walking. Wes was a big guy like Tom but with a beer belly at twenty-six. Tom had told me how Wes put the screws to contractors and put the squeeze on the laborers who worked for him, and how Wes intimidated those who got in his way. I had been forewarned. As I reached out to shake his hand, Wes grabbed my arm. I turned to face him.

"What are you doing here?" He screamed into my face. His father came up behind him. The smell of alcohol was hard to miss. "You don't belong here! Are you sorry now?" He grabbed my jacket. "I want to know why you brought him into that place, that neighborhood? Why the fuck was my brother dying . . . alone in an alley . . . in that ghetto . . . while you sat in a bar with the broads!?"

"Tom told me to wait. He said . . ."

"Yeah, and he got killed. You brought him into that drug den and got him killed!"

"I'm sorry!" I almost screamed it. And I was sorry. "I wish I'd gone outside with him." As I turned away, I saw his father, his face red and contorted, charging at me.

"You got him started on this drug thing . . ."

"No, sir!"

Mr. Dolak waved a meaty fist in my face. I had no interest in defending myself.

By this time Frank had stopped and turned around. "You okay, Danny?" He came between Ed and Wes and myself, grabbed my arm, and pulled me away.

Wes yelled after me, "Some fucking friend you are. My brother's dead!"

Frank, an arm around me, led me back toward his car.

*****

A few weeks later, Catholic Central devoted a Mass to Tom. It was celebrated on a Saturday evening at the chapel in the rectory next to the school, but it would have been held more comfortably in the gym.

Clare did not attend.

People were standing along the side walls and in back, and many more waited in the hallway or in an adjoining room, where a table was set up with coffee, soft drinks, and snacks. Most were guys from our graduating class, some from the baseball team. Several players from UD's college team were also present. A few of our teachers—Fathers Franco, Donoher, and Helmer, and others--were there. I sat next to Mr. Smith, the cross-country coach I once feared. He was especially kind.

"I remember how you whipped that boy into playing shape, McPhail. You were good for him. So sorry about this, son."

There were many others present whom I did not know or only vaguely recognized. Males and females from Tom's old neighborhood and from Precious Blood were on hand. I met and spoke with a few of them; everyone had something kind or funny to say about Tom. No one, it seemed, knew the complete Tom Dolak, the things that bothered him, how he suffered, and how he alleviated his suffering.

I took my place with the CC boys, most of whom I had known only from a distance. We shared Dolak stories. They recognized me as someone other than his sidekick. One of the guys recalled the time Tom pinned Big O against a wall for harassing our disabled classmate, Ray Frentz. "I was there, too," I said. "Nobody messed with Ray if Tom was around." Everyone nodded.

It had been five years since I began running with Tom. I was hurting that night, still traumatized, still in mourning. I mourned even the side of him that I had sometimes loathed. I noticed that night that I was not the same kid who did not speak, did not join, did not make friends. I spoke with Fathers Donoher and Helmer, two favorite teachers who I had shied away from in high school. I was surprised that they remembered me.

I would never be the life of the party, perhaps, but I was losing my fear. Was my stutter an effect of fear? I never thought so, but I was losing it, finding my voice. And I could look to Tom as an agent in my growth.

15

One night not long after the funeral, I drank six or seven beers in a west side pub, watching my brother play rhythm guitar effortlessly, with his eyes closed it seemed, in a folk-rock band. Another night, I chugged beers with Chuck and Will, guys from the block, on a tour of the old hangouts, including the Totem Pole on Woodward Avenue. Some nights I would go for a spin in my Valiant with a six-pack of Old Milwaukee or Pabst. I would drive, and park, and drive some more, listening to rock music on the radio, on the lookout for cops. I got wobbly, water-logged, wasted, but I never got so bad that I could not find my way home.

One August Saturday following the memorial for Tom, I trudged through the park to the library, needing to cram for a passing grade in my one summer class. I had hoped to get back to some kind of normal, a routine, a resumption of my life. I sat at a table facing a wall. Concentration did not come easy.

It was not long before Clare appeared at my side. I had hoped she might be in town that weekend, her summer semester ended. And if so, she might hit the old library, to study or perhaps to look for me there. I wanted this and dreaded it. I did not know why, separated as I was from my heart.

She sat alongside me and opened a book. She began to read as if this were just another Saturday, that we might continue as if there had never been a Tom Dolak.

"How are you, Danny?" she said after a while. She said it like she really wanted to know.

"Oh . . .." I had never heard of post-traumatic stress syndrome. My culture had never taught me how to examine my feelings, to dialog about them in a calm, reasonable way. The only living person I knew who had some expertise at this was sitting right there next to me. I knew that she was safe, that if I were to bawl uncontrollably in front of her, she would respond with respect and compassion.

She put her left hand over my right. "It's okay, Danny."

"Well, it's been hard," I managed to say, fighting for control.

She squeezed my hand. "Me too, Dan. Me, too."

"Can I meet you at the spot?" It was rare for me to propose a meeting. She was still Tom's girl. And in the history of our friendship, I did not arrange our meetings. I did not declare myself for Clare. At first, because I was afraid; later, because she belonged to Tom. I hated my confusion. Yet, a part of me knew that Clare was my friend, and we had shared a major trauma. Maybe we would somehow help each other.

"Ok. I'll leave you alone for now," she said. "See you around closing time?"

"At our table." I had checked; our picnic table stood waiting under the oak tree, behind the outfield fence of Diamond #1.

*****

Clare was there when I got there. I sat across from her, but found it hard to meet her sad brown eyes.

"It's just that everyone's so oblivious," she said. "My roommate is already setting me up to meet some guy. People are walking around like nothing . . . they don't want to hear about my fractured life. They would rather I take it all to a shrink, like for an hour a week, and then get back to the party."

"Yeah, well, I understand. I mean, my God . . . .." I tried to think about what I was feeling, but it was no use. Then I blurted something. "Everything is upside down. I seem to be in a cloud, or a fog. Am I numb? I'm afraid . . . if I try to bust through it, to explain, I might cry, out of frustration . . .. No, I'm just sad."

"Come over here, Danny, please."

I came around the table and sat on the bench next to her. She leaned into me. I put my arm around her. We sat quietly for a long time.

Across the fence, we watched a baseball practice. At home plate, a coach was hitting grounders to infielders, who scooped them up, threw to first base or back to a catcher. On the right field foul line, another coach was hitting fly balls to outfielders, who then threw to a relay man who tossed balls back to the coach. There were yells and chatter and the sounds of balls being batted and caught. A few of the outfielders were close enough that we could hear their conversations.

We watched quietly, while I hung onto Clare, her curls tickling my neck. At some point she untangled herself from me.

"Walk me home?"

We walked through the park to Cloverlawn.

*****

The '67 Detroit riots began late that Saturday night. The next day, on the way to a Tigers' baseball game with my dad and brother, we saw smoke coming from the ghetto.

"It looks like the city's on fire," Frank said, curious.

We had no idea until later that day that the civil disturbance had begun. By the end of that week, seven thousand National Guardsmen were on the scene as rioters looted shops and set fires in several city neighborhoods. Black people rightly claimed that they had been denied access to the freedoms and opportunities that other citizens enjoyed. Forty-three Detroiters had been killed that week. Whole neighborhoods were ruined or vandalized.

Clare and I both felt deeply about the issues and the chaos that was taking place in our city. But in this time of deep mourning, we had little room in our hearts for the daily reports of violence.

She called me toward the end of that week. "Have you ever been to that Irish pub in Royal Oak? They say the music is good and, uh, we could have a beer. So, will you take me there?"

"Tonight?"

*****

Four Green Fields was a raucous pub in a strip mall, not a good choice for talk. We found a table, and I ordered a pitcher of something on tap. The live music was entertaining, and I was in the mood for drink. If I was alone, I'd have made a quick study of that pitcher. As it was, I guzzled two shells before Clare suggested we find someplace quieter.

We walked unhappily along the dark storefronts until we arrived at a little garden area between two shops. It had a paved walkway to a rear parking lot, and a few benches. We sat. I wondered: if we were to have any kind of relationship, what would it look like? I wanted her more than ever, but nothing felt right, except that she was here with me.

"How are you, Clare?" I was the first to speak.

"Today? Right now? I am angry." She was holding herself tightly. "He lied to me, okay? He lied about the drugs. He lied about his inner life, his feelings for me, his plans, his activities." As she said this, she fought back a sob. And then she sobbed.

"Yeah," I agreed, placing my hand over hers. "I often think he only befriended me because I was gullible, weak. If I confronted him or called him out, he'd apologize, but then he'd turn around and do the same shit."

"He didn't mean it, though, you know?" Her feelings were changing by the minute, as were mine.

"I know. He was troubled."

Just like that, we alternated through moods of anger, blame, compassion, denial, shock, and hopelessness. We would sing Tom's strengths, and then remember how he hurt us. But we did not

169

experience our moods together. Often, our feelings were not on the same page. Still, I could not forget our old picnic table spot near the ball field, where earlier I felt like the man Clare needed. I had enjoyed the role of comforter, of lending my strength to her weakness.

But I was not strong, nor was Clare weak.

We sat for a few minutes. Then she said, "I'm getting some help."

"How's that?"

"I'm seeing a shrink. I don't know if he's a certified shrink, but he's a mental health counselor in Ann Arbor. I see him for an hour every week. It's through the school."

"Oh. And how is it? Are you feeling . . . is it helping?"

"I don't know. It's too early to say. Wayne State has a counseling service, too, If you want something like that . . ."

"I could find out about it."

But I never did find out about it. It wasn't that I was too proud, or too ashamed. I would not have known where to begin.

"He asked me—the counselor, I mean—asked me to begin a journal. To write in it every day," she said.

"A diary, you mean?"

"Yes, but a journal goes deeper. It's more exploratory, like of ideas and feelings and goals. A diary is only a record of events, I think."

"I don't know if I can write my thoughts. It'd be something to try."

But I did not try. Not until much later, during a time when I may have quietly experienced a nervous breakdown. Off and on since then, the journal has become a trusted resource.

I put my arm around her, and she nestled into my ribs. As comforting as this may have been for both of us, it was clear that our time together was not happy. Happy was down the mall at Four

Green Fields, or anywhere two people reveled in each other's company. Our time was one of refuge, or worse, habit.

I took her home. Clare would be back in Ann Arbor on Monday. I was enrolled for fall semester at Wayne. In her driveway, I kissed her cheek and promised to write.

"Great," she said, putting a hand on my arm. "And come out to visit one of these weekends. I'm sharing an apartment this year." She paused, and added, "I love you, Daniel."

I bent to kiss her again, but she was out the door.

While Clare got therapy and emoted and wrote in a journal, I climbed inside my head and heart and isolated there. Clare brought me out at times. I was a patient listener, and I often responded, albeit carefully, tentatively.

And I drank. One might guess that my best friend's addictions would steer me clear, but I found solace in beer. And Smirnoff. Tom had left a parting gift, the remains of a pint of vodka under the passenger seat of my Valiant. He would hand me the bottle and say, "it leaves you breathless," quoting the ads in Sports Illustrated. It seemed true that vodka breath was not as overwhelming as that from other distilled drinks. It worked for me. It fit nicely into my growing repertoire of lies.

Having acquired the beginnings of a taste of the spirits from Tom, I began to build on it. At first, a swig or two from that first bottle. Then bigger swigs and gulps from its replacements. I knew all of Tom's tricks. I was careful around my family, all of whom had become as careful around me. I knew how to hide booze, just as I knew how to hide my feelings. I couldn't unravel or detangle the mix of grief, guilt, desire, fear, affection, and concern that blended so chaotically in my heart.

16

A week after our get-together at the Irish pub, I got another call from Clare.

"Are you at school?" I asked.

"Yes. But I have a few days off. I need to get away, Danny."

"Let's go. I'll take you somewhere."

"Ipperwash is only a few hours north. You know, that Provincial Park on Lake Huron, on the Canada side?"

"How about I pick you up in the morning? I'll bring a tent and sleeping bag," I said.

"I'll be ready," she said.

If she had said Mexico or the Azores or anyplace this side of the Iron Curtain, I'd have been all in. But I wondered if the Canada idea was a hint from Clare about the military draft. Thousands of young Americans were migrating to Canada, so serious was their opposition to the Vietnam War, or to war in general.

*****

We left Ann Arbor at ten Saturday morning, took the freeway through riot-torn Detroit. We saw little of the carnage that had taken place from the recent "civil disturbance," as it was more properly called, but we had seen video and photos in the local media. Clare cried as we skirted those sections of the inner city where, we knew, stores had been looted and burned, and people had died. I put a hand on her hand.

I drove to Port Huron and we crossed over the Blue Water Bridge into Sarnia, Ontario. Luckily, the pint of Smirnoff's I had hidden behind the back seat was undetected by Canada's border security. We cruised up the east shore of Lake Huron to Ipperwash Provincial Park, where we set up the tent and laid out our sleeping bags. A few miles up the road at Grand Bend, we ate a late lunch at a diner and stopped at a grocery store for more food, and beer for me.

We spent the rest of that afternoon on the beach. Standing among the waves, letting them knock me about and wash over me, felt like a purification ritual. Eventually we returned to the campsite, changed into cutoffs and t-shirts, and ate grilled hot dogs with a side of potato salad before getting back to the beach for a walk along the shore, where the sun was slowly moving toward the water.

I was still in confusion mode. Most of me was aware of the context: Clare's boyfriend, my best friend, had been dead for six weeks; my friendship with her had been one of deep sharing, loving hugs, and some physical closeness in our grief; our trip's purpose was escape—escape from the mayhem of the Detroit riots, from the pressure of classes and jobs--especially escape to further share our grief over Tom.

But a chunk of me was on an outing with the woman I had always loved. It was a chance to declare myself, to get closer in a tent under the stars. Males of the species, so I thought, would have considered me a fool to think otherwise, given my feelings and Clare's blunt invitation.

The sun floated over the lake like a big pink grapefruit. "If you get drafted, Danny, would you consider moving here?"

I had not yet decided. "Sure. I think about it. But I don't know that I could actually leave the country."

"You'd fight in Vietnam?"

"I don't know. I'd like to think I would fight for a cause worth dying for, but you know I don't believe in that war. Still, to dodge the draft or become a deserter, those are big steps. There's no returning from Canada, Clare. I'd be arrested at the border and sent to a federal prison. And I can guess what my father would think, or your father. They're both proud war veterans."

"Whatever you do, I would respect your decision Danny," she said. "If you were to leave the country or register as a conscientious objector, I'd support you."

Even though I thought of war as detestable, I believed that some wars had surely been necessary. Most Americans would agree that World War II was a necessary war. To file as a conscientious objector, one had to claim that war, all war, is morally wrong. I had heard the arguments; Martin Luther King had spoken eloquently for non-violence. But I could not in conscience agree.

For me, then, Canada was an option, if not an easy one. Either way, my life was about to change.

Clare had always been vocal about her own opposition to Vietnam. I did not doubt her sincerity, but I did not know exactly how far she would go to support me if I were to refuse to serve. I had even considered a quid pro quo: *Come, let us be lovers in Canada.* Maybe I'd go if she were willing to come with me.

I put an arm around her shoulders. "Thank you, Clare. Your support means a lot."

We watched the sunset and walked back to the campground as darkness set in. Clare went off to the bathroom to change into sweats. I changed into my own in the tent and waited.

In our respective sleeping bags, listening to crickets and the chatter from nearby campsites, we lay there talking about Michigan and Canada, and that lovely great Lake Huron that separates the two. A lantern from a neighboring campsite offered barely enough light to see the shapes of our faces. Meanwhile, my competing versions of our relationship vied for my attention. I knew to keep my hands to myself, but I needed to come clean.

In the dark, I mustered my courage. Placing a hand on her shoulder, I said, "I want you to know how I feel about you, Clare."

She faced me, inches away, propped on an elbow, and waited.

"Ever since that summer after tenth grade when your family moved onto Cloverlawn and we became friends, I've been, well, very fond of you."

"That's sweet, Daniel. We go back, don't we? I've been fond of you, too."

"I've always wanted to be more than a friend, but . . . we were both so very unready. I was immature and fearful in those days. I was afraid I'd jeopardize it. I'd lose our friendship by . . . by telling you how I really felt. And then Tom came along and I'd lost any . . ."

"Oh, Dan!"

"And now, I don't know. Tom was my best friend. And you are my . . ."

"You are dear to me, Dan. You are *my* best friend, too. We've been through so much together. And now Tom."

I leaned in to kiss her mouth. She turned away slightly. I found her cheekbone. We laughed.

"You should know, Dan, I *so* look up to you. You're wise and funny. You're like the brother I never had."

"Oh." I closed my eyes. *Brother* was not the word I had hoped to hear.

"You've always given me your time, Dan. Always. And we're getting through this, whatever this is right now, getting over Tom. I'm in no —I have no room in my heart for anything more than our friendship. Not so soon after . . . you know."

"Of course," I said. "I'm sorry I—it was insensitive of me to tell you of these feelings. But . . . I hope you understand."

"I do. It's okay. I should not have done this with you. Here, in this tent. It gives us both the wrong impression. I'm the one who needs to apologize, Dan."

We forgave each other. We lay there listening to the chatter of other campers. Some were partying, some getting ready for bed. But the noise in my head was deafening. I had been brought back to earth, back to the reality that I knew all along, the reality that in a weak moment I had failed to acknowledge.

*****

Sometime after midnight, after lying awake, I crept out of the tent. I had a few beers left, and that pint of Smirnoff's was still under the rear seat. I longed for that burning in the mouth that I could trace all the way down to the pit of my stomach. I had to move a few things around to clear the seat so I could dig behind it for the bottle. I filled a six-ounce cup and stashed the bottle. I remained there, afraid to close the creaky car door and awaken Clare.

But after a while Clare emerged through the mesh flap of the tent. I think, now, that I wanted her to catch me in the act. I wanted her to know that I, too, was suffering. Not only from the horror of Tom's murder, but from the reality that she was unattainable.

If she knew the contents of my cup or of the desolation that drove me to it, she said nothing. She stood there, slender but desirable in her wild hair and baggy sweat clothes, and waited. I climbed out of the car. We walked to the picnic table, where I opened a warming bottle of Pabst, and sat.

"I couldn't sleep."

"Me too, Dan. Are you okay?"

I looked at her. "Yes . . . I'm embarrassed about what happened in the tent."

"You did nothing to be ashamed of. You expressed true feelings. I expressed true feelings. I love who you are, Daniel. I don't wish to hurt you."

"Yes, I know that."

We sat quietly until, when I finished my beer, she said, "Let's get some sleep."

*****

The following morning, after grilled hot dog buns, fruit, and coffee, we drove to a nearby park on a creek that emptied into Lake Huron.

We walked a trail that took us to a tower of sorts with an observation platform from which we could see down the creek to a patch of Huron. Michigan was too far over the horizon to spot.

Clare gave my shoulder a playful shove. The platform had a sturdy guard rail, but I faked almost flipping over it. Then I returned the shove. We laughed at ourselves. We had returned to that platonic level of physicality.

"Has this trip done what you were hoping for?" I wondered aloud. "I mean, getting away from Ann Arbor, away from the red, white, and blue, all of that?"

"I don't know, Dan. I'll know when I get back to school. I have a paper due on Tuesday, and a test, I think, on Thursday. It feels like I'm getting some perspective here. Maybe this time away will help me get serious about my classes." She was quiet for a bit, and said, "I think you are blaming yourself over Tom. If you are, It's misplaced, you know."

I was not so sure. Not only had I not protected Tom, from himself or from his murderer, I had coveted his girl and had made a play for her just weeks after his death.

"Once upon a time it was my job to get Tom in shape for baseball. I've always felt some kind of responsibility for him."

"But you were never really . . . .."

"No. I wasn't a coach or a mentor. But I never had many friends. And I've worried about the friends I have. Tom. You."

"Danny. Tom knew how you felt about him. He never thought you let him down. I think we--I mean me, but you too—we need to let him go."

"And you, Clare?"

"I'll be okay," she said, misinterpreting my question: *You, too? Do I need to let you go?*

✶✶✶✶✶

We left the park that afternoon, both Clare and I having had enough of Canada, and perhaps of each other. We listened to music on the return trip to Ann Arbor. Jefferson Airplane, Janis Joplin, The Moody Blues. We talked religion, politics, movies, and the hot topics of those tumultuous sixties: war, race, women's rights.

When we arrived at her apartment, it felt like the end of something.

"What will you do, Dan?"

The question sounded too ominous to attempt an answer. I could think only of the immediate future. "I gotta get back to Cloverlawn. I'm pulling a shift at the shop in the morning. And I go from there to my class at Wayne."

"That sounds something like what I'll be doing. My heart won't be in it, though."

"Nor mine."

"Daniel. Will you remember that I've always loved you, and I will never stop loving you?"

"I won't forget. I hope you know I feel the same." I would remember, but I would puzzle over our sort of loving.

We hugged. She kissed me on the cheek and said good-bye. I watched her until she closed the door of her apartment building.

17

My induction notice came two months after that trip to Canada. I spent a year in Kentucky before my tour in Vietnam. Although I felt for all my countrymen who suffered and died in that war, I came away also with feeling for those in the middle, the peasants, those in hamlets once peaceful, once removed from the mad business of the outside world.

I spent my tour in a good place, at a time of relative peace-- for that place. I was a clerk, and when I was not sitting at a desk twelve hours a day, seven days a week, I was sitting in a bunker behind coils of barbed wire with a rifle and a mounted machine gun. If an alert was signaled, I took a position in that bunker. But I fired those weapons only in training.

*****

A few months after my military service ended, I drove out to Colorado to visit a guy I'd served with overseas. He was living in a village on the eastern slope of the Rockies, in the shadow of two great mountains. John Sartorre, bred in Queens, had often spoken of a longing to sidestep the urban chaos. We corresponded after his discharge, which was not long before my own. He and his beautiful wife, Louisa, had bought a split-log cabin outside a village at eight thousand feet.

I drove out to meet him with a sleeping bag and enough clothing for a week. I stayed a month.

It was spring of 1970. John and I, often joined by Lou, took long late breakfasts at the Tanager. We fished a nearby trout stream or hiked backcountry trails. I helped him with maintenance on the cabin or gathering next-winter firewood under permit on federal lands.

After dinner, cooked on a stove heated with aspen, pine, and a few lumps of coal, I would venture to the outhouse, where the wind whistled through pine-sheathed walls decorated with cartoons tacked up by Louisa. I would sometimes stand and have a cigarette under as many stars as I had ever seen and in a land so quiet that I could hear the blood coursing through my veins. When the wind came, it rustled down the canyon, coming my way, stirring the aspen grove just uphill, continuing through me and past me.

I didn't know where to go from that place. I'd thought about school back in Detroit, but as was the case before I was drafted, I had no career goals. Besides, a taste of an independent mountain culture, elevation 8,500 feet, was showing me that I needed to find my own sense of efficacy, a way to survive in a simpler world than I had previously known.

John suggested I take a northern route home, through Montana to US Highway 2, traversing the border country into Michigan's Upper Peninsula, then over the Mackinac Bridge and back down to Detroit.

I picked up Highway 2 somewhere east of Glacier National Park. The Hi-Line, as it was also called, was mostly a two-lane road. Towns were few, but several Indian reservations marked the way. The terrain in Montana and North Dakota was relatively flat or rolling prairie, land where buffalo once roamed. A river was sometimes in sight, as was a railroad line. Traffic was light. I had a couple of 8-track tapes: a Dylan, a Hendrix, and the new Rolling Stones tape, *Let it Bleed*. "Gimme Shelter" always hit me hard.

I'd had no contact with Clare Cassidy since that day in Ann Arbor when I'd dropped her off after our short Canada trip. She had written a few letters to me in 'Nam that, for a reason I never understood, I never got around to answering. Somewhere in Minnesota's north woods, during a phone call home, my sister Kate called said she had heard from Clare's sister Maggie that Clare was still in Ann Arbor, engaged to a med student.

That night, I pulled into the old Great Lakes port of Duluth, where I drank rye whiskey like an old mariner. My lust for alcohol and drugs had waned during my time in the Army, where I became acquainted with several habitual juicers and dopers, and where I kept the vow I had once made over Tom Dolak's grave. Luckily, addiction was not in my DNA. But I had hoped all along, a hope that I had no right to harbor, that I might see Clare Cassidy again in Michigan.

The news of her engagement sent me to the nearest barstool.

The morning after, my hangover reminded me that drinking rituals do not wash away grief. As if I had a right to feel such a thing.

Continuing east, I broke from Highway 2 near Porcupine Mountains State Park and continued to Marquette, a college town on Lake Superior. I sat in a coffee shop and picked up my Steinback novel. *East of Eden*, an old Clare Cassidy suggestion.

A quartet of Northern Michigan University coeds came in and sat at a nearby table. Scrubbed clean and perky, they could have been from the cheerleading squad. I felt to be twice their ages, but when I heard them celebrating a twenty-first birthday, I realized I was only a few years older.

In the bathroom, a poster hung on the wall over the toilet tank: "War is not healthy for children and other living things." I had seen it in Clare's dorm room. I learned good values from my mother and father and from my Catholic school background, but it was Clare who impressed upon me that life is sacred, and that I have a responsibility to honor that sacredness.

"Everything connects, Danny," she would say. "But it's more than that: everything is one with everything else. And the all is God." To Clare, God was another word for love. "We are not greater or lesser, Dan. We are only in or out of harmony with the Creator."

I loved the pure spirit that was Clare, but for a long time after Vietnam I could not imagine the linkage of all things that she sometimes spoke of. I saw crippled children, children selling their bodies. I saw the effects of napalm, a liquid that burns people like no fire ever could. I saw the dead and the living dead. I stopped imagining.

*****

The road east from Marquette was rugged all the way to Grand Marais, where I landed. That place was far enough away from everyone and everywhere to be where I thought I needed to be. To find my center. To find out if I had a center. To sort things out for myself. To begin again.

I tented for a few weeks on a little ridge over the Sucker River, a few miles from Grand Marais, but winter comes early in the UP. I had no idea how I could survive there. I had little money, no possessions, and no reason to be anywhere. While in the Army I longed to be free, but up there I experienced the terror of having no idea what to do with my freedom.

18

After a few days of woeful indecision, walking trails, fishing the Sucker River with a rig bequeathed by John Sartorre, rationing my pennies, I went to the one bar in town. It was crowded with football fans. I bought a beer and a burger and watched the Detroit Lions lose to the Green Bay Packers on TV. When I got bored, I put a quarter on the pool table where a handful of guys were challenging winners.

I shook hands with the fellow next to me, who introduced himself as Jaako Toivonen. He was fifty-five years old and the uncle of one of the pool players, a kid named Ari who, when he wasn't playing, sat on Jaako's other side at the bar. Jaako's grandfather had come to Michigan from Finland to work in lumbering camps. Some of his people were miners and fishermen.

"You're from Down Below," he said, meaning from south of the Mackinac Bridge.

"Detroit," I said. "But I'm thinking about staying here."

"Yo," he said, but his expression said *don't even think about it.*

When I told him I'd been recently in Vietnam, he winced. "You ever heard of Hue?"

"Never been there but I flew over it once. It's an old capital city."

"My son . . . his name Almari . . . was killed there."

"My God! Tet of '68?" I asked.

Jaako looked intently at me. "January 30, 1968," he said, his broad face a study in pain.

"I am sorry. He was a Marine?" I knew that most of the defenders of Hue were Marines.

"First of the First." First Battalion, First Infantry Division.

"Yes." I'd heard about the heavy casualties they took at Hue.

"You are a survivor, then," he said.

"Yeah, well, I got drafted," I explained. "Didn't see combat."

It didn't matter to Jaako. From that moment on, he insisted on seeing me, an unwilling participant, as comrade-in-arms to his son.

After some conversation and a beer or two, Jaako grabbed a dry napkin from the bar and drew a parabola on it. "A life," he said.

"Looks like a rainbow."

"Ain't no pot of gold at the end of a life." He drew a crude cradle on the left end, and what appeared to be a gravestone on the right. "This line is the life we are given."

With a right hand that could have crushed a skull, Jaako put three hash marks on the curve, two of them left of the peak and one on the right, closer to the end.

"That's me," he said, pointing to the right mark. "And this broken one on the left is Almari. His best years were stolen from him. And next to him is you, see?"

"Okay," I said, reluctantly. "But—"

"No buts, Danny." He pointed to the hash mark closer to the gravestone. "I worked for The Company, see." I later learned he was referring to Cleveland Cliffs Mining Company. "The undergrounds. I worked with my father on the Gogebic Range, and then I moved to Ishpeming and worked the Marquette Range. Empire Mine. A mile long and a thousand foot deep."

Jaako paused, pounded his chest with his left hand, of which two fingers were missing at the first knuckle, and the index finger was mangled. The pounding produced a harsh cough. "Taconite dust," he said. "It was hazardous work, you see. Some of the men didn't live to retire. Now, I was laid off two years back, but too late."

"I'm sorry."

"Don't be sorry. I tell you that as I tell about my Almari--not for your sorrow. Look at you, son." He pointed to my mark on the parabola. "Your peak is away up there, see? You got fifty, sixty years of livin' to do. You want to stay up here in the north?"

"Sure."

"You're young, but there's nothing in this town for you. No future. Go to Marquette or the Soo. Get your degree. Learn a trade. Start a family. You got a girl, Dan?"

"No."

"Do you know Marquette?"

"I was there a few weeks ago. Nice town, but—"

"Lots of young women there, Dan. You could find one." He smiled and poked at my chest.

"You overestimate me, Jaako."

We laughed.

"My brother lives there, too. You see Ari?" Jaako pointed to his nephew bending over the pool table. "Ari is student. His father Pekka can look after you, get you job. Ari here is a good boy and he will be a help, too. He'll be back in Marquette on Sunday. You can get work there and go to college, see? Northern. This town is good, but it does not hold futures."

He reached into his wallet with his good hand, pulled out a fifty-dollar bill. "You can spend it on your new lady-friend in Marquette." He wrote a phone number on my napkin, above the crest of the parabola, and stuffed the fifty with the napkin into my shirt pocket.

When my game came up, I played Ari. He beat me two of three. We shook hands. I put on my coat and reached for a handshake with Jaako.

"Where you going?"

I shrugged my shoulders. It was too late to subject my car's suspension to that unpaved road all the way to Marquette. Out the window, snow was falling on the street.

"One more beer, Danny," he said, raising a hand for the bartender. "You'll come home with us. We have extra bed."

I slept that night in the bed of Jaako's dead son.

19

The ride back to Marquette was on the same treacherous unpaved excuse for a road I had taken to Grand Marais. That road brought my Valiant to the brink of extinction.

I began to understand that I could meet my doom in the UP, where the winters are legendary for heavy snowfall and below zero temperatures. I would need work and lodging soon, and wondered if this brother of Jaako—Pekka--or his son, Ari, could or would help me. My immediate plan was to scour the employment ads in the Marquette newspaper. I had no marketable skills, but after meeting Jaako I had no desire to work in a mine or a lumbering camp.

Next night, in the lounge of a homeless shelter, half-watching Monday Night Football and half-reading my Steinbeck, I looked up to see Ari. He said Jaako had told him to look for me.

"Why is your uncle doing this, Ari?"

"You were in Vietnam with Almari. He can't do anything for 'Mari."

Ari told me about his father, Pekka Toivonen. Pekka owned a septic tank service, a couple of dump trucks, a front-end loader, and was a builder. He also owned and rented a half-dozen houses in the Marquette area, mostly to Northern students. A third brother, who Ari called Uncle Kim, owned a farm near town.

"You mean stuff *grows* up here?"

"It's a short season, but yes. Uncle Kim has an apple orchard and goats. Cool guy." So there were three brothers, Jaako, Pekka, and Kim, or as I later learned, Joachim.

Next morning, I followed Ari out to Pekka's house. Ari ushered me into an office in the rear of the home. His father was there, on the phone, his back to us.

"Isäa . . ." Ari used the Finnish word for "father."

Pekka turned around.

"This is Dan McPhail, Isäa," Ari said.

Pekka Toivonen introduced himself. His hand was the meatiest I had ever shaken. "What can you do for me, Dan McPhail?"

I told him I was a hard worker, and that I followed directions well. He chuckled, as if to say, "Is that all you got, kid?" He could not promise me full-time work, not with winter coming on, but I later learned that his brother Jaako had called and asked him to look out for me. So Pekka had a proposition for me. He had recently taken possession of a ramshackle house near the university. It was a handyman special in sore need of repairs, and Ari would soon be working on it.

"It's very rough, Dan, but we could give you a partially finished bedroom and bathroom with heat and water in exchange for your help in restoring it." Pekka said that if I "worked out," he would also keep me in mind for help with other projects. He added that his brother Kim needed help on the farm from time to time.

I moved my laundry bag and sleeping bag into that house, to an insulated room with a wood stove and adjoining bathroom. I had no wood, but I had access to a woodlot and Ari's pickup truck and tools. Ari chuckled when he saw me struggle with the chainsaw. And that was just the beginning.

Snow continued to accumulate. I worked for Pekka, but more directly with and for Ari, who was three years younger than I was, but who proved to be an instructive and forgiving supervisor. With assistance from the GI Bill, I signed up for a night class at Northern for the term to begin in January.

*****

I spent most of that winter and spring working on the house I was living in. My Valiant was usually buried in snow. I walked to school, where I took a night class on the GI Bill and spent idle hours reading in my room and at Spirit Ground, the coffee shop I had discovered on my first visit to Marquette. It was three blocks from the house. Sometimes a folk singer or combo from the university or the community would entertain.

I eventually realized that I had come to the UP to disappear, to be as far away from my country, my culture, my past life, as I could manage. It was as if I was attempting to reset my internal operating system and begin again. I wanted to learn the kind of self-reliance and self-esteem I had witnessed in Army friends, in John Sartorre's Colorado mountain village, and in Upper Peninsula towns like Grand Marais and Marquette.

I never mastered any of the skills that Ari and Pekka so effortlessly practiced, but I became a reliable hand. True to my self-description that first day in Pekka's office, I worked hard and followed directions well. I was not a quick study, but I learned much.

I lived in Pekka's would-be rental until the following August. Ari and I replaced or repaired much of the ceiling and some of the walls, stripped and refinished the floors, updated the kitchen floor and cabinet space, and replaced a few windows and a door.

Trimming one bedroom door was an embarrassing experience. I was asked to fit the door to the frame, but I cut the wrong end. I was relieved that Ari laughed more at the sight of the ruined door than at the guy who had handled the table saw.

When we finished the fixup in time to rent it to four college students, all from the Detroit area for fall semester, I moved on. I found an efficiency over a garage in the same neighborhood. The house was owned by an elderly French-Canadian couple, Marcel and Elaine Caron, who deducted money from my rent for helping with snow shoveling and other chores. They would invite me for dinners of soups and stews, fish and potatoes, which I sometimes ate with their visiting children and grandchildren.

Since finishing the house, I'd been doing odd jobs for Pekka and for his farmer brother, Kim. One afternoon, winter on the way,

Ari posted a note under a wiper of the Valiant. It was my pink slip. I was laid off, but Pekka had put in a good word for me with the plant manager of a machine shop in a growing manufacturing operation near the city.

Another Finn, as I suspected. The shop, managed by a friend of Pekka, was my entry into skills that would serve me well for the rest of my working days. I began as a helper but was getting some valuable training.

*****

During the year I spent with the Carons, my second in Marquette, I began to come out of my self-imposed invisibility. I still wrote regularly to my parents and siblings, but my only friends had been Ari Toivonen, his father, and his uncle Jaako in Grand Marais. I remembered Jaako's suggestion that I should find a woman in Marquette.

I discovered a twelve-mile trail along Lake Superior that began at a park near town. I had always enjoyed running alone, but that fall I joined a running club. When the snow fell, I bought cross-country skis. And when I could see the soil again, I got back to running. Alone or with others, the practice of putting one foot in front of the other was good for my soul.

I was also increasing contact with my family. My parents and two youngest siblings were still on Cloverlawn, while Frank and Ruth were buying a home in Detroit, and Mary was sharing an apartment.

The job, the Caron's, Ari's family, my family, a few acquaintances, and the return to running were all signifying a return.

To what? I didn't know.

190

20

One Saturday evening that May, I walked up to Spirit Ground and sat with a book while listening to songs played and sung by a young pianist. I'd heard she was an instructor at NMU. As the café became crowded, I prepared to leave the table for three that I'd been hogging. Then someone yelled, "Hey, it's a McPhail!" and I looked up to see a Cloverlawn kid, June Farley, sitting at a nearby table. June was a friend of my sister, Mary. Her brother Chuck was one of my friends back in the neighborhood.

She brought her coffee over and sat down.

"I *knew* I'd eventually see someone from the block up here," she said. Cloverlawn is everywhere! Hey, I heard you were in Vietnam."

"I've been out since, uh, a year or so. Are you a freshman?" I remembered June, what little I knew of her, as brash and outspoken. During the short time I was home before my trip to Colorado, my mother had discovered a little baggie containing weed in Mary's dresser. Mary confessed and named June as her source. Now here was June in bell-bottom jeans with holes in the knees and a tight sweater. Her long black ponytail hung beneath a stocking cap.

"This is my second year, but my first up here. I went to OCC last year. What about you? I suppose you know Clare is married?"

"I heard." She married the same med student. He was probably a doctor by now.

"Come and sit with us." She was at Spirit Ground with some kids from an environmental science class to see their teacher, the woman at the piano. One of the girls at June's table was a roommate, Lizzie, a kid from Minnesota. The other was Paula, a local girl and off-and-on student who worked with Lizzie at St. Luke's Hospital in town.

When June and Lizzie went outside to smoke a joint, Paula and I were alone.

She was a blond beauty, the only child of an often inebriated, rarely employed Finnish lumberjack. She was bright and sassy and funny, and I was ready.

*****

I married her a few months later, and after a year in the UP we moved downstate. I got a machine maintenance job in a Ford plant. We bought a two-bedroom home in the Detroit suburb of Ferndale, only a few miles from Cloverlawn, where we hunkered down to raise two beautiful kids, Nora and Sam.

All seemed well, at first. Paula and I were in love, but as we grew and our children grew, conflicting ideas about money, lifestyle, and success grew us apart. I was content, in those days, to live in a small world. I never had much interest in finishing my education or striving for the highest possible income. Areas of achievement like sales or management or competitive corporate toil were of no interest to me. I'd been learning skills that I hoped would lead to economic security for my family, skills that served me well enough in those days.

My sense of enough, that what we had was sufficient, was fueled by a sour attitude toward what I thought of as the American Dream. I wanted no part of the hungering-after, the desperation, and the isolation that I sensed in my dog-eat-dog culture. I was wanting peace, as well as family and community. I hoped to eventually leave Ford to find work in a quieter, less stressful environment, but I had no idea what that might look like.

It was also true that I had not yet outgrown the reticence and social anxiety that kept me from being totally present in the world outside my comfort zone. Not many years before, I had been a boy of little affect, lest it might cause me to be seen. I no longer stuttered, but I was still discovering who I was and what I wanted to say.

I was attracted to Paula's childhood of economic hardship. Perhaps I thought that, given her background, she would demand little of me. But underneath her humility of breeding lay toughness and pride, and while I was also attracted to those qualities, I noticed her developing a need for a life of plenty for our family. And why not? It was natural enough to want what most everyone else wanted.

Over time, though, Paula's once-simple tastes drove our little family into a world of debt. I was making good money in a union shop, but Paula would buy only at top-tier stores—Hudson's, Winkleman's, Victoria's Secret--for her clothes, and our kids had to have the best and the most. She became frustrated with me. Our modest home became a symbol of my lack of motivation. I became *not-enough*.

By the time our divorce became final, she had already scored a husband-in-waiting. George Duggan was an acquaintance of Paula's back in Marquette who had taken the helm of his father's commercial real estate and land development business and was, in the seventies, staking claims in the more lucrative Detroit area market. George was bred and bankrolled for success, and he had made it no secret that he was on that gilded stairway to the Good Life. George has always treated me very well—like any good salesman would treat a prospective client.

One of George's claims became Paula, who knew what to do with George's money. Not long after they married, George brought Paula and the kids back to Marquette. I became a long-distance father. I kept in touch but was pushed to the margins of parenthood by my kids' new home, 450 miles upstate.

*****

About the years between my divorce and October of 2013, there is half-a-lifetime, in which nothing much happened. After surviving a few years of grief, I recovered. I should say that I am still in recovery. I continued like a single man in that little Ferndale bungalow. Eventually, I moved in and out of a few good relationships. If there was an opportunity to remarry, I missed it, but I made friends, bought another home, and worked a modest but honest career.

I never revisited my old Smirnoff escape. I had work to do, and the project was my *self*. I began journaling, like I had heard Clare mention, in search of my own authentic voice. I read a few good books, got counseling, got my degree, learned to relate freely and honestly to others, and continued to care for and about the people in my life.

Until they were out of high school, distance defined my relationship with Nora and Sam, but I always stayed in contact. For a time, my daughter wanted no part of me, so I waited for her. Sam had a difficult relationship with his stepfather, but he grew to trust me. Like his father, he found satisfaction in running. We also shared a love of the outdoors, through which we came to know each other. Over time, both Nora and Sam grew to see all three of their parents with mature eyes. They accept us, flawed and wounded as we are, as those who unreservedly love them.

21

It was Autumn of 2013 when I volunteered as a shelver at the Ferndale Library. A four-hour shift with a twenty-minute break, three days a week. The outdoor patio was a good place, weather permitting, to escape the mustiness. It was fitting, given our histories of library patronage, that this was the scene of Clare Cassidy's re-entry.

To say that she rocked my world would be an understatement. At sixty-seven years old, I had begun to think that my life was settled and done with, that there was nothing left of me but my home, a few good friends, and visits with the kids and grandkids . . .

"Well, by God, it's Flash!"

I looked up from my newspaper, squinting. Only one person on this earth had ever called me that name. I did not particularly like its dismissive connotation, like Speedy or Lightning or, God forbid, Zippy. But I had long ago forgiven the offender.

I heard the husky laugh. The silhouette before me was indeed Clare.

I rose and we embraced. She cried in my arms. "My sister heard you were working here. Oh, Danny."

"It's really you," I said, dumbstruck. I did not want to think about how long it had been. I took her hand and guided her to the cement bench of the patio, sat alongside her, turned to her. Her young-girl face and shape were gone, of course, but she looked good: bright-eyed, rosy cheeked, fit and casual in a jacket and jeans. Her hair was still long and wavy, bordering on frizzy, the dark brown gone gray. She wore only a touch of make-up. She never liked putting on much mascara or eyeliner or lipstick.

"So. You're a librarian?"

"Look at you. Just as pretty as ever. But no, I'm a volunteer. I've only been here since July."

"You're retired."

"Between jobs. I've applied for Social Security, but I'm not ready to retire." Truth be told, I could not afford to retire. "Are you working?" I asked.

"Yes, I live near Dexter, but I'm in the Histology Clinic at the VA hospital in Ann Arbor."

I noticed the absence of a wedding ring. "What brings you into the city?" I asked.

"My son lives in Dearborn. I'll be there 'til Friday, babysitting."

"Will you have time for a lunch or a coffee? I need to get back inside, but—"

"I won't keep you, Dan, but I was hoping you'd ask," she said. "I know a picnic table . . . ."

*****

I spent the twenty-four hours before our meeting in a state of rising anxiety. Unsettled and of my center, I conjured up scenarios of relationship with Clare. I was ready to sell the bungalow and move to Dexter, or Ann Arbor, or the Alaskan tundra or Kazak steppe. For the awakened dream of Clare. I had to slap myself to stop the noise and think of something to wear. I did not sleep or eat well. My stomach churned. My mind was tripping over the present, playing tapes past and future.

But next day, I rode my bike to the park. It was a cool but clear day. Leaves were beginning to change. The neighborhoods, including Cloverlawn, had become much more racially and culturally diverse. The expense of energy was exactly what I needed. It served to relax me and—thank God—to clear my delusional imagination and bring me back to my reality.

The park looked much the same, but I noticed a newly-paved pathway and state-of-the-art playground structures. I found a picnic table very near our old spot near the tree and the outfield fence, and dragged it to where it belonged. It was not made of wood but of plastic-coated steel. I leaned my bike against our tree, taller and grander now but trimmed of its lowest-hanging limbs.

I watched Clare pull into the lot and park. She came looking healthy and happy, carrying a sack with two cups of coffee and cookies.

We hugged. She smelled fresh, like always. Then we sat across from each other at the picnic table. Exhilarating as it was to be in her space, the bike ride and the face-to-face was shaking me out of my dream of her. I wanted only the moment. She looked at the tree, the fence and ball diamond. The nearby skating rink was now enclosed in a large building. She smiled at me.

"You could stand to put on a few pounds," she said, handing me the cookies. She nudged a Styrofoam cup toward my side of the table. "Double cream?"

She remembered.

"My son is at a conference," she said, "so I'm baby-sitting for my granddaughter Ginny today. But I get to go out and play until I pick her up from school."

"So. What shall we play?"

"Well, we can go climb on the train," she said. "Did you see the huge playground train on the other side of the park?"

"That train is famous around here, I said. And they've made some serious upgrades in this park since our day. But it's not too late. We're back!"

That laugh again. I could listen to it all day.

"Hey, Dan." She looked down into her cup. "Just to say . . . I've been aware you were working at the library for a month now, but I've been putting this meeting off . . . thinking about how it would be good to see you again, but then I got scared. I mean, I didn't feel ready to revisit those halcyon days of my youth."

"I get it, Clare. Funny, I understand exactly how you feel."

"I thought you might be able to relate."

"Oh yeah." It was all such a long time ago. My truth about us seemed to evolve over time. I wondered about Clare's truth. I would have guessed that, like me, she was not eager to talk about Tom. Or about us. But here she was, always the brave one.

"We had more than a friendship, didn't we, Dan?"

I was not sure what she meant. "It was precious," I said.

I took the lid off my coffee and took a sip. She was wearing the same green field jacket she wore the previous day. But today she also wore a touch of make-up.

She nodded to the bike. "You rode a long way."

"Three miles, not so much."

"You were always the athletic one," she said.

"Are you getting me mixed up with Tom?" I said it with a smile.

"No, Danny. Tom had power, but you had endurance."

22

We talked Obama and Afghanistan and the economy, now going strong again after the recession. She had been getting updates about the Cloverlawn crowd from her sister, who was still in touch. I had attended the Cloverlawn reunion the previous summer, so we shared news and memories about old friends on the block.

She asked about my siblings and my children. I told of my physical therapist daughter in Colorado and her three kids. And of my wayward but fascinating then-unmarried son.

At some point, I pulled the bookmark she had given me, long ago, from my fanny pack. The Serenity Prayer. "It's getting to be very ragged, but I still have it."

> *God, grant me the serenity to accept the things I*
> *cannot change,*
> *The courage to change the things I can,*
> *And the wisdom to know the difference.*

"Wow," she said. "I remember. It was my aunt Pat's. Do you pray it?"

In my twenties, my Alanon experience brought me into familiarity with that prayer. But it got lost in a book, and I lost my connection to it. A few years before that reunion, I was looking through some old things, and there it was.

"Yes," I said.

I was curious about Clare's story. Her husband, a surgeon, had been dead for ten years. She had two sons. The one in Dearborn, one out West, and four grandkids. She mentioned a man in her life, a retired cardiologist.

"That's wonderful," I said. And I meant it.

*****

We sat across from one another on the cool pine bench seats. I looked into her brown eyes, listened to her voice, and remembered those days: my invisible childhood and blocked adolescence. My two best friends, Clare Cassidy and Tom Dolak.

I sensed that Clare had come to see me for a reason, and that I, too, suddenly had a mission to carry out. But I did not know the reason or the mission.

"What happened to us, Danny?" she asked, looking at me, waiting.

"Um," I finally said, "was there ever an *us*?"

"No, not . . . but . . . we had something real."

"I've always had feelings for you, Clare. We were too young. And then Tom came along. And after Tom . . . it was not a good time for us. What could I do?"

"And I had feelings for you, Danny. But we never had a chance to work through any of it."

"We weren't ready. And I . . . when a man dies, his brother can't . . ."

"You were not Tom's brother."

"I was his friend."

"And me, too," she said. "I was—we were the only ones who knew him as more than a jock. And we cared for him."

"Mrs. Dolak," I said, wanting to be sure about something. "She loved Tom."

"True. But I don't think Ed or Wes Dolak really knew him. Ed and Wes saw him only in relation to the business. They didn't know what he was going through, and they didn't care. That was why they put the blame on you, Danny. The said *you* got Tom into drugs. *You* were the slacker who distracted Tom from his classes, his conditioning, his team, his job. You dragged him into that ghetto

200

dive-bar, which was nothing of the kind. Why did you let 'Dolak and Sons' do that to you?"

"What are you saying, Clare? I had no control over what the Dolaks wanted to believe. Tom's drug dependency began before I met him. He had allergies, sinus problems. He used pills and inhalers to clear his sinuses at first, and then later to escape from the pressure of . . . family expectations."

"I was there. Tom's dad was a pig. And Wes was always showing off for him. They killed that boy, and then they needed someone to blame, Danny. It made them feel better about not loving Tom."

"But I couldn't save him! And then I . . . I gave up on him." As I said those words, I felt that I was, for the first time, voicing a guilt and frustration that I'd been nursing all my adult life.

"That's not true."

I formed a fist, placed it gently on the table. My eyes were wet as I tried, as always, not to cry. "How can you know what was in my heart?"

"Daniel. I was a witness. You did everything you could. Tom knew that. I was the one who gave up. But that was after he gave up on *himself*!"

For a full minute, we sat quietly. I became aware of the crisp early fall day. How perfect it was! A kid jogged across the outfield grass with a book in hand. Maybe he was on his way to our old library. My baseball dream was born here, my dream of Clare was nurtured here.

"I found out you'd left for the Army from your sister. Do you know how that made me feel?"

"I was . . . not in a good place. We'd lost Tom. And then it felt like we had each other. It was good, but . . . it was too soon. I needed to let you go. I knew you wanted that."

"I was in still in shock after Tom," she said. "Those days with you . . . do you remember our little camping trip? You'd been drinking, and hiding it."

"My Smirnoff days. I dropped my classes that semester. Couldn't concentrate. Then the draft board got me. Basic Training dried me out."

"I did not want you to go to that war. I was worried about you. I wrote you, Danny."

"I remember how you felt, but I had to make that decision myself."

"And the letters?"

There were two. "I carried those letters in my pocket." I thumped my heart. "Read them a dozen times." Hundreds of times. I knew them verbatim.

"But you never wrote back."

It was true. I tried, but I couldn't get it done. "I have often wondered, if I ever saw you again, would I get a chance to say I am sorry? I was in a state of—I was shut down at the time, Clare. Anything I said would . . ."

"Would be false?"

"Or trivial. To pretend things were okay. It was selfish of me to . . . I was stuck. I could not show true concern for anyone because I was stuck in myself." It was true, but I was also trying to forget this girl who had denied me, who was lost to me, who had always been out of my league. In Tom's league. "I'm sorry, Clare. For any hurt I caused you."

She was quiet for a while. She seemed sad. Then she looked up at me. "I forgive you, Danny."

I put a hand over hers.

"And then I heard you were living in the UP," she said.

"And it wasn't long before you were married."

"You got married, too, Daniel." She sounded indignant.

"At Saint Christopher's in Marquette. But it was not a marriage made in Heaven."

"Nor was mine," she said, and changed the subject. "Hey, remember the time we kidnapped him?"

I nodded.

She turned her hand and laced her fingers into mine. "We were gonna force him to go Cold Turkey."

"But he escaped."

"Or did we let him go?" she said and looked at me. I'd been laughing, but I wonder if she sensed that I was also crying.

"It was a few weeks before . . . that night," I managed to say.

"Yeah. The House of Tom was caving in on itself. You saw what he was doing, how he brought it all on himself."

"Of course," I said, "but . . . he was suffering."

"I still go in and out of blame, compassion, frustration . . . but he lied to me, Danny. He was more honest with you. He loved you, Dan."

And I loved you. "Maybe, but you were the one. He was afraid he would lose you, and I was afraid that would kill him, if his coke habit did not kill him first. That was why I asked you to stick it out with him. Maybe I had given up at that point, but . . . I'm sorry. Again, that was wrong. I had no right . . ."

"I don't even remember that," she said. "I remember being indecisive. But we didn't see all that much of each other that year. Don't apologize, Danny. You were a better friend to him than I ever was."

"I'm . . . just saying . . . maybe I could have done something different."

"Me too, Danny. We tried, but it was bigger than you and me."

*****

Our conversation did not last much longer. We turned to updates, pleasantries, and news of the larger world. We still shared a compassion for victims and those suffering in remote corners of the globe. I walked her to her car, my hands on the handlebars of the bike. Clare wound an arm through my free arm and held on. When we got there, I held her for a long time. She offered no resistance.

"I love you, Clare," I said, leaning on the door of her car.

"And I love you, Daniel." As she drove away, I was no longer confused by what I meant, or what she meant. It was Clare who taught me, and I think she still believes it, that all life is connected, that we are all parts of a divine whole.

And the glue is love.

23

It has been over ten years since that time when all seemed settled and done with, when I might have died in my sleep out of sheer indifference.

Not long after that meeting with Clare, I canceled my Social Security application and went back to work for a small metal stamping facility in Hazel Park. The job was just okay, but close enough to home that I could walk or ride my bike.

I bought a pair of conga drums. I fished lakes near and far with my newly married son and my brothers. I posted photos and a bio online, and began to chat up and meet a few women.

I had not become suddenly enlightened or inspired. Change for me comes slow, and often with a fair amount of pain. But sometimes I look back to that last meeting with Clare and wonder if she unlocked something in me.

After five years, I retired from the plant, stopped in at the local library, and got my volunteer book shelving job back. One morning, while shelving biographies—with a Dewey Decimal number of 921 plus the first three letters of the subject's last name—I helped a woman find a biography.

We still argue about the title. I say it was Amelia Earhart. My wife insists it was Beryl Markham. We agree that it was a female airplane pilot.

We are both in our late seventies, together four years now. I am settled. But there is no room in my life for indifference.

Blue Derry

1

No one knew where the name came from. Blue said it was his mother. As a toddler he often wrapped himself in a blue blanket and carried it around the house with him. His father said he began calling his son Blue when the boy sank into dark, volatile moods that came and went seemingly without cause. When he got to school age, he did not answer to George, his true first name, but told teachers and students to call him Blue. In the neighborhood, his brothers John and Jim warned everyone not to call him George. And when someone warned you about Blue Derry, you needed to take heed or get ready to run.

Blue was the quintessential brick shithouse. He was not tall, about 5'8", with smallish feet, short legs, and long torso--a primate in city clothes. His width and girth were of legend, and he was stronger than any man on the block. He once pulled an engine block, without cylinder head or transmission, out of a car and carried it to a bench. It was my car, a '59 Ford, and I was there.

While the men of Cloverlawn argued the relative greatness of Mantle, Williams, or Mays, in baseball. or of Dempsey, Marciano, or Robinson, in boxing, until Muhammed Ali settled the issue, kids tossed around names to settle this question: who is the toughest? On the block, in the neighborhood, in the whole damn city? Street fights were cited as evidence. On Cloverlawn, we knew Blue Derry was, hands down, the strongest and meanest son of a bitch of all.

Leo Cohen was a neighborhood bully who lifted weights. He earned a letter in wrestling at Oak Park High. He loved to taunt the Cloverlawn boys at every opportunity. Leo wore tight t-shirts, boasted of his bench-press numbers, and even entered teen body-builder competitions. A jab to the upper arm from Leo would cause days of pain. He loved to give us nicknames, "Pencil-neck," "wimp-ass," "jellyfish," but he never came near when Blue Derry was in sight.

Most of us Cloverlawn boys played baseball, football, hockey, and basketball, in season. We played on the street, in backyards, and in the park at the end of the street. We followed the hometown Tigers, Lions, Red Wings, and Pistons, as well as local high school and college teams. Blue Derry knew nothing about sports or sports teams. We never saw him run or jump or throw a ball. If he were to engage in a sport, it would have been an individual activity: off-roading, skydiving, bungee jumping, kickboxing. Blue was never a team player.

His primary residence was across the street from our house with his father and brothers, but he also spent days and weeks at a time at his mother's home on Orleans Street, in a rough neighborhood on Detroit's East Side. His sister Bet also lived there. Mrs. Derry and Bet did not visit the family on Cloverlawn, so we knew little of them. When he attended high school, which was not often, Blue was enrolled at Oak Park High, from which he never graduated. He was not fond of textbooks or anything or anyone that had an air of authority. This group included parents, teachers, employers, cops, and judges. When he came of age and was in the presence of a judge, it was strongly suggested that George—cops and judges called him by the Christian name on his license, when he had a valid license—join the Army, which was thought to be a source of discipline and responsibility. But the Army wanted nothing of Blue Derry.

The kids on the block sensed there was something wrong in the Derry family. The parents, with four children, did not live together; that alone marked the Derrys as different. Most of the Cloverlawn families were nucleus-intact, striving and thriving. But John and Jim Derry, the two youngest, wore ragged clothing and worn-out shoes, and they looked to be malnourished. Both were under weight, with blotches on their arms and legs. John, who was my age, was a sickly, pale-skinned boy. He often had a blueish cast to his lips and fingers. He was weak, with little stamina for running or jumping.

Spending time at his mother's house may have explained why Blue, while never well-dressed, looked to be well-enough fed. But he had a hungry, anguished look, a James Dean, Dana Andrews look. A midwestern Dean Moriarty, he walked with a hidden purpose, which may be interpreted as an implied threat. His hair was thin and combed back, his face older than its years.

*****

The adults on Cloverlawn suspected that Mr. Derry was negligent. Lance Derry seemed like a nice guy, but too often was seen with a beer bottle in his hand and a Lucky Strike between his lips. He was usually friendly when interacting with John and Jim, but he would not have been considered an available parent. He worked during the day as a mechanic and spent his evenings in the backyard garage, a two-and-a-half stall workshop that was better equipped than his house. He built racing engines, drank long-neck Old Milwaukee, and entertained a steady stream of coworkers and friends.

Mr. Derry's lifestyle left his sons, especially the two youngest, to fend for themselves. Yet, neglected and home alone as they were, neither John nor Jim had behavior issues. The mothers of the block fretted over them. The Cloverlawn kids, naïve and non-judgmental as they were, accepted John and Jim, barely suspecting that they were different.

"Do you ever get to see your mom?" I would ask John Derry.

"Yeah, but she never comes here. She stays on Orleans with Bet."

"So when was the last time you saw Bet?" I asked. It was late spring. We were walking through the park to school.

"Um, Dad dropped us off over there on Christmas. But I saw Bet after that. Blue took Jim and I to see her after school one day. My mom had to work overtime."

"But your dad didn't take you there?"

"Nope." It seemed that Blue had more interest in seeing his sister than Mr. Derry did in seeing his daughter.

If Mr. Derry was not the best father for John, Jim, and Bet, his relationship with Blue was openly contentious. No one on the street understood why Blue fought so fiercely and unrelentingly with his father. Despite Mr. Derry's lack of attention, John and Jim did not seem to bear any resentment toward their dad. But Blue refused to listen to Mr. Derry and sometimes violently opposed him. And Blue was a formidable match for his father.

The Derrys moved to Cloverlawn when Blue was fifteen. No one understood the back story: the divorce, the relationship of Derry boys to their mother and sister, Blue's reasons for moving back and forth from Detroit to Cloverlawn. We did not know why Blue was so enraged, so lost to the world around him, so hopelessly alienated.

I was sitting on our front porch the night Cloverlawn got its first taste of the ferocity of Blue Derry. Mr. Derry and Blue got into a very public exchange that included punches, loud swearing, and a visit from an Oak Park police cruiser. It was early enough in the evening to generate a sizeable audience. No one knew what had caused it. The fight began in the garage, then moved to the house before ending on the front lawn. Mr. Derry ended up with a bloody nose—he had to wear a splint for a few weeks—and a shredded shirt. Blue finally calmed down at the pleading of John and Jim, but it was best, everyone agreed, that two armed Oak Park cops arrived at the scene.

2

In seventh and eighth grades, I had a morning Free Press paper route. Papers for the neighborhood were dropped off about six blocks from our house, in a little strip mall that held several Jewish-owned businesses: Dexter-Davison Market, New York Bagel Baking Company, Mertz's Bakery, and Hi Horenstein's Delicatessen. A half-dozen kids arrived on bikes at 5:30 in the morning, folded and stuffed their papers into canvas saddlebags, and pedaled off in near-darkness to deliver them.

For me, those mornings were an enjoyable time. The paperboys would chat and kibitz while folding their papers. The streets were strangely quiet, save for a few early-birds leaving for their jobs. Cloverlawn was on my route; I could imagine my friends and their parents asleep in their beds or fixing breakfast. If the kitchen light at my house was on, I could almost smell a brewing pot of coffee, my father and siblings getting ready for the day, my mom getting a bit more sleep.

Every detail of the route was automatic, every stop long memorized, so I delivered the morning's news in a near-slumber. Some of my lazier customers wanted their paper inside a screen door or under a mat, but most papers were rolled and tossed from a moving bicycle to a stoop. I performed these maneuvers without thinking, which set my mind free to wander.

When I was thirteen, one of my customers was asphyxiated in her enclosed garage. Mrs. Kipp had left her car running; the cause of death was carbon-monoxide poisoning. She left behind a husband and three children, two of whom, twins, had been in my classes for years. The previous summer, Kenny Kipp and I had been on the same Little League team, the Lions. Until her mom's death, Kenny's sister Jenny, who was pretty and friendly enough to make small talk with, sat next to me in homeroom. After the funeral, I never saw Kenny or

Jenny again. This accident, which we eventually realized was no accident at all, was the talk of the neighborhood for weeks thereafter. It was my first knowledge of the danger of CO, an odorless, invisible gas that could kill.

My carbon-monoxide vigilance was a factor in my first run-in with Blue Derry. Blue had recently got his driver's license, and soon afterward was in possession of a '55 DeSoto Firedome. It was pink, with a white top and a white stripe that flared out behind the rear wheels. By the time Blue owned it, that car was near the end of its run: badly rusted, blowing smoke, and needing a muffler. He always parked it on the street in front of his house. Sometimes I would see him bent over the engine or working underneath the chassis.

On one of those dead-quiet weekday mornings, I was cycling through the route in my semi-conscious dream when I turned the corner onto Cloverlawn. The only parked car on the street was Blue's DeSoto. As I approached, I could see blue smoke rising from the tailpipe. The car was not only running, but burning oil. The radio was on. As I passed by, I saw Blue in the driver's seat, slumped half-over with his eyes closed.

My first thought was carbon monoxide. I did not know Blue, but I knew of him as John Derry's older brother, and I feared him greatly. I stopped the bike dead in the street and ran to the driver's window to get a better look. No movement. I knocked on the window. Still no movement. I knew then that I must act quickly to save a life from the deadly gas. I yanked open the driver's door and violently shook Blue's arm to wake him. Then I put my mouth to his ear and called his name.

As Blue jerked to consciousness, he reached for me, not to thank me for bringing him back from the grave, but to hold me still while he beat me senseless. Realizing that I had awakened a raging beast, I slipped from his grasp, hopped on my bike, and pedaled down the block. Blue charged after me but only for a few steps, too groggy or hung-over to continue. I had believed that I was saving a life, but only later did I realize the stench coming from Blue's car was of alcohol. I had been rousing a drunk.

For many days afterwards, I was on guard every time I saw the DeSoto at the Derry's curb. But it was not there for long. One night that fall, Blue got drunk, hit a parked car, and abandoned it at the scene. He escaped trouble for this because, I had heard, the car was hot, registered to a driver in another state.

My reckoning came on a day that winter when I was walking down the block toward the park. Blue grabbed me by the shoulder and spun me around.

"What were you thinking that morning you scared the shit out of me, kid?"

I took a step back, anticipating a slap or worse. "I thought you were in danger of carbon monoxide, Blue. Mrs. Kipp died from it, you know."

"Mrs. Kipp."

"She lived on Church Street. Everyone knew about it."

"I'll bet you ten dollars Mrs. Kipp was in a closed-up garage, sitting in her car with the windows open. My car was sitting out on the street."

"But you had the windows closed, Blue, and you were out cold. You could have been asphyxiated." I had learned that word, *asphyxiated*, and I hoped Blue was impressed with my pronunciation of it.

As he seemed to consider this idea, I got ready to run. But he surprised me.

"What's your name, huh?"

"Gary. Gary Bauer. I know your brothers."

"Oh, I see. You about John's age?"

"Yep."

"And you have a sister plays piano."

"Ann."

"She's good. Sometimes I like to sit on the porch and listen to her. I've heard her play this tune, a Bach thing. Would you tell her I love the way she plays it?"

"Sure, Blue. I'll tell her."

"I have a sister, too." He said. "Lives on the East Side."

"Yeah, John and Jim told me about Bet."

Blue's face tensed up. "What did they tell you about her?"

I didn't know what to say, but I blurted something out. "I have a little sister, Melanie. She's the baby of my family, even though she's almost nine. We treat her different, I don't know, like we spoil her, I guess. She gets a lot of affection from us. So, um, John and Jim talk about Bet that same way. Like she's special, cute and, uh, cuddly." I took a deep breath. Everything I said was true, but I had no confidence in my ability to articulate it. Not with Blue staring me down.

He paused as if to consider all I had said. My CO concerns, however farfetched they may have been. My friendship with his brothers John and Jim. My piano-playing sister, Ann. My little sister, Melanie. Blue's sister.

He smiled. It changed his face. I felt like I had walked the trail of hot coals and come out the other side. I smiled back.

3

Blue had a soft spot for my sister Ann. It appeared he would try to transform himself into the kind of guy Ann might fall for. But these attempts only made Blue look foolish. Ann said that he was a fixed idea, a hopeless case. Later, as I began to think of myself as Blue's friend, I feared that I was simply an avenue of access to Ann. Blue had no reason to like me. I was two years younger, an innocent kid and a good student, a Cub Scout, a Presbyterian. I got along with everyone, even, usually, my parents.

Blue? He was a train wreck. Trouble.

But he sought me out. The first time this took place was in the park. The Oak Park Municipal Park is a sixty-acre tract of land that was undeveloped until the mid-to-late fifties, when the city gradually installed ball diamonds, a skating rink, a swimming pool, tennis courts, and a building that held a library and community center. In the middle of all this, about ten acres of dense woods remained untouched: mature trees, deep thickets, and two shallow ponds—we called them Twin Ponds--separated by a narrow path. Dirt trails, most of them created by kid traffic, provided access in and through. The woods was a glorious, semi-private, unstructured playground. And it was at the end of my street. Without the park and its woods, my Cloverlawn was just a flat, barren, working-class suburban wasteland. Cookie-cutter tract homes, each with a nondescript sapling by the curb.

The park was where Blue approached me.

Since we had already met, I was no longer terrified by him, but he was not an amiable or approachable guy. Something seethed in him, some deep hostility that he carried with him everywhere he went. He had no friends on the block, but was sometimes seen with neighborhood toughs. One afternoon in the winter, after my asphyxiation fixation, I was crossing through the park on my way home from school. Blue appeared from out of nowhere, walking purposefully toward me in his ape-like way. I had the feeling he had been waiting for me, and that he might want to punch me out, or worse.

"How's it hanging, Gary?" he said. He came up close to me, closer than was comfortable.

"Okay, Blue. How ya doing?"

"Good, good. Looks like you got some homework to do tonight, eh?" He sneered at the sight of my books, which, in those days before bookbags and knapsacks were common, kids carried under an arm.

"Yeah," I said, looking down at my load.

I was not practiced in the art of small talk, especially not with an intimidating older kid. I also sensed that he was not interested in me, that he wanted something from me. Eventually, after an awkward attempt at politeness by us both, he got to the point.

"Lemme ask you, man, I mean . . . tell me about your sister."

"Ann? My older sister?"

"Yeah, well, uh, what's she like?"

I did not know how to answer such a question. Ann was sixteen, I was fourteen. She was much more sophisticated than me. I think she felt duty-bound to look after me, but it was more natural for her to look down on me as a rather uncouth example of a teenage boy. Ann was getting attention from guys her age and older, while I was trapped in adolescence, that awkward age for boys, after puberty but less mature than girls my age, too young to drive, yet old enough to feel the angst of approaching young adulthood. I was very conscious of the fact that my voice was changing from little boy to bigger boy, and this defect did not embolden me to speak. It took me a while to answer.

"Uh, she has some nice friends, and she'll be taking driver's training next semester, and she, uh, made the honor roll. But, um, I don't know what you want from me."

"Just curious," he said. "I seen her here and there. She's interesting. I hear her on the piano. Did you tell her I like the way she does the Bach?"

"Yeah," I lied. "She was surprised to hear you liked it. She said to be sure to tell you, 'Thanks.'"

"Listen, Gary. Do you think she would go out with me?"

"I don't know." My first thought was *no way*, but I chose a safe answer. "I don't think she dates guys. I mean, she has guy friends, but, uh, she doesn't really know you, Blue."

"Well, maybe if you brought her here, we could get acquainted."

"You mean here to the woods?"

"Sure. It's a good place to talk. You don't have parents and all that."

I knew there was a better chance that a tree would fall on me than my sister would consent to meet Blue Derry in the woods, but I said, "I don't know."

"Well, could you ask her for me?"

"She doesn't come through this way from school. She takes the service road with her girlfriends."

"I could meet her on the road, then. But I'd be grateful if you would ask for me."

Ann was pretty, and if not rebellious, independent. She fit in with the other girls on the block and at school, and she could do all the dances—the Hand Jive, the Boogie Woogie, the Stroll, and when she Jitterbugged, everyone else stopped dancing. And she was a leader. She didn't tell kids what to do, but they saw something in her that they could look up to. She had *boy friends*, too. She wasn't afraid of guys and could verbally spar with anyone. She wasn't fooled by fools, and she could easily dispatch an overly flirtatious boy or a bullying female. But she wasn't dating yet, and it was not only because our parents forbade it.

Blue was correct: Ann played the piano beautifully, still does. Not long before that conversation in the park, Ann said that Blue knocked on the screen door while she was playing. She stopped and answered the door. He asked if he could come in and listen to her. She told him *no* because a parent was not home, which was not true. Blue had hung his head and walked away, Ann said.

When I approached her about Blue's idea of a meeting, Ann was adamant. "What does he want with me, Gary? Will you tell him I'm not interested in meeting that gorilla? Not in the park or anywhere else."

"I think if you tell him how you feel, he'll respect that."

It took a bit of coaxing, but she eventually gave in. "Okay," she said. "I'll tell him."

"But go easy on him. He means well."

"What? Are you friends with that cretin?"

"No. Just relaying a message. But I don't think he takes rejection easily."

"You mean he'll punch me out if I tell him how I feel?"

"No. He's just a guy who admires you and wants to meet you."

"Tell him to meet me by the drinking fountain in the park. Around 3:45, tomorrow."

The drinking fountain was near the service road, where it wound around a picnic area beyond the outfield fence of the ball diamond. I got the message to Blue through his brother John.

The next evening, I was at the kitchen table doing homework when Ann sat down across from me.

"Well, I told him."

"You mean you talked to Blue, and it went okay?"

"He was nicer than I expected. He had a nice shirt on, but it was kinda small for him. But his hair was combed. He smiled a lot, but he looked nervous. He asked about the Bach, if I could play any of the fugues. I told him not yet, but I'm working toward them. He said Bach opens up his soul. I thought, 'whaddaya know, the guy has a soul.' I asked him if he played, and he said 'a little.' He didn't go into detail."

"Did he ask you out?"

"He asked me if I like Alfred Hitchcock. I told him I saw 'North By Northwest,' when it came out, but I didn't understand it. Well, there's a new Hitchcock at the West Side Drive-In, 'Psycho.' He said he saw it the other day and wants to see it again. I heard it's really scary, you know, a horror movie. And he wants to see it again? And take me along? Are you kidding?"

"So you told him no?"

"I told him I'm not ready to go on dates. He seemed kinda hurt. He said he'd respect me. He wouldn't '*try* anything.'" She said this in a weak imitation of Blue's voice. "Try anything! He better not try anything!" Ann laughed. "It was weird, Gary. He asked if I was afraid of him. I told him I'm not sure. You know, I was more afraid of him yesterday than I am now that I met the guy. I told him it was sweet of him to ask me out and I thanked him for the compliment on my piano, but I do not want to go on a date with him. Not to a drive-in movie, no way. Not with Blue or anyone else, for that matter."

I nodded. I would not have expected Ann to say anything different. She reached out and ruffled my hair. "Look at you, Gary," she said. "You're getting muscles, and your voice is changing. It won't be long before the *girls* will be wanting to date *you*."

4

Not long after my sister told me that Blue admitted to "dabbling a bit" musically, a couple of friends told me a story that made me more curious about him. In a house several doors away from the Derrys, a younger kid, Frank Abrams, was given a drum set for his birthday. It had all the components—a bass drum, a snare, three toms, and several cymbals--but it was cheap, little more than a toy. Frank invited a couple of kids, Will Miller one of them, to see his present. The kids took turns sitting at the drums, pounding away to pop music on WKNR. The result was anything but musical.

Blue heard the commotion, followed his ear to the source, and knocked on the door. Frank got scared when he saw Blue and promised to keep the noise down, but Blue said no, he only wanted to see the drums. Frank was hesitant to let him in the house with no parent home, given Blue's growing reputation as a "hood" or trouble-maker. But he was also afraid to refuse Blue, so he let him in.

Blue watched and listened to the kids' playing for a few minutes. They were apologetic at their lack of skill, but Blue gave them smiles and encouragement. After a while, Frank handed Blue the sticks. Blue turned the radio off, then sat down and tinkered with the setup. He adjusted the foot pedal on the kick drum and the wires on the snare. Then he tested the cymbals, adjusting positions as needed. After situating the chair to his satisfaction. He sat at the skins and broke them in properly. He began slowly, playing a simple beat on the snare and gradually filling in. It did not sound much like music at first, but Blue was *listening* as he kept that beat. Then he slowly increased the tempo and adding more embellishments. The boys said it sounded like rock and roll at first, but then it became something more complex that they could not identify. The guys said they had never heard anything like it. After thirty minutes of playing, Blue just got up and thanked them all for letting him play, and left.

I talked to Will Miller later that day. "You shoulda been there, Gary," he said. "Blue was amazing! There were four of us there when he started playing, but five or six more kids came in when they heard the commotion. They were all jammed into Frank's bedroom. Blue would go along nice and soft-like, but then he would jump to a louder and faster pace, almost scaring the kids, and then he'd soften it into something like a lullaby."

*****

One afternoon not long after this, I was sitting at my sister's piano. I had never taken lessons, but I tinkered. I had learned how to make a few chords with my left hand and melody notes with my right. I would play, slowly, a song like "You are My Sunshine" or "Love Me Tender." These tunes were slow enough and simple enough for me. If I encountered a difficult chord, I would play the major version of it, which was close enough for me. I rarely took the time to learn correct fingering or time signatures.

It must have been Spring by then, because windows were open. I answered a knock at the door and it was Blue, just standing there. By then I was no longer afraid of him, but he seemed out of place in our well-kept house, as if not fully domesticated or suitable for a family environment.

"I figured it was you, playing," he said, taking a seat on the edge of a chair. It was not a compliment. Ann would not have been playing those songs, and if she had been, they would have sounded truer to their originals.

I nodded. The last thing I wanted to do was perform in front of Blue. So we sat there awkwardly until he asked if he could "try something."

"Oh, you play?" I asked.

222

"Not much, but when I went to school on the East Side, it was called Pershing High, they had an old piano in the detention room, and I was a regular there." We laughed. "I'd write numbers and letters on the keys in pencil to help myself remember the sequence of pitches that would make a melody. I later found out that my system don't agree with the standard A through G with flats and sharps, but it was close enough for me."

I got up from the bench. Blue sat down. "But these keys ain't marked!" he said, laughing. "Oh, well." His hands were not big. They were meaty, thick fingered. But they remembered.

Like I had heard about the drum set, Blue seemed to be listening to something only he could hear. And when he caught up with it, he played it. I didn't know what jazz was in those days, but my sister was aware of it. As he was playing, our car pulled up the drive, with Ann and my mom in it. When Ann walked in from the kitchen, Blue was at the keys facing away from her, engrossed. Ann stopped dead before sitting down in an armchair, looking shocked.

It took him a while to find his way, but it was worth the wait. When he was done, Ann and I applauded. Blue turned around, saw her, and blushed.

"Sorry," he said.

"Sorry? That was cool! What was that?" she asked, genuinely curious.

"It's something like, um, do you know Grant Green?"

"I've heard the name," Ann said.

"Well, he does this tune, uh, but I got lost, took it in another direction."

My mother came into the room. She looked even more shocked than Ann to see Blue sitting there.

"Mom, this is Blue Derry," I said.

"Hello, Mrs. Bauer," Blue said. "I'm a fan of your daughter's playing."

"So are we," Mom said. "We don't know where she got her talent from."

"Are you making any progress on the Bach?" Blue asked.

"A little," Ann said. "I'm still working on the Preludes, doing the Prelude in C almost by heart."

"Not so many flats or sharps to consider."

"It's his easiest one, but I have a long way to go."

"Keep a window open. I'll be listening," Blue said.

We had little else to talk about. Sensing his time in our house was up, Blue rose from the piano bench. "I gotta split," he said, and slipped out the door. Our living room seemed quiet and spacious without his Neanderthal girth at the piano.

"Why did you let him in?" my mom asked.

"Why not, Mom?" I said. "He lives directly across the street. Blue is our neighbor."

"Isn't he dangerous?"

I didn't know what to say to that, and Ann was no help. My mother had a point, though. Stories had circulated about Blue. He was said to be a powder keg. Lately he had got into a fight in the park, bloodied a guy's nose. He had also been in another shouting match with his father, which upset the neighbors. And the muffler on his car was shot; his every entrance and exit onto the block intruded on our eardrums.

Yet there was the underlying sensitivity of Blue Derry. I did not seek him out, but I felt drawn to that quality.

My mother stood pat. "I don't want him in here," she said. "Not with Ann or Melanie. I don't think he should be in here at all. He needs to show me he's as civilized as . . . as we are. Let him get his own piano."

"Who's Graham Green?" I asked Ann, after Mom had gone back to the kitchen.

"*Grant* Green, silly. He plays piano. Jazz."

"Have you ever played that kind of music?"

"No. Mrs. Lerner would kill me. But it sounds like it'd be fun to just play, I mean, without a piece of music or any rules on a page in front of me."

"And Blue has an ear for it." I told her what I'd heard about Blue's session on Frank Abrams's new drum set.

"Wow," she said. "I wonder what lessons would do for a guy like him."

5

The Derrys were *different*. No mom was in the home, and Mr. Derry was not a typical dad. And Cloverlawn was leery of the loaded gun that was Blue. We pitied his brothers. They were good kids, but John and Jim rarely saw the insides of our homes.

John Derry was an albino in rags. His skin was very white, his hair whiter than blonde, his eyes a pale blue covered by a big pair of glasses that he was always pushing back onto his nose. His baggy pants were held up by a long belt, the end of which wrapped half again around his waist. A threadbare shirt ballooned over that belt. His leather shoes, devoid of color or polish, were tacked and taped together. They hindered his step as much as his lack of stamina did. John walked as if carrying something heavy on his back.

John was a neighbor and a friend. He sat in front of me in Social Studies class at Clinton Junior High. He was agreeable but not a bright student. He was one of those kids who learned little but got passed from one grade to the next. Because of his poor health, he did not regularly attend school. And because he had no support from a parent, he had little motivation to succeed in his classes. Sitting behind him, I had his back, literally. I often helped him with routine paperwork and short assignments.

We would walk home from school with groups of kids. The route was about a mile. We would cut through the park to the neighborhood. Not a strong kid, John would need to stop to catch his breath. The larger group would continue without him, but I would wait with him until he was rested.

One day near the end of the school year we stopped at a picnic table near the park's service road. A public drinking fountain was close by. We sat alongside on the bench, our backs resting against the hard cedar table edge, our feet splayed before us. John picked a cigarette out of the crumpled pack in his shirt pocket. It was a Camel, bent, almost broken, with no filter. He straightened it best he could, packed the bits of tobacco by tapping on one end, and produced a match. He lit the soft end while inhaling on the packed end. Then he handed it to me.

"Where'd you get it, John?"

"Eddie owed me." Eddie Friedman, who lived on the corner, was a grade behind us.

Until then, I had only watched my parents or older kids smoking. My father was not a heavy smoker, but, because of my mother's objections, he would have a puff in the back yard. He had an old Zippo lighter. It smelled of butane and had a US Army insignia on it. He would smoke that Marlboro down, then scatter the tobacco from the butt over the dirt in the garden before dumping the filter into our aluminum garbage can.

I looked at the rising thread of smoke. *Someday*, I thought, *I'll be a smoker, too*. But John? I had warned him about the danger to his health.

In imitation of my father, I took a serious drag on the Camel. It did not go well. Choking on an inhaled piece of tobacco, I stumbled to the drinking fountain. Someone had stuck a twig in the spout, which restricted the fountain's flow so that it spurted up into my face and onto my jacket. After I'd gargled and coughed up and swallowed enough water to sooth my throat, I sat back down. John passed the cigarette to me again.

"If that's what smoking's about, no thank you."

"First puff's a surprise. You get used to it," John said, pushing his glasses up on his nose.

"I'll get used to it some other time," I said. I waited until he stubbed out the cigarette and put the butt back into his pocket for later. Then I emptied the paper bag that carried the remains of my lunch, a fried baloney and cheese half-sandwich and an orange. The sandwich was on "enriched" white bread, the Wonder Bread brand we got from our home delivery bread man. John watched me put the sandwich on the tabletop between us.

"Hungry?" I asked, offering it to him.

"Sure," he said. "But you gave me some of your lunch last week."

"I had the other half at noon. You can have this one."

He dismantled the sandwich, then removed the crust and nibbled at the soft white bread before eating the meat and cheese. "Your mom makes a good sandwich," he said.

I peeled the orange, threw the skins into the weeds, and gave him half.

After he ate, he finished smoking the butt, picking bits of tobacco from his lips. Then we resumed the walk home. As we emerged from the park, a 1955 Chevy wagon turned into the gravel parking lot, making a racket before skidding to a stop. Blue reached over to roll the passenger window down.

"Get in, Johnny," he said.

"Where we goin'?"

"Orleans." The street where Bet lived.

"Can Gary come?"

"No! Get in, dammit!"

John got in. Stones flew as Blue U-turned and sped away, gears shifting and smoke blowing.

*****

I had heard mention of Bet. John and Jim spoke of her with undisguised affection. At first, I thought she must be a baby or toddler, but later I realized that she was older than John, thus also older than me. I wondered if she might be as old as Blue. I didn't know where she fit in the Derry family birth order.

Next time I got a chance to talk to John, I asked about the visit to Orleans Street. He shook his head. "Blue wanted to check on Bet.

Mom was working late, so he fixed dinner for us. Then he got her clothes ready for tomorrow."

This puzzled me, but I chose not to ask why Bet did not get her own clothes ready.

"Does Bet go to school?"

"Sometimes. She takes a special bus."

"What grade is she in?" I asked, fascinated by this girl I had never seen.

"I don't know nothing about that. You better ask Blue."

Did John not know much about Bet? Or was he told not to say anything? Why was John's mother not in John's life? Divorce was rare in those days; the Derrys were the only broken family on Cloverlawn. Then, as now, kids blamed themselves for their parents' conflicts. I wondered if the unseen weight John carried was due to his fractured family.

6

I saw little of Blue Derry for the next two years, my last years of high school. No longer in school, Blue was spending more time at his mother and sister's house on Orleans Street. The few times I did see him pull up in front of the Cloverlawn house in a battered car, I got no more than a nod from him. Jim Derry, two grades behind John, looked up to his brothers but had his own set of friends on the block.

John and I were still friends, but we were growing in different directions. Oak Park High in those days was mostly Jewish kids, and many of them were college bound. The graduation rate and the percentage of kids who went to college were high. I also took college prep courses, but John was now shuttled into shop classes, "general education," and "special education" classes. He once told me that a teacher called him a "slow learner," a category that included brain injured, dyslexic, and developmentally or perceptually disabled kids. With his easygoing nature John made friends in his special classes, but because of his physical frailty he was not very active and did not participate in sports.

Because of our different school curricula, I spent more time with the other so-called "normal" guys on Cloverlawn. I played baseball, football, and hockey with Will Miller and Chuck Farley, who were my age and in some of my classes. I also played a lot of baseball with Dan McPhail, who went to Catholic Central High in Detroit. We played pickup games and on Rec League teams. Except for Danny running track and Will playing football, the Cloverlawn kids were not varsity jocks.

John told me he had been working parttime in a machine shop owned by a friend of his father. The money he made gave him a feeling of freedom and security. He could buy food and cigarettes. One winter, he bought himself a winter coat that was so heavy, he appeared more stooped than ever.

John was picking up some basic auto maintenance skills from his father. And he made friends with Eddie Friedman and Louie White, both of whom also smoked cigarettes and worked on cars. John bought a disk sander, with which he could feather in the Bondo he used to patch rust holes in fenders and rocker panels on his buddies' cars.

*****

During summer break, big pickup games were played at Diamond #1 at the park, which was the best field in the city. Kids would arrive around 8:30. By 9:00, captains would emerge. Elaborate coin tosses and bat-handling contests would determine which captain got first pick, after which they would take turns filling out their teams. The loser of the coin toss would get first bats. We often had so many kids that some weaker and younger kids ended up on the bench, chasing foul balls.

An alternative to picking sides was Jews vs. Goys. We Goys outnumbered the Jews and tended to be better athletes, so we gave the Jews one or two of our guys to even the odds. We often sacrificed Jim Flynn, a good player who lived in a heavily Jewish neighborhood.

We never saw any of the Derry brothers at these baseball games, but a Cloverlawn street game that brought out all the kids regardless of age, gender, or religion was Kick-the-Can. The game was usually played in the evening during the warmer months, after dinner dishes were washed and dried. The *can* was often a Maxwell House Coffee can, which was placed in the middle of the street.

Younger kids were most enthusiastic about the game, screaming and laughing as they ran from the "seeker" or charged the can. Most of the older kids had fun, too, but Blue Derry, my sister Ann, and one or two others had outgrown Kick-the-Can.

The game begins when a kicker puts a leg into the can from its spot on the pavement. Everyone runs except one kid who is "it." This kid, usually determined by a rock-paper-scissors elimination,

231

charges to retrieve the can while the others scatter for hiding places within preset boundaries behind or under cars and shrubs, between houses, and even behind the skinny saplings that lined the avenue.

When the "it" kid, or Seeker, returns the can to its position, he or she can find and capture others by tagging them, thus putting them in "jail." But if the Seeker strays too far from the can, one of the hiders can charge the can, kick it, and free all the prisoners. The game ends when only one kid, the winner, remains uncaught or when the streetlights go on. The next Seeker, if time allows, would be the first person to be put into the jail when the game ends.

That first prisoner was often John Derry, but we knew better than to let John become the Seeker. John was too weak and slow to catch anyone. His brother Jim would step up and volunteer to help him. Everyone agreed with this solution.

*****

Chuck Farley was one of the first kids in my circle of friends to have a car. Chuck's dad traveled a lot for his job as a sales rep for an auto company supplier, but he made good money and bought Chuck a '62 Pontiac. It was a great car, but it was not long before Chuck complained about a slipping clutch. John Derry urged him to bring it to his father, who adjusted the clutch for free.

One late August day while Will, Chuck, and I were hanging out in the park, John came up. He looked distressed and out of breath. "Hey, Chuck," he said, "I need a ride. Gotta check on my sister. I can give you a couple bucks for gas." At twenty-five cents a gallon, Chuck stood to come out of the trip with plenty of fuel to spare, but he refused the money.

"I owe you one, John," Chuck said. He was willing to help, and was curious, as was I, about John's sister. Chuck, John, and I piled into Chuck's car and headed for Orleans Street. Will opted out, needing to get to football practice.

As we drove east on Eight Mile Road, Ron explained that Blue had called him from his job. Their sister Bet was home alone and needed some help.

"You mean her mom needs a baby-sitter for Bet?" I asked. John had told me that his mother worked at Lynch Road Assembly, a plant that turned out Plymouth sedans.

"Sort of. Mom's working overtime, and Blue can't get there 'til tonight."

Bet, and presumably Mrs. Derry, lived in an older neighborhood that was well integrated, as the growing Black population from inner-city Detroit expanded toward the city limits. Coming from a lily-white suburb of newer, if lesser, homes like Oak Park, Orleans appeared to be a tough street, its kids less friendly.

As we rolled up to the house, a group of kids hanging out on porches glared at us. Three guys standing *in* the street did not budge, so we slowed down and squeezed past them. They did not smile or wave. We parked in front of a house that looked to be uncared for. The grass was dead, and no attempt at landscaping had been made. The house needed paint. The screen door had no screens in it.

"Wait here. Bet's kinda shy," John said, as he went in.

Chuck and I sat on the stoop, feeling uncomfortable under the looks of the street kids.

"Do you think John's mom is in there?" Chuck asked.

"No. She's at work."

Finally, John came to the door. "I had to check on her first. Bet don't get many visitors. Come on in."

The living room was dimly lit. It smelled of nicotine and dirty underwear. Bet was sitting very straight in a far corner. She was beautiful, in her own way. She had short blonde hair, high cheekbones, and a very light complexion, like John. She looked thin and scared in pajama bottoms and bare feet and a simple white blouse. Sometimes she would rock gently in her chair. Neither Chuck nor I said anything. I guessed her to be about my age.

"Are you sure it's all right? We can wait outside." Chuck said.

"It's okay." John said and turned to Bet. "Bet, this is Chuck. He gave me a ride over here. And this here's Gary. Say hi to my friends from Cloverlawn."

Bet gave us a shy smile, but did not look directly at us.

"Can you fellas wait until I fix Bet a little dinner?" He looked at her. "You're hungry, aren't you, hon?"

She nodded.

Chuck rose from his chair, clearly uncomfortable in that house. "We can wait on the porch or in the car if you think--."

"I just need to warm her dinner and get some food in her. Then we can go."

Chuck and I sat awkwardly in the living room. Bet walked, mostly on her toes, between us and into the kitchen. John opened the refrigerator door and rooted around for food. He fired up a gas burner to heat something. When Bet tasted the food John had prepared, she said "too hot." John said, "It's ok, Bet. I tasted it." She repeated "too hot," in a voice that sounded younger than she looked.

"All right, Bet," John said. He poured a bit of cold water over the food and stirred. He sat and prompted each bite while Bet ate slowly, rocking a little.

Sensing that Chuck and I were the cause of Bet's anxiety, if it was anxiety, I rose from my chair and started for the door. Chuck followed gladly. As we exited the house, we got the attention of some kids standing on a lawn across the street. One kid said something which prompted the group to laugh, and they continued to look our way.

We sat on the porch steps, while the chatter and laughter across the way continued. I heard someone say something that included the word, "retard," followed by more laughter. Chuck stood up and glared at one of the kids. He elbowed me as he said softly, "asshole."

Later, John tried to tell us about Bet as we drove back down Eight Mile toward Oak Park. "She gets, like, swamped by too many things to do. She's, uh, different. I mean, a little slower than everybody else."

"I think Chuck and I upset her by being there," I said.

"Maybe, but I wanted her to meet you guys. I wish she had more good people around her. She doesn't have no one."

"She has your mom," Chuck said.

"Yeah, but Mom doesn't, um, she doesn't always know what Bet needs."

I wanted to press John for clarification, but it was clear he was not comfortable talking about his sister. Or his mother.

"How old is she, John?" I asked.

"Seventeen. Bet's a year older than me, but she's like a little sister."

When Chuck commented about the asshole kids on the block, John asked us not to mention them to Blue. "Don't tell Blue you were there. Please. I probably shouldn't'a let you guys in, 'cuz Blue, ah, he might get pissed about it. And those kids. It's best if he doesn't know what they were doing. He might want to talk to them about it. Know what I mean?"

We knew.

7

My parents wanted college for me long before I wanted it for myself. I came up at a time when parents—mine and many others—wanted their children to have more opportunities than they did. This was the American Dream of so many who had come up through the Depression and a world war. They wanted higher education and better jobs for their kids, whether their kids shared these goals or not.

My father made a decent living working long hours as a machinist and tool and die maker. He helped my sister with her tuition at Wayne State in Detroit, where she majored in Music Education. Dad wanted me to try for a degree in mechanical engineering. I thought about that, but I realized as I got closer to high school graduation that I had no interest in any math beyond basic calculations and geometry.

So, I wasn't sure about engineering school, in which calculus and other advanced math was said to be a requirement, but since I was expected to go to college, I tried in eleventh and twelfth grades to raise my GPA and get admitted to a school like Michigan State, where I hoped my parents would pay at least part of my way.

My two best Cloverlawn friends, Will and Chuck, took college prep classes, but neither was serious about school. Will hoped his success with football would earn him a scholarship somewhere. Chuck talked about joining the Navy for training in electronics or mechanics, after which he might have the option of college on the GI Bill. There were others in my classes and on the block—Dan McPhail was one of them—who seemed to be set on college, but I wondered if I had the drive or desire to earn a college degree.

During those last two years of high school, we male children of Cloverlawn grew. Our voices changed. We noticed girls. We rebelled against our parents and authority in general. We discovered the Beatles and the Rolling Stones. We skipped out on church. My dad cosigned for my first loan and I bought a car, a 1959 Ford Galaxy.

A few weeks after I bought that Ford, which I found through an ad in the newspaper and bought from a private owner, I noticed the sluggish pickup, the bluey-white smoke, the smell of burning oil, and the low oil level. The situation worsened over the next weeks until I stopped driving the car altogether. Most of the money I made from a parttime job was spent on car payments, so I was grounded until a low-cost solution arose.

John Derry, who knew auto engines as well as any of my friends, said I'd been ripped off. He suggested I needed at least a head gasket, and possibly piston rings or valves. I thought he would recommend his father, Cloverlawn's own backyard mechanic, but John told me that his dad was no longer doing engine work that might require a hoist and someone younger and stronger to do the heavy lifting. He recommended his brother.

John told me that Blue was working at an auto repair shop on the East Side, not far from his mother's place on Orleans, and that Blue had access to this shop on evenings and weekends. I hadn't seen Blue in months, and was hesitant about him. His reputation as lazy and unpredictable was growing, and I couldn't afford the prevailing rate for engine work.

A few evenings later, after hearing from John that Blue was willing to look at the car, I drove it to Stan's, a small auto repair shop on Joseph Campau in Hamtramck. Enroute, the car stalled out several times and was smoking badly. I could not get it to go faster than 35 mph.

*****

I saw a light on in one of the bays, so I knocked on a high garage-door window. A minute later, Blue emerged from an entry door.

"Sorry," he said. "I was in the middle of pulling a carburetor." He was wearing the greasiest pair of coveralls I had ever seen. He

237

looked under the hood and signaled for me to start it up. "Well, you got it here," he said, waving at me to shut it down. "A tow would have cost you plenty."

"Yeah, and I don't know how much this is gonna cost, so—"

"Cool it, Gary. We haven't even looked at it yet. And I'm not worried about the money right now. Maybe later. Let's see what it needs."

He told me it would be best if I waited in the office. He would call me if he needed help.

"I got to call home," I said.

"Phone's in there." He pointed.

"I have homework to do. Is that okay?" I said.

He laughed. "Yeah, go ahead, schoolboy. Knock yourself out."

The office consisted of an old wooden desk, two metal chairs, a Playmate of the Month wall calendar, and an advertising poster for Ford's newest arrival, the Mustang. The ad left no doubt that the Mustang was designed and built for baby-boom kids, who, it was said, had more disposable income than any crop of teenagers anywhere, ever. Standing behind the sleek yellow car were two blonde, white, affluent-looking teens.

The desktop was littered with barely recognizable auto parts, repair manuals, half-filled coffee cups, and food scraps. A 12-inch diameter ash tray was filled to overflowing with Pall Mall and Lucky Strike butts. I cleared a spot on the desk, opened my World History textbook, and tried to make sense of the Tudor Dynasty. I learned that night that Henry VIII had six wives, two of whom he beheaded.

Blue came back after about an hour and a half.

"What's that you're writing? he asked.

"Homework." It was supposed to be an essay, but it was mostly a summary from my history book.

He sat in the chair across from the desk. "Will you read it to me?"

"Uh, okay." I began reading. About halfway through the first paragraph, he asked me to read louder. I stood up and read it as if I was reading to the class.

Blue listened carefully, at times asking me to slow down or repeat a sentence. "It's interesting," he said when I finished. "You write well."

We went back into the repair bay where I could see my car, its engine partially disassembled. "I can tell you right now," he said, "it needs a PVC valve and it'll need a head gasket, but we gotta pull the engine to get a look at rings."

I looked around the room for a hoist. "How—?"

"Stan isn't set up for this kind of work. He farms it out to another shop. Let's worry about it tomorrow. I got to get you home. Good thing it'll be Sunday. Stan don't want cars here overnight."

*****

On the drive back to Cloverlawn in Blue's '55 Chevy, he asked about my sister.

"Ann's doing okay. Going to Wayne State. Still playing the piano."

"How's she's doing with the Bach?" he said.

"I don't know."

"Is she seeing guys?" I suspected that question was coming. I also suspected that Blue might be thinking *quid pro quo*, a kindness to get into Ann's good graces. It irked me that he might see me as nothing more than useful, but I was desperate. My father had cosigned for a two-year auto loan on a car that had little value, as it sat. Still, I had to tell the truth about Ann.

"I think she has a boyfriend now."

"I'll bet he's a frat boy."

I laughed. Frats and Greasers were two distinct teenage cultures, poles apart in behavior and style. Greasers were more likely to be seen in jeans, pointy shoes, and a black leather jacket. They put

Brylcream or Vitalis in hair that they combed all the way back into a duck tail. They were more likely to get in trouble and drop out of school. If Blue had identified with a group, and he had not, it would have been the Greasers. I was not aligned, but I had more in common with Frats.

"The kid dresses like a Frat," I said. "Madras shirts, loafers with a fake bow tie on top."

"Oh, no! Does he wear those white chinos with the buckle back?"

"Probably. But I don't think he's in a fraternity."

"You sure Ann wants to date this sucker, pass up on a true gentleman like myself?"

"I don't know, but your name doesn't come up in our dinner-table conversation very often."

"That's your job, boy. You need to tell her about my, uh, sophistication, my skills under the hood," he said, and winked. He was still wearing that greasy jumpsuit, and his face and hands were covered with grime.

"Ok, I'll work on that." I said.

I'd been thinking about Blue's sister, Bet. I had not seen her since that visit to Orleans with John and Chuck, one year before. I felt pity for her, which I now understand is a rather judgmental version of compassion. That day with John and Chuck, I was curious. Bet was pretty, with a nice shape, but I also found her vulnerability attractive, even though I would never have admitted that. I did not spend enough time with her to know just what afflicted her. Maybe, I thought, she *was* mentally retarded. But it angered me that kids in her neighborhood were laughing about her, calling her names. I wondered if those punks might hurt her in some way. I wanted to be on the side of her protection. That day on her porch with Chuck, I wanted to confront the kids who insulted her, but Chuck and I were outnumbered, and we were not the type to get into fights.

"What about Bet?" I said. "How is she?"

Little did I know, I'd pulled the pin on a hand grenade. Blue pulled his car to the side of the road and faced me. "How do you know my sister?"

"I don't know her, Blue. I only met her once. With John."

"What are you saying. John took you to Orleans?"

"No. John asked Chuck for a lift, and I went along for the ride."

He was quiet for a while. I think he was deliberating whether he could trust me.

"I only asked about her," I said. "Is she doing okay?"

"I try to give her what she needs. She's happy and comfortable, no thanks to her mother. Or her old man. She don't have nobody in her corner, okay? Not her parents, not her neighbors, not the government people who want to lock her in a warehouse. But she's taken enough shit from the world. Anybody who messes with Bet's gonna hear from me. Got that?"

As he spoke, he fingered a knife that he had pulled from his pocket. When he finished, he flicked it at me so quickly that I barely had time to jerk back. I'm certain he never intended to cut me, but he came close enough. The knife tore what looked like a single thread in the arm of my shirt. I reached for the door handle and backed out of the car. We were near the corner of Eight Mile and Wyoming, a few miles from home. I began walking.

Blue stopped his car alongside me, got out, and ran up to me. "Shit, Gary, did I nick you, man?" I shook my head. "I'm sorry. God, I never hurt anybody with that thing. It's just that I been practicing, see? And I'll do anything to protect Bet."

"But I would never hurt her, Blue. You got to trust me on that, okay? And I'm not about to get back in that car with you right now."

"Somebody came in and tried to rape her, okay? I don't know exactly what happened, but when I find out . . ."

"Wait, Blue. You know a little bit about me. I don't . . ."

"God help me," he said. He looked at me and at the knife. "I'm so sorry, man." He reached back and heaved the knife onto the road. We watched several cars pass over it before a truck smashed it where it lay on the pavement.

"Dammit, Gary, will you forgive me? And let me give you a ride home."

8

My parents were waiting for me when I walked in the door. I had called to say I'd be late, but late did not mean 1:30am.

"We don't want you going around with Blue Derry. That young man is trouble. Got that?" My father was given the job of speaking for my mother. I explained that I had taken the car to a shop on the East Side of town where Blue happened to work, that he was getting me a great price, and that I needed to get back to the shop tomorrow to see the job through. I had to assure them that I was not "going around" with anyone but that John Derry had recommended Stan's Auto Repair to me. I also stressed that I wanted to get the repairs done to protect my dad's investment in me, and that I would not be relying on financial help from him or anyone else.

They were skeptical, as was I, but, my engine in pieces, I had no choice but to give Blue, who had very nearly sliced my arm, a chance to finish the repair and put the pieces back together again.

*****

The following afternoon, I walked the two miles back to Eight Mile Road and stuck out my thumb. I had heard stories of kids hitchhiking. Dan McPhail told me that he sometimes hitched four miles to Catholic Central High. Others I knew begged a ride to get to a ballgame in downtown Detroit, or to get out to Plum Hollow or Franklin Hills, in the suburbs, where they caddied during the summer months.

I got a ride to within a half-mile of Stan's and walked from there. I knocked on the same window, and soon Blue came out in those coveralls, carrying a big wrench. He led me to the office, where he had two cold bottles of Old Milwaukee in the icebox. He put down the wrench and handed me a beer.

"I'm embarrassed about last night, man," he said.

"Okay, but you should know I would never hurt your sister."

"I know. I'd been practicing with that knife. Getting to know it well. Thinking about how I might use it on certain people. You are not one of those people, Gary, but my imagination got the best of me. I'm glad I got rid of it." He reached out that meaty paw, and I looked at it. Then I shook it.

"So does this mean my date with your sister is out of the question?" he said.

We laughed and carried our beers out into the shop.

"I may need you soon," he said. I was shocked to see my car, its wiring and hoses hanging free, its radiator and grill work removed, its transmission and exhaust manifold disconnected. A repair manual for my car was lying open on the bench. "The next step is motor mounts. Then we pull it."

I happen to be very good at hiding my emotions. The skill has helped through some tough situations, but it has also made a liar out of me. But here was a time to put on my best poker face. And pray. I was not in the habit of asking for help from above, but the situation called for it.

"What can I do?" I said, as Blue tossed the last mounting bolt to me.

"After I get it out of there, you can get your hands under the pan--here." He handed me a crud-infested pair of canvas gloves, showed me where he wanted me to stand, then stepped into the engine bay with a rusty old blanket tucked into his shirt, got the block into his arms, and lifted it out. Once he was out, I helped him walk it to the bench, which had been cleared. I knew little about engine work before that and less since, but the few friends I told about Blue and that engine were incredulous. Will Miller called me a "lyin' liar."

As it turned out, Blue found part of a grommet that had heated up, crystallized, and broke apart. A tiny piece of hardened rubber had blocked the rotation of the oil pump.

"But the pump doesn't need replacing," he said. "We'll just soak it, and clean or flush everything else. But we do need the PCV, the grommet, a hose, and a few gaskets. Then we'll put new oil and fluid back in it."

"So it'll take another day?"

"I should have it at your place by noon tomorrow."

"What will I owe you?"

"We'll talk about that some other time."

"What about Stan? He'll find out the car has been here, won't he?"

"Stan can't fire me 'til I get this thing out of his garage."

*****

I was at school, but it was about two o'clock the next afternoon, my mother said, when Blue pulled up with my car, parked it at the curb, and rang the bell to give her the keys. When I started it, it purred like I'd never heard and was no longer smoking. I found a note on the driver's seat:

be at Stans Saterdy at 6 if you can. You ow me diner. Blue

*****

During those days in the fall on 1963, I dated a girl from school named Penny Singer. She was my first girlfriend. She lived on the other side of the park, so the park was a convenient place to meet after school or after dinner.

The city had recently built a state-of-the-art fenced-in playground with numerous safety features for kids. On a base of sand and wood chips, the play structures were made from hard plastic and splinter-free wood. Brightly colored, with vinyl coatings, rounded edges, and rubber surfaces, it took a year before parents realized that here was a space where they could safely bring their toddlers and younger kids.

At first, Penny and I had it all to ourselves. We would take positions on the teeter-totter or the swings, or huddle together on the soft ground under a play structure. Penny was smart and funny. We would talk, and when it was getting dark enough and the coast was clear enough, we'd make out.

When I first got my Ford, I took Penny to a wacky comedy at the West Side Drive-In, *Who's Minding the Store*, with Jerry Lewis and Jill St. John. I don't remember much of the movie, but I still remember the thrill of putting my arm around her shoulders and inching my hand toward forbidden regions below. Our relationship, though, was doomed by the fact that Penny was Jewish. She could not invite me into her home. She knew her Orthodox parents would never approve of a non-Jewish boyfriend.

But her stated reason, and reason enough, for breaking up with me was the car, which by then was smoking so badly that the oil smell got into our hair and clothes. When Blue finally got my car running, I called Penny with the news. She was happy to hear the car was fixed, but she had moved on to another guy.

9

I arrived at Stan's at six that Saturday, my Ford still running like new. Blue had changed out of his work clothes and his hair was slicked around to the back of his head, but he still had the hands of an auto mechanic.

"Hot wheels!" he yelled, sliding onto the bench seat. He suggested a nearby Clock Restaurant on Eight Mile Road. As we looked at menus, the first topic of conversation was Blue's family. John had recently decided to drop out of school so he could work fulltime in a machine shop. I was surprised to hear that Blue, also a dropout, was concerned about him.

"I told him it's not too late to stick it out," Blue said. "He's not strong enough for the life of a shop rat, and it'd be nice to have someone in the family who can read and write." Blue smiled as he said this, but I could tell by now that his smiles often had a bitter edge to them.

"I hear Jim is a good student," I said.

"Jimmy," he said, shaking his head. "My youngest brother is what, fourteen years old? He's a survivor. He has the best excuse in the family for being a fuckup, yet he has more sense than the rest of us put together." It was true. Jimmy was a bright and surprisingly grounded boy, with neither the rage of Blue nor the indifference and sluggishness of John.

The diner was not busy, so we got waited on right away. Blue ordered a BLT, home fried potatoes and a soft drink. I had a ham and cheese and a glass of water, hoping I would have enough cash to pay our bill. I had been prepared to claim an upset stomach if Blue ordered dinner, a drink, and dessert. Besides, I wondered how much Blue would charge me for the engine work on my Ford. Parts may have run only $15-20 dollars. But labor? Whatever that debt might be, how would I pay it?

The conversation came around to Mr. Derry.

"My old man is, well, keep this to yourself, okay? I don't know if he is really my old man or some guy named Lance that my mom married after she had me."

"You mean –"

"Yeah, I was born before my mom married him. She once told me that it could have been someone else."

I was shocked to hear this. "Can they prove it with a blood test?"

"No. I mean, sometimes they can show a probability. But if the kid's blood group is wrong for both so-called parents, you can know that the kid must have a parent other than one of those two. So a blood test might tell that Lance is not my father, but it can't be used in court, so it can't prove nothing.

"But Lance says he's my real father, see? I don't know, I don't see him in me. I *do* see my mother in me. He never legally adopted me, and he won't take a blood test. He says he raised me, and the rest is just paperwork, which don't mean nothing. And it don't. So he's maybe my step-father, but I would be generous to call him a father. Keep all this to yourself, hear?"

"Sure. I won't say anything." And I never did. Until now. It wasn't until 1984 that DNA testing was discovered that would prove paternity, and DNA wasn't used in courts until much later.

"Look, Lance is living in fantasyland," Blue said. "He don't want to think about his family, so he drowns himself in beer and work and his friends."

"Does he see very much of Bet?" I risked the question.

"Are you kidding? He doesn't want to be reminded that he fathered that girl. And he went and had two more kids, only to prove to himself that Bet was a freak of nature.

"And her mother," he paused to gather his thought, and I could sense his emotional state ramping up. "Our mother, that is.

She thinks Bet is a punishment from God. Like, she thinks God put a demon into Bet. So she feels guilty and hides her guilt in alcohol. Whiskey is her game, and her job at the Chrysler plant is another escape. She don't want to look at Bet. She tries, when she's home, to be a mother, but she's so gone that she don't know that Bet needs more than Spaghetti-O's and a weekly bath. And she don't realize that Bet isn't dumb. I'm no genius, but I know she's very smart, she just learns a different way, and Bet doesn't have natural skills with people. Sorry, man, I'm getting worked up. I promise not to take it out on you."

He laughed. I laughed cautiously.

He pulled folded-up papers from his shirt pocket. "Look, Gary, you say you get decent grades in school. You told me about that paper you were writing for your history class, the one about King Henry. Would you look at this stuff for me, and tell me what it says?"

"You want me to read it out loud?" I asked.

"You don't need to do that. Just give me a sum up."

I saw about four pages, two letters. The first was about six weeks old. It was a request to visit the family of Elizabeth Mae Derry on October 20, which was two weeks in the past. The visit would be an assessment of Bet's "home atmosphere" and "treatment needs." The visitors would be a doctor and a representative from the Child Welfare System of the State of Michigan. The letter included an acknowledgment form and a reply envelope.

The second letter was a follow-up to the first. It was not a request but a notice advising that an assessment visit would take place on November 10, the following Friday, at 3pm. "Failure to comply," the letter read, could result in "parental custody relinquishment" to the child welfare or juvenile justice systems.

I remembered what Blue had said a few days earlier about those who would harm Bet or lock her in a warehouse. They were the people he might protect her against, with the thrown-away knife he had not, I hoped, replaced. Those were the people who had sent the letters.

"It looks like your mother ignored the first letter," I said. "The second letter says a doctor will come to see Bet on Friday at three pm to examine her. They want to know how she's doing and what she needs."

"That's what I read, too," he said. I wondered to what extent he was illiterate. "Do you think they'll try to put her away?" He was able to use the auto repair manual at Stan's, but I suspected he only studied the diagrams.

"I don't know," I said, "but they *could* take custody of her if you and your mother are not home with Bet on Friday. You should be ready to show these people that Bet is in good hands."

Blue nodded, but then he took the pages out of my hands and ripped them in half. "Someday," he said, "with the right kind of guidance and teaching, Bet could have a job and her own place in the world. She knows a lot about flowers and plants and stuff. She loves animals, too. And she can draw. But once the state gets a hold of her, she'll never be anything more than she is right now."

I looked again at the first letter. "They say that if they see 'neglect' or a 'disruptive home environment,' they could take her, or start court proceedings to take her."

"It makes me crazy, Gary, knowing I don't do enough for her. Not as much as I should. A few weeks ago, a neighborhood guy tried to rape her. Did you know that?" he asked, his voice breaking.

"You said something. Is she . . . is she okay?"

"I think so. She won't talk about it. She says she fought him off. She gave no name, but I found out who it was, and I will take care of it."

I shook my head. "Call the cops, Blue."

"No, I can take care of anyone who hurts her at home, but I can't do anything if the state gets her. I know what they do with kids like Bet, and I won't allow it."

"Okay, but hold on, Blue. Will you listen to what I have to say?"

"Go ahead, dammit."

"If you and your mother play ball with those people, listen to them and take their suggestions, and you show that you're willing to cooperate, they're likely to leave your sister alone. I'm just sayin' don't antagonize them."

"Yeah, I hear you," he said. "But Gary, I don't even know if my mother will be there. I'd feel better about all this if she's *not* there to mess things up. And we know that she disregarded the first notice. I don't think it'd upset her if Bet's out of her life."

"Your mom needs to be there, Blue," I said. I was done talking, but then I remembered one more thing. I pointed a finger at him. "Please, Blue. Don't go after the guy who tried to molest her. If you have evidence, take it to the cops. Hear me?"

He nodded, but said nothing. I thought Blue got the message.

Up to that point in my seventeen years of living, I had few occasions to care deeply about things. I remember being scared when my grandmother had a stroke and was paralyzed on her right side. My parents took me to see her. Her face was drooping and she could barely speak. She could not walk or feed herself. I could see that she was in pain. Not long after that, she died. My parents said they were relieved as well as sad. I was not at all relieved.

When Mrs. Kipp was found asphyxiated in her garage, I felt afraid for Kenny and Jenny Kipp. I couldn't imagine what it would feel like to lose a mom.

But most of my childhood had been carefree, all about safety and sameness. There were my family and the Cloverlawn kids and my schoolmates, and a park where I could play until the streetlights came on. I had no reason to feel deeply about anyone or anything.

Now Blue Derry was ushering me into a new age of caring and feeling. Not long after he had slashed at me with a knife, he was trusting me with revelations about himself and his family, and he was listening to my opinion. People, it seemed, were not either good or bad, not two dimensional. They were, like Blue, mysterious.

10

Sometime after my meeting with Blue, I saw Jim, the youngest Derry, at school. I asked him how John was doing. He said John would come home from his machine shop job too tired for much else but sleep. Then one day after school I was walking toward the park when John drove up in Blue's Chevy. I'd heard he had bought the car from Blue for $70, and that Blue may have got the best of the deal. John reached over to open the passenger door, a cigarette dangling from his mouth.

"Gotta stop and get some sandwich meat. Want to come along?"

"How's the job going?" I asked. His hands were dirty. His work shoes were crusty, but they were a cut above the previous pair I had seen him in.

"Got me a few bucks in my pocket," he said.

We went to the Jewish market, Dexter-Davison, and I went in with him. I had heard that a girl in one of my classes, Carol Urbanski, was working there. I saw her cashiering at one of the registers and walked up to say hello, but she shooed me away. "Can't talk right now," she said. As I walked away, I saw a store manager watching me.

A year earlier, a stock boy and a cashier had been caught working together to steal money from a register. No one knew the details, but the two employees were fired and prosecuted. Before and after that incident, kids who worked at the market were saying that the store owner and managers were suspicious, not only of their non-Jewish employees, male and female, but also of young non-Jews who came in. The bosses were hard on the lookout for shoplifters.

On my way out, I stopped at the bagel shop. It was always possible to tell which of the available flavors was the freshest. The shop's stock of salty, salt stick, raisin, egg, cheese, and plain was on

253

display in Plexiglass bins. As I walked in, the baker dumped a basketful of egg bagels from the oven into a bin. Twelve cents later, I had a paper bag with two hot egg bagels.

When John arrived at the car, he looked flustered. "Some guy checked my bag and my receipt," he said.

"Figures," I said, embarrassed for him. Shuffling in, in work clothes, with dirty hands, they would suspect John, but they left me alone.

"I was the only one he stopped," he said.

"Maybe it's time to take our business to the A&P."

As we drove home, each of us with a bagel in hand, I mentioned that Blue had never charged me for his work on my Ford, which never ran more smoothly than it had been running lately.

"If he didn't say nothing, you don't owe him nothing," John said.

"Well, at least I can pay him for parts and fluids. Did I tell you I hired on at Walt's Hardware? It's only parttime, but it's a paycheck. I can pay him for parts right now. Later, I can give him money for labor."

"He gets parts with Stan's discount."

"Is he still living at your mom's place?"

"Got a pen? I'll give you the number."

"What if Bet answers? How is she, anyway?"

"Bet's fine. She can take a message."

"She writes?"

"Not very well, but she'll pass the message."

"Blue was afraid she might get taken by the state," I said.

"Blue needed money to get Bet ready for that state doctor, so he sold me the car. Only $70 bucks. Then he bought her some clothes and stocked the icebox with food for her."

"Really?"

"That seventy bucks was my first paycheck. But Bet's my sister, too. I'm giving this rig back to Blue soon as I can pick up another one. Got a line on a Merc belongs to a guy at the shop."

"Sounds like Blue is working hard to keep Bet at home."

"Yeah," John said. "He even got my mom to take the afternoon off work that day. But the doctors want to see some changes in Bet's diet and I don't know what-all else they told him."

I was stunned. Blue had taken my suggestion. So much of what I was learning about him was in contradiction of everything I thought I knew.

Then John said, "I hear you told him I took you to Orleans."

"Sorry, it kinda slipped out. Was he as upset with you as he was with me?"

"He was pissed at you, too?"

"Quite," I said, deciding not to mention the knife incident. "When you see him, will you tell him I'm working now?"

*****

I didn't call Blue at Stan's or at his mother's place. I fell back into my school routine. The job at Walt's gave me after school and Saturday hours. Walt taught me to cut replacement glass and do screen repair. He also called on me for deliveries. The job put gas in my car and a few dollars in my pocket, but it did not leave much time for "running around," as my father would put it.

Ann was living at home while attending Wayne State, so I had no expectation that my parents would foot the bill for MSU or any other out-of-town college. I planned on going to Oakland Community College, where I could also continue to live on Cloverlawn, and, if my grades were good enough, I hoped could spend my junior and senior years at a four-year college.

The rest of that winter, I didn't see much of the Derrys. Once, I saw a car that might have been Blue's, and I saw him walking through the park one day, but he didn't acknowledge me, and that was okay. I never heard anything about my debt to him, and I was grateful for that but hesitant to approach him.

My eighteenth birthday was in May, a month before graduation. A few days later I registered for the draft. The fighting—it was not called a war until much later--in Vietnam had not yet been requiring large numbers of guys to be drafted, and I had no firm ideas about it. I had no interest in politics, did not read the newspapers, and stayed away from conversations about Vietnam, God, communism, and everything else I considered to be "heavy." But early that summer I registered for a full load of classes at OCC, which gave me a student deferment from my draft board.

At the time, being called into the Army would have been a very big inconvenience. I wanted the freedom to earn money and go to school. I had also met someone that summer. Spending time with that girl, Jane Beckwith, became my top priority.

11

Back when I was thirteen and fourteen years old, Jane's house had been a stop on my morning Free Press route. When I rang her bell for the weekly bill collection, Jane would answer the door. "Mom, it's the paperboy," she would yell, before receding back into the house. We were kids, Jane a year younger than me, but there was an unspoken connection, sealed only by smiles.

Suddenly it was 1962 and I had just turned sixteen. I played third base on a recreation league baseball team that summer. Our sponsor was One-Hour Martinizing, a dry-cleaning establishment in town. Two other Cloverlawn kids were on the team: Chuck Farley was in the outfield. Dan McPhail played first base.

One night, we were playing at Diamond #1 in the Oak Park city park at the end of the block. Early in the game, I noticed Jane and a few other girls standing along the third base line, behind my team's bench. I had to look twice; Jane had grown.

When I went to the on-deck circle for my first at bat, I noticed her walking toward home plate. After I got into the batter's box, I saw her standing directly behind the chain-link backstop. I felt self-conscious, knowing she was watching me. It was not often that I had an audience. In those days, it was not so common for parents to watch their kids' games. So I was eager to make an impression on Jane Beckwith.

I swung late on the first pitch, and on the second, I swung at a ball that was way outside. With two strikes on me, I stepped out of the batter's box, realizing that this girl was distracting me from the task at hand. After taking a few seconds to wipe sand on my hands, I heard her say, "Take your time, Gary. Make him work for it." I looked her way and saw her smiling, then looked toward the third base coach, who gave me the "hit" sign. I stepped back into the box and fouled off a pitch, and then looked at several more pitches that were off the plate before hitting a ball hard into the outfield for a single. Standing at first base, I noticed Jane clapping at her spot behind the backstop.

She lived several blocks away and went to a Catholic School, Shrine of the Little Flower, but Jane was entering my orbit. We had different sets of friends, too, but when we crossed paths, I always got a smile or hello out of her, and although I was not dating girls yet, I had a good feeling about her that went back to the paper route and that night at Diamond #1.

It was not until my senior year, fall of 1963, that I began to meet my first girlfriend, Penny Singer, at the park playground. My fling with Penny was doomed by my religion and/or the oily fumes that were coming from my Ford, but by the summer after high school graduation, girls were the biggest blip on my radar. I had no expectation of a serious relationship, but as I got to know Jane, it became clear that she was not interested in a meaningless fling.

"Summer of '64," we call it now. My Ford's engine had been restored, and my hours at Walt's Hardware had been expanded for the season. I saw Jane almost every day. We hung out with a group of kids, often at the park, and I spent much time with her family. We were on budgets, saving for college, but I did not miss out on anything that summer. I had Jane.

One day, walking through the park with her, we came upon Blue Derry. He was sitting at a picnic table, bent over a guitar.

"Hey, Blue," I said, as we approached. "This is Jane."

"You Jane, me Blue," he said, scratching his ribs, aping the Tarzan movies, before returning to his guitar. We stood before him expectantly, but Blue was not in the mood for people.

"Okay, well, see you around," I said, finally.

"You know that guy?" Jane asked, as we continued walking.

"He lives across the street. Or he did."

"I hear he's trouble."

"He has a reputation," I said, "but it's not all that way. I mean, he's not a bad person."

"Did you recognize the song he was playing? she asked. "Green Fields."

"Really?" I said. "I recognized it, but . . . wow! Isn't that a folk song?"

"It is, but he changed it into something else."

Blue was an enigma. I had once begun to think I had a friendship with him. He'd done some serious work on my car. We'd had a serious talk about his family. My warning to him about the Child Welfare system may have helped to keep Bet out of an institution. But now he didn't seem to want to know me, and I wondered why.

*****

One afternoon toward the end of that summer, a police car pulled into the Derry's driveway. I was at work, but my mother saw two officers knock at the door. They waited for a while, but drove off after finding no one home.

A few nights later, I was walking through the park when Blue appeared. He walked up close to me in his intimidating way. He was carrying a knapsack with a bedroll or blanket attached.

"How's it hangin', man?" he said.

"I'm okay, how about you?"

"I need a little help right now."

"What it is, Blue?"

"I'm going to California, and I'm askin' for fifty bucks."

"I don't have much, but . . . when can you get it back to me?"

"I just need some cash to get out there. I'll be making good money in LA. I figure I can send you the money in a month. Two on the outside."

Was he running from the cops? Was he leaving Bet to fend for herself in that house on Orleans? I had only a twenty in my pocket. I was not in the habit of lending money, and I wondered if I would ever see it again. While I pulled out my wallet and hedged, Blue said, "You're like *them*, aren't you?"

"Uh, like who?"

"You know who. The cops and judges. The doctors and lawyers. The people who run everything."

I did not know what to say. I had never considered myself to be like *them*, but I had not thought about it much. "I don't know, Blue," I said. "I only got a twenty on me. I just don't have a lot of money to lend."

"You can trust me for the twenty, Gary. Can you get me more?"

I did not know that I trusted him, but I was afraid to say no. I didn't want to be on the side of the cops and judges.

"Do you have a car?" I asked.

"Sold it to brother John." He had sold it for money to buy clothes and food for Bet.

As I gave him the twenty, I said, "How is Bet?"

"I lost her, man. We were doing good until that little punk came in and tried to . . . you know. He took advantage of a girl with . . . of an innocent . . . my sister. The cops didn't care. They said the victim would need to come in. They said it was a private matter. But I caught up with him. I should have killed him, but I only messed up his face. Maybe I broke his nose. Then Child Welfare found out about it."

"So, the state took Bet to a home for . . .?" I didn't know how to complete the question.

"I got to get her out of there. They do shock treatments that take the spirit out of you. They tie the fallopian tubes of girls so they can't have babies. People don't get better in those places, man. So I got to get her back. But right now I gotta get moving 'til things clear over. Can you get me thirty more? I swear I'll get it back to you, but I gotta split, Gary."

He stood in the dark with his hands in his pockets, his expectant face inches away from my own. I wanted to help, but I wondered if he would make a fool out of me.

"Listen," he said, "I got a buddy in LA, works in a high-class restaurant. He can get me in as a waiter. He says those movie people are good tippers. I'll work my behind off, man. I just need a little time to make some money, and . . ."

"The cops'll arrest you when you get back here, you know." Blue's anger may have been justified, but he was responsible for the trouble he was in and for Bet's removal from her home.

"I think I've persuaded that pervert to drop charges," he said.

I went home for more money, and brought my car to the park. I also made up a self-addressed envelope, complete with four-cent stamp. When he jumped in, I said "where am I taking you?"

He raised his thumb. "I-94. I'll be in Chicago by morning."

12

That fall of 1964, Walt cut my hours at the store back to parttime. I took courses at the community college. My idea of fulfilling my father's dream of an engineering future had petered out. I no longer knew what I wanted to be, but I knew I wanted a life with Jane. I wanted a home and family with her someday, and I would need a career of some sort so that I could provide for them. I wasn't ready to share that dream with Jane; she had just begun her freshman year at Marygrove, a Catholic girls' college in Detroit. We were too young to consider marriage, but the only future I could imagine had Jane in it.

My father had been an infantryman with the 30th Division in western Europe during the war. The 30th, which he called Old Hickory, landed at Normandy after the initial invasion, and they fought their way across France and helped to stop the German offensive in the Battle of the Bulge, before chasing down German units in mop-up operations throughout Germany. My father didn't talk much about his war experience, but I knew enough about the war to revere him and all the Allied troops who fought and died. Like most of my friends, I played with toy soldiers, watched combat movies on television, and dreamed of someday becoming a soldier.

But my dream of life with Jane, and the reality of the escalating war in Vietnam, turned me around. I knew that I might be drafted someday, but I wanted to keep my student deferment. Although I was not as serious a student as Jane, I came to enjoy the college life. I did not choose a major right away at the community college, but I took psychology and social studies as well as science and humanities classes, and I hoped to transfer to a four-year university as a junior.

Most of my Cloverlawn friends, those who were my age, were now in college. Will Miller did not get the football scholarship he'd hoped for, but he got accepted to Wayne State, where Dan McPhail was also attending. Clare Cassidy, a very smart girl, was at UM. Chuck Farley, who got a job at a Ford plant in Sterling Heights that summer, was still thinking about joining the Navy.

I talked to John Derry in the street one day, around Christmastime. He seemed tired, more so than usual, and attributed it to working forty-eight hours per week. He was still doing piecework on a drill press at the same shop he'd been working since quitting school. John said Blue had called from California, where he was working in a restaurant. I did not expect to see Blue or my fifty dollars, but I was glad to hear he had made it to LA and was working.

John said he and Jim had visited Bet at a sanitarium southwest of Detroit called Eloise. Bet was doing well, working in a greenhouse there. Come spring, he said, she had a chance for a job at a farm on the premises.

Where, I wondered, did Blue get the idea that Bet would be mistreated or abandoned, or worse, in an institution? Do people in a place like Eloise get better? Could a girl like Bet get out someday and become an independent adult? I did not know enough about her to identify her disability. In those days, anyone with a learning or developmental problem was thought to be mentally ill and labeled mentally retarded. Many people with disabilities, and their families, were ashamed, like Bet's mother, or embarrassed or guilt-ridden, like her father, and many disabled became shut-ins, like Bet. They and their families feared the labels and ridicule that came from people who hated and feared them.

Blue had made the case that Bet could not have a fulfilled life in an institution. I agreed, but I realized that, for some who are not able to function independently and are not able to learn, a place like Eloise might be best if it helps the patient achieve his or her potential. It seemed, listening to the Derrys, that Bet could learn, if not in the ways many others learned.

In January of 1965 I got a ten-cent Christmas card from Blue Derry with a fifty-dollar bill enclosed. He signed the card but there was no note. Of course, I thought: Blue cannot write. Then sometime toward spring, Walt came into the back room of the store where I was cutting glass for storm doors. "Take a break, Gary. Guy named Blue is here to see you."

*****

He looked good. Leaner, tanned, healthy. We sat on wood crates in the back room. He told me about his travels.

"I worked at a bar, place called The Frolic Room, on Hollywood Boulevard. Lots of action at that place. And the money gets thrown around there! I met these movie people. Lee Marvin, who just finished making 'The Killers.' And Shirley MacLaine. I had a conversation with Ingrid Bergman, too; now there is a fine lady. And I made some good dough. Might even hold on to some of it."

Fat chance of that, I thought.

He showed me his car, a red two-year-old Olds Ninety-Eight convertible with whitewall tires and a big white stripe down the side.

"Drove this thing all the way back to Michigan. Check out the leather seats."

"Did you get to see California?" I asked.

"Yeah. Came up the coast to San Fran on my way home. I saw the Big Sur. That's on the ocean, with cliffs and rocks as big as a house, waves crashing in on 'em. Slept on a few beaches up there. I met a guy at the Frolic, an actor, Phil, from a little town, Aptos, near Santa Cruz. His parents ran an artichoke farm there. They had me driving tractor for a few weeks before I came home. Pickin' 'chokes in February, ain't that crazy? Too cold in Michigan to pick yer *nose* in February." He laughed. "I got to work with some Mexicans, migrants. They were families, and every member of the family helped. They

264

fed me, showed me a lot about 'chokes. How to know the good ones, all that. But I got in a fight with a guy, had to leave.

"After that job, I spent a few days in the mountains. Redwood country. People talk about God? That's where I found him, in those trees."

"You found God in the trees?"

"Yeah, well that's how it started. But then I discovered him in here." Blue tapped his breast with a fist. "He was in there all the time. I only just didn't know it."

It was the first time anyone had spoken to me about this God inside us, all of us, connecting us at our deepest core. "Good to see you back," I said, "but . . . have you seen your sister?"

"She's doing good. She growed up a little since I was gone. Eloise is better than I ever hoped. I want her out of that place someday, but she's learning stuff."

"Taking a class?"

"No. A woman, another patient, older lady, is looking after her. Sitting down with her, getting her to talk, teaching her things. They spend a couple hours every day together. The lady, her name is Julie, this Julie treats her like she's her own kid. Bet never had anyone like that, someone who really cares and puts in the time. She's learning more about nature and gardens and stuff."

"Does this Eloise place have books?"

"Yeah. Must be a library. She has some kid books, not little kid books, but, like, books with pictures and writing about animals. And Julie was reading this one book, The Magic Stone, about these girls who find an old sword that belonged to King Arthur . . . and Bet was listening to every word!"

"Wow, I'm glad for her."

"Look, Gary, the reason I came in here. You're a writer—"

"That's not so."

"Okay, but you can write, and I'm . . . I have some thoughts about Bet that I want to write to her doctor at Eloise, and I was hoping I could get you to put them down on paper for me. For Bet, you know."

"I could try . . ."

We walked out to Blue's car, stood on the sidewalk. I was still not a smoker, but I liked one on occasions. Blue offered, so we smoked. I supposed that Blue was still using me, wanting me to write a letter, but I did not care. I owed him—the engine in my Ford was still purring, even as the alternator was almost shot and the quarter-panels were rusting out.

"Gotta split, man," he said. I'll be in touch about that letter. Hey, are you with that Jane girl?"

I nodded.

He smiled as he ducked into his car.

13

In the summer of the following year, 1966, John Derry was working at his drill press in the shop when he collapsed. His coworkers called an ambulance, but he was dead on arrival at Mt. Sinai Hospital. Cloverlawn was in shock as the news spread. We were all aware that John was sickly. His general weakness, shortness of breath, chest pains, and fainting spells were written off as asthma or chest colds. No one questioned John's family history. We had said little while watching him struggle all the years he lived on the block.

A funeral service was held at Sullivan's in Royal Oak. All Cloverlawn, it seemed, showed up that night. Some of his coworkers and old classmates were there, too. We spoke in subdued voices. "Too young," and "he suffered so," and "he's breathing easy now." We talked about his gentle nature, his work ethic, the way he struggled.

Mr. Derry, in a suit that was too big for him, sat despondent in a corner, nodding to those who approached him. It was good that some of his work friends stopped in to sit with him, Jane said. He did not have friends on the block.

Blue Derry, meanwhile, was not present.

Jim, the youngest Derry, now eighteen, stood near the casket. He was subdued, but he represented the family well, greeting visitors, accepting condolences, and fielding questions about his brother's death. A doctor had told Jim that John died of cardiac arrest, possibly due to a genetic heart condition. To me and others, this news raised the question: was this condition ever diagnosed? Was treatment available? Had John ever been treated?

Jane and I greeted Jim, who briefed us on John's death and escorted us to the casket. Neither Jane nor I had ever seen a dead body up close. Jane knelt, while I stood at her side. John was death in white, that pale body with wispy ultra-blond hair in a starched dress shirt. After a minute, I took Jane's elbow.

Jane had been aware of John from the neighborhood, had met him several times. Once, she had told him in her way, not pushy or controlling, that he should stop smoking. John seemed shocked and embarrassed that someone would care so much for him. He thanked Jane, told her he would try, but he was unable to take the advice. Beer and cigarettes had become comforts. We suspected they had played a role in his death.

While I huddled on folding chairs with Jane and a few others, Chuck Farley elbowed me. I followed his gaze to an entry door, where Jim was approaching a young woman.

"Who is she?" Jane asked.

"John's sister." She was about twenty-one by now, looking taller and more fit, more confident than she had seemed four years before. Her face and figure had filled out. Her hair had grown in waves down her back.

"John's sister? Bet? I thought she was at Eloise," Jane said.

"Me too. How did she get here?"

Bet stood at the casket with Jim for a long time before he turned to greet someone. After a while, Jane saw that Bet was looking lost, sitting alone. "I'm going to introduce myself," she finally said.

"Let's go." Suspecting that Bet would feel more at ease if a female approached her, I had been hoping Jane would lead the way. It was the kind of thing Jane did, and still does.

"Do you remember Gary?" Jane asked as we stood before Bet.

She smiled. "I remember his face." She looked shyly back at me. "You were John's friend. He brought you and another boy to meet me."

"Good memory. So sorry to see you again under these sad circumstances, Bet."

"Yes."

"We heard you were living at Eloise," Jane said.

"Yes. They gave me a pass to come for this . . . to see my brother."

Bet was still quite shy but seemed to be making a conscious effort to raise her head, to face us. She seemed more confident with Jane than with me, but she looked at me to speak.

She asked me, "Are you the Gary who walked to school with my brother?"

"He told you? Yeah, I live across the street. John sat in front of me in homeroom."

"He said you were a good friend. And you helped him with his taxes?"

"I did," I said. "He would bring me his W-2s. Math isn't my best subject, but John said I was better at it than he was."

"Can you tell us about your time in the hospital, Bet?" Jane asked. How do they treat you?"

"Well, first they took me to Pontiac State Hospital. That was very bad. It was hot in that place. Then when cold weather came, it was too cold. They made us sit in wood chairs for hours at a time, and we couldn't get up or get warm or do anything. The attendants there were mean, too. They beat people up and called us names, and the food was bad. I lost a lot of weight there, and then I got sick. My brother helped me get put in Eloise."

"You mean John got you transferred?"

"John helped. He told George what they were doing to me. George was in California. He called a lawyer from Protective Services. They got my records to show that I'm in Wayne County, so they transferred me to Eloise."

I had not heard anything about this, but it made sense that if she was officially living on Cloverlawn, in Oakland County, she should be sent to Pontiac. Blue must have convinced this lawyer that Bet was sent to Pontiac in error, that her true address was on Orleans in Detroit, in Wayne County. I had no idea that Pontiac State Hospital was as bad as Bet described it. Later, I saw that the Detroit Free Press did some investigating about that hospital. That reporting confirmed Bet's comments.

"So, Eloise has been good for you, you think?" Jane asked.

"Yes, it is better," Bet said. "I have a friend there. Julie King. She was a teacher. I work with her every day. And we help in the garden. Julie teaches me. We read and do math, and we study nature."

"Do you get visitors?" I asked.

"My brothers have been there. John and Jim come on some Saturdays, and George came to visit when he got home from California."

"Your brother, George. We call him Blue."

Bet smiled. "His name is George."

"I thought we might see him here."

"He brought me, but . . . he won't come in . . ." She looked over her shoulder at the man sitting alone in a corner. "Not until my father is gone."

"I see."

"Excuse me," Bet said, nodding in Mr. Derry's direction, "Is that my, um, my father I mean, in the corner?"

Jane and I nodded, amazed that Bet would need to ask.

"You go to him, dear," Jane said. "I know he would love to see you."

We watched as Bet moved across the room to the corner where Mr. Derry still sat, sullen and unresponsive. But when he saw the young woman in front of him, he rose to his feet. Bet, as tall as her bent-backed father, took his hands and faced him and spoke, nodding. Then Mr. Derry brought his hands to his face and cried. Bet put a hand to his arm and continued to speak, still nodding.

"She's a remarkable girl," Jane said. I had told Jane that Mr. Derry, for a long time—I did not know how long—had refused to acknowledge her. I suspected Mr. Derry may have also refused to accept John's heart condition.

*****

As the service neared closing time, some of our Cloverlawn friends planned to meet for a drink. Jane and I decided not to participate, both of us having early start times the next day. We filed out to the parking lot, where I had almost forgotten about Blue. He was leaning against the front end of my car. It was evident that he had been waiting for me.

I had not seen him since proofreading the letter he had written, or tried to write, to Bet's doctors at Eloise. Blue's intent in the letter was to ask Eloise to release Bet back to him and his mother, promising to "treat her right" and prepare her for an independent life. I rewrote the letter and mailed it without showing him the revision, a toned-down appeal for occupational training, with the same goal of independence.

As I got closer to him, his elbow slipped off the hood of my car, and he almost lost his balance. Then I got a whiff of some kind of whiskey he'd been drinking.

"Remember Jane?" I said, coming face-to-face with him, aware of his explosiveness. I felt like one of those Yellowstone tourists who insist on a close-up of a cute old grizzly.

He nodded to Jane, then looked hard at me.

"Where's Bet?" I asked.

"She's in the car," he said, nodding toward his Olds. "Can you believe she wanted to see him here?"

"Who?"

271

"Her father!" he growled, as if I should have known. "A man who pretended she never existed, that she was a mistake. Same man who allowed his own son, my brother, to die. Can you tell me why she would have mercy on good ol' Lance? As he spoke, he staggered toward me. I raised my hands, afraid he might take a swing at me.

"No. I can't tell you, Blue. Are you okay?"

"I'm not okay. Not any more. Not with John dead in there," he said, nodding toward the funeral home. "He was twenty years old. And he never had a chance."

Jane stepped between Blue and myself. I tried to nudge her out of the way, but she shook me off. "Your sister needs to be back at the hospital by ten o'clock, and you, Blue Derry, are too drunk to take her there." As she touched Blue's arm, he flinched. "I understand you are grieving and angry, but Bet told me she will be punished if she reports late."

Blue looked at her dumbly. "Uh, sure, we better get moving. I'll get her back there on time."

"Maybe you can drive, Blue, but you're not going anywhere with that girl in the car. Gary and I will take her back to the hospital. You need to settle down before you do something foolish."

Blue looked at me. I nodded and said, "I'll take her."

"She's in the D building, down at the end . . . she'll show you."

"Blue," I said, "you should get out of this lot before your father comes through that door. He'll be with Jim. This isn't the time or place, if you want to talk to him."

"Oh, I'll be talking to him soon enough. You can bet on that," he said, and turned back to his car. His Olds had been in a front-end accident since he brought it back from California. Its hood was tied down with what looked like a coat-hanger. When he started it, a headlight looked to be out of alignment. Jane had taken Bet to my Ford. I reached for my keys. "Take care of yourself, Blue," I said. "We'll take care of Bet."

14

We were only twenty years old, but Jane and I had become a couple. Our lives revolved around school, jobs, our families. And each other, of course. Jane was pulling close to a 4.0 grade point in the Nursing program at Marygrove while working short shifts at Lou's Deli, which was across the street from the college. What was it that kept me coming back to her? That night at the funeral home, she looked after a girl she did not know and put a menacing drunk, Blue Derry, in his place. *That* was the Jane I came to love.

During my two years at OCC, I watched my instructors at work. I noticed how they approached their coursework and their students. I observed their methods and the success or failure of those methods. As I participated in class projects and discussions, I noticed a growing interest in the workings of a classroom and of the ways kids learned. I grew concerned about learning, and the things that got in the way of learning.

A history professor during my first year, Mr. Grossens, took an interest in me. It began with a question I asked about migrant workers during the Depression. I remembered Blue's comments about the migrants, and had read *The Grapes of Wrath*, the John Steinbeck classic novel, about the Okies who left their own barren land for a dream of plenty in California, a dream that, in most ways, went sour. I was caught up in the tensions between workers, labor unions, farmers, and government, and how those tensions affected a family.

"If you aren't busy, come to my office," Mr. Grossens said. "I'll fix us a cup of tea. We can talk about it."

It was the first of many visits. I always felt I was learning along with that man. I wished that a teacher like Mr. G had reached me in high school. I discovered an interest in history that had lain dormant in me. During my time at OCC, the idea of becoming a high school teacher, one who approached his students and learning like Mr. G, took root.

Near the end of my second year at OCC, I was accepted in Wayne State's College of Education. My first semester at Wayne was Fall Quarter of 1966. My parents worried; in those days, teachers made about $8000 per year in Michigan. My father knew I could make much better money in the auto industry as an engineer. I never considered myself to be idealistic, but I was lucky enough in those days to know what I wanted, regardless of the salary. And with summers off, I believed I could get a warm-weather job that would help support a family. I also knew that my father would eventually accept any choice I made about a career.

I had two years of college to finish, and a student deferment that would take me through college if I continued to pass a full schedule of classes. But lots of guys were being drafted immediately after college graduation, and no one knew how long the war might drag on. A medical deferment would require dishonesty. I knew guys who were submitting letters from doctors for things like "asthma" (Joe Biden) and bone spurs (Donald Trump). Some essential jobs, like farming, medicine, weapons manufacturing, and even teachers of critical subjects were granted deferments. Other ways of avoiding the draft, like burning a draft card, leaving the country, or just refusing to report for service, were out of the question for me. At that point I had no fixed idea about the war. It was all about me: I did not want heroism or martyrdom or jail time.

But Vietnam was becoming a serious issue among men of draft age. Some who believed in the war joined the military to help fight it. Others joined so they could pick a non-combat role, like avionics or cooking or clerking. Every man who came of age in the '60s or early seventies has a personal story to tell of avoiding or serving, or both.

My own story brings up another means of getting a deferment. Jane and I had talked about marriage. It was a step I wanted to take, yet I was not certain that Jane or I were ready for that commitment. And while we discussed having kids as a general idea, we never talked about having a baby.

But that is how I escaped the draft. Jane and I had been seeing each other for three years. People were asking us when we would be tying the knot. We knew we would be married "when the time was right," but we were on hold, both still in college, both living at home. Something had to give.

In early 1967, just after New Years, Jane gave me the bad news and good news. She was pregnant. Bad news because it was unplanned, good because the baby would be ours, and we knew we would welcome it and love it. We made the dual announcement to our parents, that we were getting married and having a child together. We feared the reaction to come, but we did not doubt. As it happened, everyone affirmed us.

Early in the war, John Kennedy signed an executive order that granted a III-A, or hardship deferment, to men with children. So in 1967 I became a "Kennedy father," one of millions to choose fatherhood. Because I knew a few guys who did not come back alive, or came back forever scarred, I have felt guilty about my exemption, but every time I look at my daughter Grace, I feel only joy.

Some called it a shotgun wedding, but no one was holding a gun to my head. On May 10, 1967, Jane stood proud in a rose-colored dress and heels, while I stood proud at her side. It was an outdoor wedding, held at the Oak Park Municipal Park, the park at the end of Cloverlawn that was always a gathering place as well as a refuge.

The wedding took place on a Saturday. My Best Man was Chuck Farley. Our Maid-of-Honor was Jane's best friend, Mary Jo. The service was officiated by a Catholic priest, Father Dimitriou, an assistant at nearby Our Lady of Fatima, a man who Jane and I had met with several times in "pre-Cana" (pre-marital) counseling sessions. A few months later, after I attended Initiation classes, Father Dimitriou administered the sacraments that brought me into the Catholic Church.

Most of Cloverlawn, young and old, were at the wedding. The Farleys, the Millers, the Elkins, the McPhails, the Colangelos, Sheldon and Melvin Weiss, the Cassidys, all ten Cunningham kids with their parents. Even the Greens, the oldest couple on the block and rarely seen, were there. Ann played Gershwin and Cole Porter on an amplified keyboard before the wedding, and then accompanied Father Dimitriou during the service. Afterward, she accompanied one of the Cunningham girls, who sang "Baby I Need Your Lovin'" and "The Very Thought of You."

Mr. Derry was not present, nor was Blue, but Jim Derry, now nineteen, brought his girlfriend and his sister Bet, who was still a patient at Eloise. Jim told me that after her good friend and mentor Julie died, Bet was adrift for a time, "regressing," Jim said, but she got some counseling. An occupational therapist who saw her as potentially independent began working with her. Jim said that Bet was also getting supportive phone calls from Blue, who had been housed in the Oakland County Jail for the previous eight months.

During our wedding reception, held on a section of Cloverlawn that had been blocked off for the occasion, I asked Jim if he had heard from Blue.

"He called me about a month ago. You probably know this, Gary. The worst thing you can do to my brother is put him in a cage. I think the confinement is getting to him. But I hate to admit that jail is where he belongs right now."

"True," I said. "I'm hoping he can get straight and come out of there with a good attitude." As I said this, I had little confidence that it would come to pass.

"My brother is lost right now," Jim said. "He is as low as I've ever seen him. He has some forgiving to do, and some repenting, patching things up. I don't know if he can humble himself, though. He'll need to find a way to get through this and begin all over again."

That was Jim, a nineteen-year-old kid with an uncanny wisdom.

15

Blue's meltdown occurred almost nine months earlier, in August of '66. The scene was Cloverlawn. Since John Derry's funeral in June of that year, when Blue had promised a confrontation with his father, Jane and I fretted over possible violence. I had not seen much of Blue or his car parked across the street. I considered that he might have been living with his mother on the East Side.

Jim said it all began with the bottle, since both parties had been drinking heavily. Mr. Derry came in from the garage to find Blue asleep on the living room floor. Mr. Derry kicked him—or nudged him gently with his boot, depending on which version of the story you believed. Whereupon Blue, seeing red, came after the old man. Mr. Derry was no match for his son, who would have killed him if not for Jim Derry, who had been sleeping upstairs.

Upon hearing the commotion, Jim rushed down the stairs, grabbed Blue from behind, and tried to calm him down, but his brother spun away from the hold and pushed Jim through the front screen door. Then he continued to whale on his father until he heard a siren and realized he was in trouble. He ran from the house and jumped into his Olds convertible, its front end still-busted-up, which was parked in the street. But before he could leave the curb, police cars were closing in from both ends of Cloverlawn.

I was home at the time. I had heard the commotion and had seen Jim Derry come crashing through the aluminum screen door, flying across his porch. My mother heard the commotion and was one of several neighbors who called the police. Knowing they were enroute, I ran out to meet Blue. He had started his car. I said something to try to calm him down, but he was in a world all his own—possessed, frantic. When I saw the police lights, I backed away from the street. As I stood on the sidewalk and watched the unfolding scene, I noticed neighbors up and down the block peering from porches and picture windows.

A policeman approached Blue's car with a long flashlight, asking him for identification, then asking him to exit the car. As Blue resisted, the cop opened his driver door. Blue got out of the car yelling. He pushed the cop away and ran into the arms of a second approaching officer, who had less luck containing Blue than the first. Not even together could the two cops subdue Blue Derry.

"Please don't draw your weapons," I whispered to no one.

A third officer, meanwhile, called for more backup before joining the fray. This meant the whole of the on-duty evening shift of the Oak Park Police force would soon be at the scene. Now there were three squad cars, with three sets of overhead lights flashing, their colors reflecting off the windows of the cookie-cutter houses on both sides on the street. These lights set the stage for fierce resistance by Blue. He punished the first three officers, then pushed a cruiser door so far outward against its hinges that it would never close again. It took the two newly arriving cops with swinging night sticks and foot-long flashlights to join the others and chase him down and trap him. One heavyset older cop, whose cap had been knocked off, hit Blue several times on the head with his stick, while the others spread-eagled him to the hood of one of the police cars.

Everyone who saw the beating agreed that the final blows were unnecessary. Blue had already been restrained.

While he was conscious, Blue cursed and raged at the cops. Later, handcuffed in the rear seat of a police car, bleeding and struggling to free himself, he threatened to kill every policeman on the force. It was a scene that no one on Cloverlawn ever forgot, but that no one seemed comfortable discussing.

An ambulance came for Mr. Derry. He suffered a concussion, cuts to his face, a permanently damaged eye, and an injury to his back which kept him in the hospital for a few days and out of work for a long time thereafter. Jim Derry suffered a broken arm and cuts and bruises. He lost six weeks on the job and the cost of medical attention. The Derry house, too, was injured. Its picture window was shattered. Its front screen door stood ajar, frame twisted, screen dangling. Inside, a chair sat on three legs.

The charges against Blue were many. Five counts of assault on a police officer (all five of the officers reported cuts, bruises, or worse), two counts of domestic assault (though Jim Derry withdrew charges), resisting arrest, and destruction of public property. A month after the event, he was sentenced to three to five years in the Oakland County Jail. To most of us on the block, it was a relief to have Blue Derry gone. We were safe. We could return to something like normalcy.

On Cloverlawn, we white folks had lived the illusion that we were immune to the violence that was said to be common across Eight Mile in Detroit, but we did not see Blue Derry coming.

*****

I could not understand, at first, how Jim Derry could find it in himself to forgive and advocate for his brother. I had seen Jim's broken arm dangling at his side the night Blue pushed him through that screen door. I had seen his father being wheeled in a stretcher to an ambulance. I had watched Blue taking on five Oak Park cops, filling the night with screams, threatening me and my neighbors.

"What if he'd got ahold of one of the cops' guns?" I asked Jim.

"I don't know. I'd like to think, to believe . . . but I don't know."

Jim spoke for Blue in court and showed up periodically at the county jail to check on him and share updates with all who were interested. Not many of his neighbors on the block were interested.

*****

Jim recovered quickly from his wound. He had been living mostly alone with his father ever since John died. He had looked up to John, even though John was sickly and slow-moving. Jim grieved for his brother without blaming his father, but John's death surely broke Mr. Derry, broke him down, exposed him for the weak, ignorant man he had been. His relationships with his ex-wife, daughter, and all three of his sons had been tales of neglect, abuse, and ignorance.

But Jim loved his father. He saw something in the man that no one else had noticed. Jim's most important task after his brother's blowup was to look after Mr. Derry. When the old man returned from the hospital, he was bedridden for weeks. He needed to be fed and otherwise cared for. Jim was his only option. Broken arm and all, Jim took care of Mr. Derry until he, Jim, was healed enough to return to work.

Bet's appearance at John's funeral had left an impression on Mr. Derry. He began asking Jim for updates on her progress. Jim told me that Mr. Derry's feelings over abandoning Bet were so intense that he began counseling with Father Dimitriou at Our Lady of Fatima. Mr. Derry had been baptized Catholic but had never been a churchgoer. His counseling prompted him to ask Jim if he could visit Bet at Eloise. There, he asked for and received forgiveness from Bet, and continued to be in touch with her for the rest of his life.

*****

As soon as Jim could drive, he resumed his weekly visits to Eloise. When Bet's mentor, Julie, had been transferred to a critical care ward at the facility. Jim walked with Bet to visit her. Later, he took Bet to Julie's funeral. He also helped to hook Bet up with an occupational therapist. Blue had convinced Jim that the goal must be to prepare Bet for a life after Eloise.

When Jim told Jane and me about Bet's nosedive after Julie's death, Jane stepped in and engaged in what turned out to be a lasting friendship with Bet. Jane did not set herself up as Bet's teacher or mentor, but she talked and read and laughed with Bet, and facilitated progress in Bet's learning, confidence, and trust. After Bet expressed an interest in succulents, a book, an article from a gardening magazine, and a Jade plant soon showed up in Bet's room. And Bet's interest in Jane's second pregnancy began a new area of learning for Bet—sex education and motherhood.

16

Bet's institutionalization had taken her mother off the hook. No longer responsible for her daughter's care, Mrs. Derry was now free to spend more time at Andrew's Pub and Kelly's, her favorite after-work dive bars. Both were in Hamtramck, not far from her home. She had recently taken up with another Andrew's regular, a fellow functional alcoholic who installed radiator hoses on Monaco sedans at Dodge Main Assembly Plant. Mrs. Derry visited her daughter from time to time, but she told her friends that she felt uncomfortable around Bet ("Them nurses won't let me do nothing for her"), and ordered another gin-and-tonic.

Bet's parents came up in a culture in which mentally ill or developmentally disabled people were stigmatized as freaks of nature. They were retarded, deficient, and best kept away from polite company. Mrs. Derry believed that Bet was a punishment from God—if Blue was not punishment enough—for conceiving and giving birth to Blue out of wedlock, and for her inability to identify his father. Likewise, Mr. Derry had taken no responsibility for Bet. He added to his wife's guilt, blaming her for the "accident" that she bore.

Blue had good reasons for wanting to shield Bet from life in an asylum. "I don't want my sister wrapped in a straight-jacket," he once told me. "And those joints use shock treatments that will mess up your brain for life."

This was true. My wife learned that seizures were induced in some patients to reduce their cognitive faculties. ECT, electro-convulsive therapy, often turned patients into compliant vegetables. By the '60s, Jane said, many psychiatrists were modifying the shock treatments like ECT by using muscle relaxants and anesthesia to gain the same mind-numbing effects.

Blue may have been the only person who saw that with the right guidance and education Bet could learn to take care of herself. His zeal to care for her backfired when he took matters into his own fists when she was assaulted. The police might overlook a sexual assault on his sister, but his revenge on the assailant branded Bet's home as unsafe, and put her in the place he most feared.

The shift to Eloise, in Wayne County, engineered by a free legal service commissioned by Blue, turned out to be a godsend. Bet was fortunate to meet Julie King, the patient at Eloise who, somehow, was allowed to become a parttime teacher and mentor. Bet also benefited from the fact that by the middle 1960s, therapy was becoming gentler. Headway was being made in the classification of many disorders and in their causes and treatments. Clinical psychologists were administering tests, and occupational therapists were working with those who showed an aptitude for independence. I do not know what those tests revealed, but much later I learned that, among other things, Bet was on the Autism/Asperger's spectrum.

In the fall of 1971, not long after our daughter's fourth birthday, Jane and I helped Jim and his new wife, Sarah, to ready a one-bedroom upper flat for Bet. We cleaned the place and gathered some secondhand furniture, including a television. From its location near downtown Royal Oak, Bet could walk to shopping and the bus line.

In November, Jane and I were there when Jim brought Bet, newly released from Eloise, to her new home. We celebrated with dinner, prepared by Jane, at Bet's very crowded kitchen table. Her landlords, the young couple who lived downstairs, were also there to welcome her.

Blue was also present that day. He had been out of prison for almost two years, was working in an auto repair shop and living in nearby Hazel Park. I had seen him only two or three times since his release. The first was in a market, where I found it difficult to make conversation with him. I suspected he might have been embarrassed by the turn his life had taken that led to his epic meltdown and imprisonment. We never did have much in common. Jane and I had two children by then, and I was teaching in Detroit Public Schools. I wondered if Blue still saw me as one of those authority figures he had come to hate.

The next time I saw him, Blue was in a car, with Jim at the wheel. "Hey, Gary," he said, "tell your Jane I 'preciate what she's doing with my sister."

The day of Bet's release, at her new flat, Blue, still called "George" by his sister, seemed quiet but emotional. I could see that he was proud of Bet, proud to tears, and respectful to everyone there, especially Jane, who was more attentive to him than anyone else. But he was subdued. I wondered how prison may have changed him, but he never spoke about it. Not then. I wished him well.

Bet's entry to a life of independence was not smooth. She had much to learn, and learning was slow. She had some support, but she needed to learn how to ask for it, and some of her behaviors were counter-productive. She was still very shy, especially around men, often avoiding eye contact. Her discomfort in social situations and otherwise stressful situations led to rocking her body or making little noises. Some loud sounds, visual cues, or even textures would cause stress and confusion, and would trigger the automatic responses of rocking and squealing.

As helpful as her time at Eloise was, compared to many less fortunate patients, she had fallen into a predictable routine there. The structure was helpful, but she would need to find a new routine for herself on the outside.

Eventually, she found a job at English Gardens, a greenhouse and garden store. She walked the mile-and-a-half to and from the Gardens, where she was put to work doing what she loved, planting and nurturing plants. The managers at the nursery saw that her customer service skills needed some nurturing, too, but over time she became a fixture, and would answer questions from shoppers with a shy friendliness and efficiency.

Bet Derry became a friend to my family. Sometimes on a holiday, Jane brought her to our place for dinner. Or we stopped by her place. Jane and I and our kids loved her. Her place was always full of plants and flowers. Jane would bring food, and Bet would talk about her job and the few friends she had made.

In the late eighties, Jim's career as a tool-and-die maker took him to Connecticut, where he is now retired, a great-grandfather. He and Sarah have been married for fifty-four years. Bet always gave us news of Jim's visits.

She also spoke of her "George." Blue did not visit much, having moved with his wife and her kids to a house in Monroe, but he called often. I have not seen Blue or Jim Derry since Bet's funeral and do not know if Blue is dead or alive.

Bet worked at the Gardens until she died in 2015 of a cancer that took her life only three months after diagnosis. Jim Derry arranged for a reception for Bet at Sullivan's, the same funeral home where John and Mr. Derry were remembered. Some of our old Cloverlawn friends, acquainted since Bet became a regular at the Gardens, came to say hello and goodbye. Funerals, it seemed, had become the only occasions for the Cloverlawn kids to see each other.

It was good to see Blue again. He was the same man, a man of contradictions, tender yet explosive, in denial yet painfully honest.

17

Almost everyone had left Sullivan's when Blue pulled me aside and asked if we could go out where he could smoke. His wife was ill and could not attend, he said. Overweight, jowly, and shuffling, I could see that he had not aged well. His sister's death had shaken him. I had not forgotten his baffling talent as a musician, and asked if he had been playing lately.

"Playing? You mean, like, an instrument. I have this Gibson. A mellow old guitar. I take it out on the back porch at night and . . . um, I listen to it. Sounds like the Spirit, you know?"

I smiled.

He asked about my sister.

"She's been married forever, has eight grandkids. Still gives piano lessons. Lives up in Leland now."

"Lotta rich people retiring up there," he said. "I had a crush on Ann, if you remember."

"You asked her out."

"I was pissin' into the wind."

He had not forgotten his unraveling, that night in 1966.

"You were there, Gary," he said. "You saw what those goons did to me. If that had been twenty years later, I could have had them fired. I could have sued the city for millions."

"You're probably right," I said. "But . . . at first they were trying to restrain you. Two people had been injured. They were responding to a call for help. It was their job to—"

"Whose side are you on, man?"

Almost fifty years after the fact, Blue still had me lined up with the cops and judges. "I was always on your side," I said. "Let me finish."

"So finish."

"It would have been wrong, but you're lucky you didn't get shot. But once they had you down, there was no need for what happened next. I saw that cop's face. He totally lost it, and what he did with that club was brutal. We did not know how bad you were hurt. We were concerned about you, as well as Jim and your father."

"My father?" Blue's face was contorted. "Lance sometimes claimed to be my father, but he never adopted me, never even got a blood test."

Despite his explosiveness, I could always be honest with Blue. "You put him in the hospital. And Jim's arm—"

"I was . . . I admit I was confused that night," he said, confronted with the rest of the truth. "I'd been drinking, sure. And when I drink I get . . . you know. Hey, nowadays they use a stun gun or electric shock, or tear gas, or a net. And some cops can take a guy who's, uh, out of himself, and talk him down."

"What was it all about, Blue? I mean, why did you go after your, um, stepfather?"

He looked down at his hands, turned them over, wrung them out. "I spent three years in OCJ, in jail, thinking about it. A few things. Big things to me then. John dying, and if he'd got the right care, he might be here today . . . and Bet, God rest her sweet soul, Lance wouldn't have nothing to do with her, 'til . . . and Jimmy. Jim wanted to go to GMI, you know, that technical college that GM runs. But he needed up-front money. The old man wouldn't spring for it." He took a long breath.

"Not long after that, I found a deal on a house. I had this idea that Bet could live with me there, like when she got out of the hospital. But my, you know, Lance—he said he couldn't risk it. He had all these excuses, and no trust.

"So, I was pissed. I went over there just to talk, you know. I was gonna give it another try, but then I ran into a buddy, and we drank a lot of something, and it was all so hopeless. And I kept thinking, the man ain't my father. What's the use in having his name? He was never in my corner. So yeah, I was feeling like, like an orphan.

"But, you know, Gary," he said, shifting in his seat, "I *am* sorry for that night, and for so many things. Bet wanted me to make up with the old man, you see. And I wish, I really wish I'd had the guts to do that before he died."

I told him I understood. It made sense to me that Blue Derry would feel like a nonentity. His father may not have been, and his mother was not present for him. I compared his life, what little I knew of it, with my own. Despite my own flaws and scars, I came from an intact family, had a good marriage. My kids are grown. I'm retired and secure. More than that, I have confidence in something solid in myself, not an unshakeable thing, but solid, even if it is deep in my soul.

"I want you to write my story, Gary," he said. "Will you do that?"

"I'm not a writer. I only—"

"But you are," he said, getting his face up into mine like he always had done. "You helped me write that letter to the hospital. And way back, remember that night at Stan's, I was working on your Ford, you were writing your history essay, and I asked you to read it to me. What was it? Henry, the King of England, and all his wives. He had two of them beheaded, remember what for?"

"Not offhand. I'm shocked that *you* remember."

"One of 'em was for not having a boy baby, someone to take over after he died. You told me then . . . about that word, I mean, what it's based on. Primo . . . genitals, or something."

"Primogeniture." I remembered, mainly because, years later, I taught European History to eleventh graders. "Succession to the throne was based on male-preference primogeniture."

"And that means—?"

"It means the oldest male child gets the throne."

"And inheritance works that way, too," he said.

"Well, not anymore. Nowadays, all the children get equal shares unless the will specifies otherwise."

"But step-children don't count."

"Not unless they are legally adopted, I think."

"I never counted, see." His face was up close to mine again, but I knew that Blue only wanted me to hear him. "I can't write my story, Gary, but I'll pay *you* to write it. Even if nobody reads it, and why would they? But I *do* have a story to tell."

"You do," I said. Everyone has a story to tell. I did not know half of Blue's story, bits and pieces only, but I knew, I saw, that he was an extraordinary man.

"I *could* write it," I said, "but I'd need material. Facts, your thoughts. I'd need you to fill me in on lots of things. Like, these last many years."

"You already know most of the important shit, Gary." That, I realize now, was true. "And you can improvise. Use the true, then fill in the false. Build on it."

"But then it'd be fiction," I said.

He smiled. "I'm okay with that."

*****

We never did get together to go over the important shit, or anything else. It was the last time I saw Blue Derry.

But I told him I would write it, and so I did.

www.ingramcontent.com/pod-product-compliance
Lightning Source LLC
Chambersburg PA
CBHW071246300726
48975CB00002B/569